CLIMATE
OF FEAR

CLIMATE OF FEAR

by

George A Smith

ABOUT THE AUTHOR

The author is a retired detective chief inspector and former head of Brighton CID. He was a senior investigating officer on many murder investigations and complex fraud cases. During his police career he also operated in the UK and Ireland with the Counter Terrorism Command. Later in his career he was recruited into the Security Service (MI5) and worked in the UK and USA with the FBI. As a young detective inspector he was involved in the interrogation of Argentine Commander Alfredo ASTIZ during the Falklands War. He has a BA degree in history and politics and is a keen photographer and motorcyclist. In retirement, with his wife, he owns and manages a woodland in West Sussex.

DEDICATION

As with my previous two novels,
all royalties from this novel are being donated to
St Catherine's Hospice (Crawley) in gratitude for
the excellent and loving palliative care given to our
precious daughter Clair Joanna, who had terminal
cancer and sadly died in 2022.

~ George A Smith

Contents

CHAPTER ONE

No Escape

There would be no escape from death. The petty criminal and drug dealer knew he was to be murdered. His death would be long and painful.

Earlier that day, he had answered a call on his mobile phone instructing him to deliver cocaine wraps to an unknown 'customer' at a lay-by on the rural outskirts of Crawley town in West Sussex. He arrived at the agreed location and waited. There were no other vehicles or people on the lay-by. After several minutes, a car approached at speed and stopped in front of him. No words were exchanged. Two men, wearing dark clothing and black balaclavas, leaped from the car wielding pickaxe handles and violently attacked him. He was bludgeoned to the ground. A blindfold was tied tightly over his eyes and his wrists and feet were bound with rope. He was kicked many times. Once subdued, he was bundled into the boot of the car and driven away at speed. The journey lasted for several hours. Throughout, and in complete darkness, he was in great pain. He slipped in and out of consciousness and knew no mercy would be given.

He woke up confused, sweating and in extreme pain. His body had been stripped naked. At some stage, his blindfold had been removed. He was upright with his wrists bound together above his head, with rope ascending to a pulley fitted high up on a wooden cross-beam. He was suspended with his bare feet swaying just above the ground. The other end of the rope was tethered to a ratchet hand winch bolted to a stationary farm trailer loaded with straw bales. The location was an old agricultural barn used for storing redundant rusting farm tractors and other machinery. There were no windows in the building. It was in semi-darkness with a cold musky atmosphere. He had no way of knowing where he was. The barn was, in fact, within a semi-derelict farming complex in rural North Wales.

In front of where he was hanging was positioned an old brown leather wing chair which had seen better days.

Looking down at his own torso, he could see large bruises and open bleeding wounds. The pain was excruciating. His shoulders were burning and felt as though they were being dislocated. In this contorted position, breathing was difficult. He did not know who had kidnapped him, or why, although various reasons flashed through his mind. However, he realised his life was in imminent danger. His injuries would require medical attention and he knew that was not going to happen.

Through the sweat dripping into his eyes, he focused as the heavy barn door on his right slowly and noisily opened. It let in a shaft of daylight along with a refreshing cool breeze. The silhouette of a man appeared in the doorway. For several minutes, the figure did not move. In his left hand, the man clasped a long wooden shepherd's crook. In his right hand, between his fingers, he held a large cigar. Slowly and deliberately, he walked towards the empty chair and sat down. He remained silent and made cynical eye contact with the shaking man. He lit his cigar. Taking deep puffs, he leaned back in the high-back chair and seemed to enjoy the spectacle before him.

The hanging victim, Barry West, was known by his nickname, 'Digger.' He instantly recognised the man seated before him. This increased his fear. West was 25 years of age but, as a consequence of his frequent drug misuse, looked much older. He had a scrawny body, with an unhealthy pale complexion, and was of unkempt appearance. In his hometown of Brighton, he was well known within the drug fraternity as a street dealer of drugs, mainly selling the Class A drug cocaine.

Increasingly, much of West's income from selling drugs had been spent satisfying his own drug addiction. In the previous month, he had failed to pay for several deliveries of drugs. When the 'enforcers' came looking for him, he had disappeared and relocated to the town of Crawley in North Sussex.

The man sitting in the chair was David Evans, known within the criminal fraternity as 'The Alligator.' He was not a man to cross. The term 'alligator' is often used as a slang expression to describe someone who is aggressive, greedy and who always wants more. Evans was the 'Boss' of the drug syndicate who supplied drugs to West. He was known for his unpredictable behaviour and violent temper.

Rolling the lighted cigar between his teeth, he held the shepherd's crook in both hands and prodded West, causing his body to swing backwards and forwards like a pendulum. As it slowed, a further prod was administered, with the semi-conscious West groaning in pain.

"Please, please help me. What do you want?" pleaded West.

"You have been a naughty boy. A very naughty boy. You thought you could steal from me, then do a runner from Brighton and hide in Crawley. Big, big mistake. My 'accountant' tells me you owe £25,000 for cocaine delivered to you."

"Please, give me a little time and I will pay you in full," whimpered West.

"That is what you promised my boys last time. Then, after they left, you packed your bags and scarpered without leaving a forwarding address!" shouted Evans.

"Please, please, give me another chance, Mr Evans. I won't let you down."

Evans stood up, slowly walking the few steps towards the hanging and shaking victim. He lifted the shepherd's crook and thrust it towards West. He hooked it around the hapless victim's neck and pulled him forward until their faces were almost touching.

"I hear that last week, the police arrested you for drug dealing. Caught you red-handed selling cocaine to an undercover copper. Is that correct?"

"Yes."

"Unusually, you weren't charged. Very, very unusual. Why weren't you charged, Digger?" shouted Evans in an increasingly aggressive voice.

"I don't know," responded the shaking West.

Evans moved even closer. "I understand they wanted to know the name of your supplier and asked about me. What did you tell them?"

"Nothing, Mr Evans. Honestly, I told them nothing. I denied even knowing you. I said I'd never heard the name before they mentioned it."

"And, I understand, they offered you a deal - grass on your supplier and your charge sheet would be torn up. Is that correct, Digger?"

"Yes, but I didn't tell them a thing. Please, believe me."

"But you were still released without being charged. Digger, you nasty excuse for a human being, why? What were the conditions?"

"The cops told me to go away and think about it, with the promise of doing a long stretch in prison if I didn't cooperate. They said they would phone me in a couple of weeks for my decision."

"And what did they say about me?"

"They wanted your 'arse.' Sorry, Mr Evans; that's the word they used. I was asked to get as much info as I could get on you. They would make it worth my while with a large handout of cash. I told them I knew nothing. Honestly, that's what I said. I would never grass on you."

"I don't believe you and can't trust you. You have been talking to others about your arrest. Your biggest mistake was telling a friend you didn't think I had 'the muscle' to enforce recovering the debt. You showed me disrespect. Big mistake. You must pay for your mistake."

Evans removed the shepherd's crook from around West's neck. He stepped back and, with his left hand, grasped the handle of the winch. He turned it slowly. West was lifted higher from the ground and hoisted almost as high as the top of the barn's wooden rafters.

West was in no doubt his life was about to be snuffed out. He had become a dangerous liability. There was no way Evans would allow this injured man to go free or to receive medical attention. Evans looked up at the crying broken man and smiled. He winched West even higher up into the rafters, causing an increased swinging pendulum effect of his body. Without further comment, Evans turned and walked out of the barn, slamming the door behind him. West continued swinging, drifting into unconsciousness. It took several painful hours before he eventually died.

The friends, associates and 'customers' of West quickly became aware of his disappearance, but none reported him missing. His mobile phone went unanswered. The police were unable to make contact with him. His body was never found. It was said he had been murdered, with his body cut up and fed to pigs. No evidence was found to confirm that assertion.

Likewise, no evidence was forthcoming to identify where, how or who had carried out the murder. Rumour suggested his 'disappearance' was related to his involvement in the murky world of drug dealing. The police were unable to secure evidence to connect Evans with the disappearance. No one was willing to speak to the authorities. However, cautiously and with a good degree of fear, Evans' name was whispered as the likely person responsible. Evans was aware of the rumours. He quietly enjoyed the kudos and status associated with the rumour; it added to the climate of fear he sought to actively promote.

In recent years, within the Home Counties of the UK, several men connected to the drug trade had been murdered, mainly by shooting. In the majority of cases, the victims had been what the police referred to as 'low-level street drug dealers.' In reality, the murders were 'executions' authorised by drug barons on individuals who had shown disloyalty or were considered a liability to the continuing success of the trade in drugs. The bodies were often left in situ as a public warning to others. None of the murders had ever been solved.

The police were acutely aware of the growing influence and control Evans had on the drug trade within the Home Counties. It was believed his organisation had been responsible for ordering many murders, with Evans undertaking some personally.

It was said he was a killer with no remorse, undertaking the ultimate punishment with a lack of empathy or guilt. He acted with callous indifference. His expanding drug empire had inflated his ego. The failure of police to establish a case against him had increased his delusions of grandeur. People regarded him as a psychopath.

Evans' success was dependent on imposing fear with swift and harsh punishment on any individual who dared challenge or refuse his increasingly excessive demands. Disloyalty was not to be tolerated. Early in his criminal career, he had learned that the Italian Mafia used fear to achieve its goals. Its tentacles stretched deep into society, with fear and the code of silence entrenched in all levels of the population. This included using payments and extortion to achieve cooperation and compliance from businesspeople, other criminal organisations, the judiciary and even the police.

As the organisation Evans headed became more profitable, with its ever-bulging war chest, he was able to offer bigger 'cash rewards' in exchange for intelligence and tasks undertaken, in essence, by paying bribes. He would often quote, "Every man has a price." His organisation now had extensive international connections with Colombian and East European gangs involved in the illegal importation of drugs.

The majority of the contacts and deals were undertaken via the dark web, the internet source that was a haven for criminal activity. The identities and locations of 'darknet' users stay anonymous and cannot be tracked due to the layered encryption, which was the process of encoding information. Together, such organisations control routes used to smuggle drugs, mainly cocaine, from Colombia to the UK and Europe.

One recent importation of cocaine from Colombia was reputed to have had a street value of £350 million. Evans' personal profit from the deal was said to have been many millions of pounds. Why would a man who had amassed so much wealth take unnecessary risks to personally deal with a low-level street drug dealer like Barry West? In his terms, £25,000 was a paltry debt.

David John Evans was 42 years of age, thick set, with a shaven head and a broken nose. He had the build and appearance of an ex-boxer. He had left school without any formal qualifications and had often played truant. From an early age, he had rebelled against all forms of authority. Evans may have lacked education, but he was very sharp-witted and street-wise, with a desire to be rich. He was a man without scruples or moral considerations. A dominant confident individual, he had acquired his wealth by involvement in crime and the enforcement of fear. He prided himself on being physically strong and constantly worked out in his home gymnasium.

His large detached six-bedroom period Georgian house, with neo-classical styling and uncomplicated symmetry, was set within an acre of beautiful gardens and grounds. The property was enclosed behind continuous high brick and stone walls, which ensured absolute privacy. In addition, the extended estate included thirty acres of countryside and woodlands, located in a remote area of Wiltshire. There were no nearby residential properties.

Access to the house was along a two-mile country lane, which led up to a set of electrically operated wrought iron gates. Once through the gates, there was a long paved driveway to the house, which stood in splendid isolation with its impressive solid oak front door. The gates were kept locked. Closed circuit security cameras and floodlights were prominent. Access into the grounds required approval via the intercom system fixed to the wall adjacent to the gates. The uninvited visitor would not be welcome.

The property deeds, lodged with the UK Land Registry, stated that the house was owned by and registered in the name of his wife, Fiona Evans. The house had been purchased for just over £4 million, payment being in cash. Under their occupation, the house had undergone extensive and expensive restoration. Within the walled grounds was situated a small cottage. This was occupied by his unmarried twin brother, Terry Evans.

David Evans did not possess a bank account, nor was there any known record of savings within the UK. He had no known financial means of support, yet he had never claimed any form of social security benefit. Neither had he ever paid any income tax. In reality, he was a full-time professional criminal. His private passion was the ownership and racing of classic sports cars. In wider society, his 'hobby' gave him an air of respectability.

When questioned by the authorities about the source of his wealth, he would simply dismiss such enquiries, whilst ensuring he had an expensive lawyer at his side. As a frequent reply, without giving facts that could be verified, he would say: "Many years ago, a distant uncle left me a nice pot of money." He would always decline to disclose the amount or supply any evidence of where the alleged inheritance was banked. However, this allegedly enabled him to finance his interest in buying and selling classic sports cars for cash. It was a hobby and, therefore, there was no requirement to pay tax. No one actually believed the story about an inheritance and an unnamed uncle.

Evans enjoyed long summer holidays staying in a large family villa, with swimming pool, in southern Spain. Again, the property was owned by his wife. Other properties were registered in the name of, and controlled by, various dubious offshore companies located on Gibraltar, Jersey, in Panama and elsewhere, with Fiona Evans recorded as being the principal director. It was believed his riches, accumulated by criminal means, had been banked with various financial institutions in foreign countries and those outside the reach of the UK authorities.

Evans grew up in the poorer part of Liverpool with three generations of his family living in the same terraced house. He had two brothers. Terry was his twin. He was slightly shorter in stature than David and with a much quieter personality. He rarely smiled or outwardly showed emotion. The young Terry had always shied away from any form of conflict, looking up to David as being the leader and his protector. In any group activity, David was always the dominant gang leader, demanding that others did what he said with the threat of violence if they did not. Terry was regarded as David's ever-present 'shadow.' He would run errands for David, often to collect or deliver items acquired by criminal means.

Their close brotherly relationship continued into adulthood with Terry being employed as David's driver and odd-job man. Terry never married and appeared content with his lot. However, his friends had noticed that in recent years, he would always wear American leather cowboy boots with Cuban heels, which gave him the appearance of being the same height as David. However, he insisted it was because he had always been a fan of cowboy westerns.

In adulthood, the twins continued to associate with men from their youth, visiting their old haunts such as the local snooker halls, social clubs and pubs. Both brothers were only comfortable mixing with their own kind. Nevertheless, when they visited such establishments, David Evans demanded, and was given, respect. He was aware that his presence generated an element of fear, and this he enjoyed.

The third brother was Larry Evans. He was two years younger than the twins. Like his brothers, he lacked much of a formal education, but from an early age, had been determined to be different. With passion, he hated his humble beginnings but was not averse to taking part in the family's criminal activities to earn much-needed cash. Yes, he participated in car theft but was more discreet, stealing only luxury high-value cars, and often without the knowledge of his brothers.

In his late teens, Larry moved from his family home to live in Leeds. He continued to deal 'discreetly' in stolen luxury cars, which enabled him to acquire the funds to establish a limited company buying and selling property. To his new friends and business associates, he was now known as Lawrence Churchill-Butler with an enhanced, most would say false, curriculum vitae. He became more refined in manner and appearance and cultivated a quieter, slower-speaking voice.

From his outward appearance, Lawrence appeared a respectable member of the community. He had become a member of various business associations, including the local masonic lodge. Senior police officers and magistrates were within his sphere of friends. Contact with his brothers was limited only to David, with an occasional brief telephone call. If there was money to be made, Lawrence would still be willing to engage in nefarious criminal activities. In essence, he was an intelligent but dishonest and manipulative individual.

For the three brothers, from birth, crime had been an everyday family activity. In the early 1960s, their grandfather had been convicted of murder involving a gangland-related feud. Their father, who had also served several terms of imprisonment, owned a back-street garage which sold cheap second-hand cars and undertook motor vehicle repairs. Local folklore said cars would be stolen off the street, or stripped in situ, with the removed mechanical parts being used to facilitate the repairs.

As youngsters, the brothers were actively involved in their family's criminal activities. Indeed, their father forcefully demanded that the brothers be involved in crime. He was an unpleasant and violent man with a short temper. He ruled his family by fear and regular beatings. He did not need an excuse to administer violence.

From an early age, the children would be forced by their father to act as a distraction when he was shoplifting, by, for example, pretending to be injured and cry. They would also be sent into shops to steal specific items on the orders of their father. On occasions, the children would be detained by staff, with their father contacted to attend and collect them. The father would then offer profound apologies for the children's wrongdoings and, in the presence of the shop owner, physically punish them. However, once at home, they would receive a more severe beating for having got caught.

Through every day of their childhood, the children lived in fear of being beaten by their father. The brutal unloving treatment David received throughout his childhood, from his father and from every other adult he encountered, undoubtedly contributed to the development of his own unpleasant and uncompromising character. At school, he was frequently caned and constantly chastised by teachers that 'the boy from the slums' would never make anything of his life. He was frequently chased out of local shops and cinemas and grew up being acutely aware that he was regarded as being on the bottom rung of society. Likewise, as a youngster, whenever he found himself in trouble with the police or appeared before the Magistrates' Court, officials treated him with contempt.

Throughout his young life, he was never treated as an equal or with respect.

When no longer under the control of his father, David was determined that he would never be dominated or humiliated by any other individual and this continued into his adulthood. He considered employing violence, instilling fear and involvement in crime as his only means of gaining respect and achieving wealth.

From his late teens, David Evans had branched out to successfully set up his own criminal enterprise, stealing luxury cars from all parts of the UK and exporting them in sealed shipping containers to Eastern Europe and to the continent of Africa.

He had also developed a profitable sideline cultivating cannabis plants in a remote abandoned barn in North Wales. The barn had been set up with all the necessary equipment to successfully grow the plants, including water tanks, fans and powerful artificial lights; the system known as hydroponics. Electricity to power the whole enterprise was obtained by illegally attaching cables to an underground high electricity transmission line from the National Grid. He had established a network to sell the dried cannabis product to local street dealers, but he never consumed the substance himself.

From dealings in cannabis, he had, in recent years, progressed to importing and dealing in cocaine, and on an ever-increasing scale. His initial foray into dealing in cocaine had taught him what a competitive, dangerous and ruthless world he had entered, and he wasn't to forget the painful lessons learned.

His first venture into importing cocaine from Columbia was, in drug terms, for a modest amount, the product being valued at one million pounds. The approach had been naïve and, no doubt, his own arrogance played a part. When arranging the importation, he had failed to take into account or negotiate with the UK competition.

Having become a successful local supplier of cannabis, Evans had assumed he possessed the status and muscle within the drug-dealing fraternity to go it alone to import cocaine which would elevate him to a different level of wealth. The shipment had been arranged direct through a personal courier and smuggled into the UK aboard a London-bound aircraft. Importation of cocaine was regarded as the lucrative preserve of international crime organisations. He had fallen foul of their code. His punishment had been swift and brutal.

Whilst at a local nightclub, celebrating the success of his first cocaine drug importation, he had been invited outside to the car park. He had gone willingly, believing it was to talk drug-related business. In the semi-darkness, he had been grabbed from behind by several men and beaten. One of his attackers made a cynical comment that he was 'being taken for a dentist appointment.' A sack had been placed over his head, his wrists handcuffed together, and he was bundled into the back of a van. He had been kidnapped.

After a journey of about fifteen minutes, during which the vehicle was driven at speed, it slowed almost to a crawl and was driven onto a bumpy unsurfaced road. After a short distance, the van stopped. The rear doors were flung open and he was forcibly dragged backwards from the rear of the van with a person holding each arm. He heard the sound of heavy doors being unlocked and opened. It appeared to be a garage lockup; there was a strong musty smell of oil. He continued to be dragged backwards over a greasy uneven brick floor. Verbal communication was brief, with the language abusive and threatening.

He was to be punished. Several men were involved. His arms and wrists were forcibly tied to a metal-framed chair. The sack was removed from his head and replaced with a blindfold. One of his abusers held him violently in a headlock whilst another forced open his mouth. A pair of pliers was used to wrench out several of his teeth. The pain was excruciating. He lapsed into unconsciousness.

Evans woke up confused, alone and shivering in the chilly night air, lying in dense damp undergrowth within isolated woodland. He had a vague recollection that he had been dumped there from the back of a van, several hours earlier by two men. His mouth was severely damaged, bruised and bleeding. Having composed his thoughts, slowly and with some difficulty, he stumbled to his feet and stood for several minutes leaning against the trunk of a tree. Patting his jacket pockets, he was surprised and relieved to find he still had his mobile phone. He cautiously made his way through the darkness of the woodland and eventually came to a road and was able to establish his location. From there, he telephoned his twin brother, who collected him and drove him home. He subsequently received private medical treatment and expensive private dentistry. He did not report the attack to the police.

Evans had been humiliated and would seek revenge. From his early youth, he had always been handy with his fists and had never been slow to punish those who crossed him or displayed disloyalty. The punishment would normally have involved a beating with no serious or permanent injury. From this time forward, the punishment he handed out would be brutal: He would ensure he was feared.

Within a month of the attack on him, Evans had paid out significant money to underworld sources to have the 'dentist' identified. Shortly after, the body of a man was found floating in a local river. He was a man with numerous criminal convictions, including for violence and drug-dealing. The police approached his death as 'unexplained.' There were several marks on his body, but not sufficient to confirm he had suffered a violent death. The post-mortem concluded that his death had been caused by drowning. Had he accidentally fallen into the river and drowned, or had crime been involved? At the inquest, it had been noted that a pair of pliers had been found in the top jacket pocket of the deceased. No one could suggest the significance of this. Perhaps one man could!

In his early life, David Evans had run-ins with the police resulting in criminal convictions. He quickly learned never to admit anything and became ultra-cautious in his everyday activities. He was convinced, and probably rightly so, that the authorities had, for many years, been taking an active interest in his activities. David did not own a personal registered mobile phone and never used the main-line telephone in his house to discuss any form of criminal business. Likewise, for any illegal activity, he never used his home computer for Internet research or email communication.

David had been married to Fiona for about twenty years. There were no children from the marriage. They had met when she was working as a model. She had been impressed by his expensive clothes and Porsche sports car. In their later years, Fiona had become aware of his extramarital affairs. However, she accepted it as the price she was willing to pay for a life of luxury.

Their lifestyle was now more of a business relationship. On paper, she headed an international property empire, buying, selling and renting properties in the UK, Spain and elsewhere. The companies were incorporated in various offshore tax havens, with complex and obscure lines of directors and accountability. In reality, Fiona had little knowledge or interest in the companies; her husband was in total control.

He was aware that a dedicated police operation had recently been established to investigate his criminal activities and he was convinced his house and car had been bugged. He would only talk 'drug-related business' when he was out walking in his woodland with one of his trusted 'lieutenants.' Such people were usually close family and friends he had grown up with. Even then, he would insist they switched off their mobile phone and left it in the house. He would then pat them down to ensure they were not fitted with a recording device.

For Evans, the word 'friend' was a pejorative term. Throughout his life, he had never been in, nor had he sought a close relationship with anyone. He was a loner who did not trust anyone and kept people at arm's length. Personal contact and verbal communication were kept to a minimum. He regarded people simply as individuals and associates who could benefit his efforts to achieve his ultimate goal of making money. Sharing his personal and private emotions with others was not part of his agenda.

However, in his late teens, he had realised the benefits of cultivating associates who could be 'persuaded' to assist him in his illegal activities. Late one evening, the young Evans had been arrested by the police on suspicion of vehicle theft and taken to the local custody suite for formal interview. As was his legal right, he demanded the presence of a solicitor to represent him and to be present during the interview. Solicitor Peter Costello, who was on the duty call-out roster, attended at the custody suite and was shown into a small unoccupied interview room. It contained a basic metal table with four chairs. He placed his folder of paperwork on the desktop and sat down.

A few minutes later, Evans had been escorted into the room and was directed to sit on a chair opposite Costello. The custody officer introduced Evans to the solicitor and reminded him of his legal rights to consult privately before the formal interview was undertaken. The officer then left the room, locking the door behind him. Peter Costello was a young recently qualified solicitor employed with the local legal firm that dealt primarily with defence work in criminal cases.

From the outset, Evans took the initiative and spoke first. He sat back in his chair, looking relaxed, and, with a smile, engaged eye contact:

"Sorry to get you out so late tonight. Obviously, you were enjoying a quiet evening… at home, or was it at a party?"

Costello appeared perplexed and frowned but made no verbal response.

Evans spoke slowly and quietly:

"When the cops come in to interview me, may I suggest you take your chair and position yourself in the corner of this room and make your notes from there?"

Costello continued to look perplexed. With an element of indignation, he simply replied: "Pardon?"

In a slow, quietly spoken voice, Evans continued:

"Cannabis."

He paused, then went on:

"You have recently been smoking cannabis. The pungent smell of cannabis is wafting in my direction."

Costello did not contest the allegation. He looked somewhat nervous and gave a weak smile.

Evans gently nodded and offered reassurance:

"Your secret is safe with me."

Before the formal police interview began, Costello positioned his chair in the corner of the room to ensure he kept his distance from the two police officers. It proceeded as a 'no comment' interview. No charges were forthcoming.

In the coming years, the young Costello developed into a mature and experienced defence solicitor. On several occasions, Evans called upon his legal services, for which he paid the solicitor in cash and frequently supplied him with cannabis. The relationship was mutually beneficial to both parties.

In the years that followed, Evans continued to cultivate and 'groom' likely useful contacts. In some cases, it was by direct blackmail; for example, where he had established that an accountant had frequently used the services of a prostitute, spending nights with her at a luxury hotel. In other cases, where he had identified a specific professional businessman target who would be important to the success of criminal activities, his approach would be more long-term and subtle. He would be prepared to invest time and money into the enterprise, including feigning friendship.

For example, Evans initially sought the advice of a local bank manager, the relationship with whom he progressed as a 'business friendship' with an invitation to lunch and picking up the bill. Then, over time, he introduced the bank manager into other social activities. The 'friendship' evolved, with small gifts given, and, eventually, payment made for the bank manager to take his family on a foreign holiday. The professional boundary between bank manager and customer had been breached. Thus, this created a need for discretion and secrecy around the relationship.

Once the bank manager had been fully compromised and made aware that disclosure would ruin his professional reputation and cost him his position within the bank, he would be asked 'favours' which would ultimately involve using his banking knowledge to facilitate the movement and transfer of money obtained from criminal activity, commonly known as money laundering.

In addition to the solicitor and bank manager in his arsenal of useful 'recruited' contacts, there was a police officer, a magistrate, a senior county council official and a customs officer. Evans ensured he acted independently with each; the 'bent' police officer was not aware of the existence or identity of the 'bent' solicitor, etc. Using similar methods of persuasion, entrapment, blackmail and rewarding with significant cash payments and 'retainers', he had also recruited other important 'players' including an aircraft pilot and lorry drivers.

Evans' most audacious recruitment operation involved calling in the services of his now longtime and trusted solicitor, Peter Costello. Evans had a reputation for rewarding loyalty very well and a frightening reputation for rewarding disloyalty with severe punishment and possibly death. He had identified a recently established charity committed to the development of community-based projects to protect the environment. It was a genuine charity, but Evans had seen the opportunity to use its name and aims as a means to further his illegal activities.

At the instigation of Evans, the solicitor, Costello, had sent a letter to the charity stating his firm had been instructed by a successful and influential businessperson to offer significant financial funds to the organisation. The principal stipulation was that the identity of the donor must remain anonymous, otherwise, the offer would be withdrawn. As an offer of goodwill, and to show the approach was genuine, an initial payment of £50,000 would be forthcoming. To launch the project, it was proposed an events agency should be employed to organise the function, with the entire cost funded by the anonymous donor.

A luxury country house hotel located in the rural county of Sussex was booked for the exclusive evening function to be held in the main conference room. In addition, several side rooms were also set aside for the comfort of the VIP guests. Local dignitaries were invited to the private event, which included Members of Parliament, senior politicians and police officers, and influential businesspeople. During the evening, much free champagne and other alcoholic drink was consumed in a convivial and relaxed atmosphere. Naturally, Evans did not make an appearance, nor was his identity known.

The charity's management, the event organisers and the hotel staff all believed the event was being held to launch, and for the sole benefit of, the worthy charity. On the direction of Evans, a small group with devious intentions had infiltrated the gathering. The group had included two high-class prostitutes and several drug dealers who were au fait with discreetly identifying users and supplying them with cocaine. In addition, the dealers were equipped with covert cameras and audio recording devices.

Prior to the commencement of the function, several concealed miniature cameras had been installed within the side rooms. The operation had been engineered to capture photographic evidence of one, and hopefully more, of the prominent dignitaries in embarrassing, compromising and illegal activities. The small group had been pleased with the results they had obtained; the criteria had been met for obtaining the necessary evidence in respect of several of the attendees. At the end of the function, not one of these guests knew what awaited them.

Whether dealing in stolen cars or trading in illegal drugs, Evans' approach was always the same. He was the elusive Boss who organised the criminal activity, from a safe distance, and gave the instruction for the crime to be undertaken. The principal characters in his 'gang' consisted of five men. They were referred to as 'The Committee.' Each member had their own group of criminals who would be called on to undertake the requested crime. Evans would meet with them infrequently, always on an individual basis, and only when absolutely necessary. Such meetings would be prearranged. They would meet at an agreed location, at a fixed date and time. The meets would take place in a crowded environment, such as a football stadium or horse racetrack, which would make any police surveillance extremely difficult.

In most cases, his true identity would not be known to those carrying out the crime. When successful, the offenders would be well paid in cash and that is what mattered to them. Evans always ensured that if things went wrong, there was a 'firewall' between him and the people actually undertaking the crime; no evidence would exist to connect him to the crime.

On the rare occasions when Evans required the use of a mobile phone, he would be supplied with a 'burner phone' resourced by his brother Terry. A 'burner phone' is an inexpensive mobile phone often used by criminals to evade detection by law enforcement agencies. Such a phone protects the identity of the user when conducting business and is untraceable. They are usually destroyed or discarded after limited use, often after only having been used on a single occasion.

As David Evans' criminal drug ambitions had expanded, conflict and mistrust between rival crime organisations increased. His response was to increase the frequency of violence to impose control and supremacy. He considered that the first sign of weakness would halt progress and begin the decline of his empire. Without the swift and brutal punishment of transgressors, others may be 'persuaded' to cooperate with the police and give evidence against him, a scenario he could not even contemplate as he had big ambitions.

Drug trafficking was the most profitable illicit activity in the criminal world. The world's illegal trade in cocaine had an estimated annual value of over £110 billion. The European market for cocaine was estimated at £10 billion, with over £2 billion illegally imported into the UK. The UK has 976,0000 users of cocaine, which is regarded as the drug of choice for an increasing number of middle-class users.

Several years back, when Evans had initially sought to enhance his status in the drug trade by importing cocaine, he had naively undertaken the venture without involving international crime organisations; he had trespassed on their ground. This had resulted in him being severely punished. Although he had achieved revenge for the attack, with the killing of the man known as The Dentist, he had appreciated that to be involved in large-scale importation of cocaine, he needed the experience, cooperation, and finance of established international drug bosses based in the UK.

Now, having been involved in several successful major importation operations, and having profited from the vast amount of money to be made, he once again had ambitions to go it alone without sharing the proceeds – to be the ultimate Boss. It would be brutal. It would be dangerous. It would involve the liquidation of former partners and rivals. He had already removed the lesser players and those who had crossed him. Now he was targeting and removing the top-level UK drug dealers.

To 'remove' his top-level UK rivals, he called on the services of 'The Committee.' The members had the available 'resources' to undertake assassinations and other acts of brutality, usually committed by men who had entered the UK by illegal means on false passports and who would depart the country immediately after committing the crime.

Evans now had the necessary personal wealth, and contacts within Colombian and Mexican organised criminal cartels, to make drug deals without having to work with other 'drug barons' in the UK. He knew how to use the 'dark web' to order and negotiate cocaine importation. He had set up shell companies, which played a pivotal role in money laundering schemes, in countries that had low or no financial regulations. Evans had become aware that in countries such as Columbia, the authorities were reluctant to aid international investigations into alleged crimes committed on their soil.

The murder of UK victims and leaving their bodies in situ had, in the past, been used as a warning to others involved in the drug fraternity. Now it would be considered too dangerous.

Within the UK Home Counties, five different police forces were currently undertaking separate murder investigations where bodies had been found. The common factor was that the victims had been actively involved in the illegal drugs trade. Tentative links between the murders and the gang headed by Evans had been established, but they had nothing positive. Potential witnesses were too fearful to cooperate with police and there was no indication that this would change.

Some months earlier, and after much effort and persuasion, one informant had been recruited by the police. He had been arrested on suspicion of supplying cocaine and, aware of the evidence against him, realised he was likely to receive a long term of imprisonment. Reluctantly, he had agreed to turn informant with the promise of immunity against prosecution and a new identity, plus a significant financial payment.

Within days of agreeing to be a police informant, he had been found murdered with his body floating in a river. He had been tortured. His hands and feet had been bound. He had been severely beaten and his tongue had been cut out. Pinned to his chest was a copy of a newspaper article reporting on the police investigation into drug dealers. This was a clear and brutal message to anyone contemplating talking to the police. A different approach would be required by law enforcement agencies if they were to develop a more specific and targeted intelligence model.

At senior police level, agreement would be reached that the five separate murder investigation teams would continue. Close liaison between the five teams would be paramount in the sharing of intelligence. This would be achieved by regular contact linking their respective HOLMES2 data bases. [HOLMES2, the Home Office Large Major Enquiry System, is the information technology predominately used by UK police forces for the investigation of major crime.]

In addition to the five murder investigations, police intelligence suggested that other people involved in the drug trade had 'disappeared.' Often, such people did not have fixed accommodation, nor did they keep within a stable circle of friends, which made it difficult to establish if they had just moved or if something more sinister had happened to them.

Police intelligence indicated that two further named drug dealers had 'disappeared.' It was likely they had been kidnapped and would be murdered. Perhaps more sinister, the two were regarded as 'major drug importers' higher up in the hierarchy of the drug dealing trade. This indicated a developing and dangerous turf war between competing UK gangs.

The two individuals were considered direct rivals to Evans, seeking to achieve overall control of the lucrative cocaine trade. Each of the drug 'bosses' was equally ruthless and capable of ordering the liquidation of their rivals. Evans considered he was also a target. The increased frequency and violence were causing public concern and demands from the media and politicians for results. A more concentrated and effective police response was required.

Public figures in positions of influence on government decision-making, and those individuals involved with the judiciary, were now targeted by drug gangs in an effort to subvert the due process of law. Recently, a male Member of Parliament, who held a senior ministerial position, had visited the chief constable for his area to report, with much embarrassment, that an attempt had been made to blackmail him.

The MP had received a sealed envelope, sent to his home address, marked 'strictly personal' and containing coloured photographs of himself undressed and in a compromising position with an attractive, much younger woman. In another photograph, he could be seen snorting white powder, which he acknowledged was probably cocaine. He assured the chief constable he had never before taken the drug.

The photographs had been taken, without his knowledge or consent, at a recent charity event he had attended. Each photograph clearly identified him, showing his full facial features. The identity of the woman could not be ascertained from the photographs. Her facial features were obscured, no doubt deliberately, by her long blonde hair. The photographs showed her in a state of undress, displaying sexy underwear and much naked flesh.

The MP remembered the early part of the evening in detail. He had been flattered by the attention of the attractive young woman. She appeared interested in his role as a member of parliament and wanted to know more. At her invitation, and with her holding a full bottle of champagne, they walked to one of the unoccupied small side rooms to relax and talk in comfort. They talked, flirted and consumed much champagne; she was extremely attentive. He acknowledged that he got very drunk during their time together and, from then on, his recollection of what took place was rather vague. Yes, pleasurable sexual activity occurred, and, on reflection, he recalled she encouraged him to 'snort' a line of cocaine. He had no recollection how the evening had ended or how he had arrived back in his hotel room.

The MP said he was now extremely embarrassed, and concerned, about what had taken place. The existence of the photographs had the potential to devastate his career and public reputation. He had clearly been the subject of a sophisticated entrapment operation, but he was not offering that as a defence for his inexcusable behaviour. Accompanying the photographs was a type-written message, simply stating: 'We will be in contact. In exchange for the original photos, and our silence, you will be required to undertake a specified task. Failure to do so will result in the photos being released to the media.' Details of the 'specific task' were not mentioned. No doubt, this would be given in a later anonymous communication.

Taking hold of the photographs, and reviewing each one, the chief constable cynically asked:

"May I assume this mysterious young lady did not tell you her name or give you her business card?"

The MP did not respond.

The chief constable subsequently reported the matter to the Home Office and liaised with senior officials at the Cabinet Office. He was able to confirm that this had been the first reported account of an attempt to blackmail a dignitary who had attended the charity event. Under the direction of the chief constable, discrete enquiries were undertaken to obtain the names of all dignitaries who had attended the charity function to establish if any had received similar compromising and threatening correspondence. At this time, it remained unclear whether the MP had been the sole target because of his prominent position in government, or if it had been a 'blanket' operation to entrap any dignitary who appeared vulnerable to the temptation of attractive young women, drink and drugs.

Evans' pursuit of useful 'recruits' had continued over a period of years. As the years had progressed, his brazen methods and ambitions to target important individuals had increased with much success and personal financial reward. His evil criminal tentacles had spread into many elements of society, and the judiciary, which made successful detection and prosecution of offenders more difficult.

It was said that he had financed witness intimidation, which had resulted in several crown court prosecutions of drug dealers being abandoned and others where juries had unexpectedly returned Not Guilty verdicts.

During one major crown court trial, which involved the prosecution of four defendants for the importation of cocaine, and in the sixth week of a trial which was expected to last for three months, the judge had been forced to halt proceedings having received allegations of jury tampering. Following careful review, the trial had to be abandoned with the Crown Prosecution Service ordering a retrial. Evans was said to have financed jury intimidation.

In that case, evidence had emerged that three members of the jury had been approached in menacing circumstances and, with the promise of a significant cash payment, advised that they should vote to find the defendants not guilty. When interviewed by police, several other jurors had recalled suspicious incidents. When leaving the crown court building after a day's proceedings, they had felt uncomfortable and suspected they had been under surveillance and followed. The anonymous individuals who made the threats allegedly knew the identities, home addresses and workplaces of each of the jurors.

In a further major drug-related crown court trial, a principal prosecution witness had unexpectedly departed the UK and declined to return to give evidence. Without providing any form of medical confirmation, he cited serious health issues. The Crown Prosecution Service had no option but to offer no evidence and withdraw the case. The two defendants, who had been held in custody and were clearly significant drug dealers, were formally found not guilty and released.

In yet another drug-related case, just prior to the beginning of the crown court trial, a female witness had been out with her pet dog walking through a local woodland when it unexpectedly ran off into the thick undergrowth. The dog did not respond to the lady's calls and could not be found. The distressed owner rushed home and returned to the woodland with her husband. After a detailed search, the husband spotted the dog in the distance. A noose had been placed around its neck and deliberately tied to the branch of a tree. The dog, gently swaying in the breeze about six feet from the ground, was dead.

The lady owner was devastated. She, and her family, were in no doubt that the killing of her dog was a warning not to give evidence at the forthcoming court proceedings. She became physically and emotionally unfit to give evidence, with the prosecution subsequently withdrawn.

With an increasing number of drug-related crown court trials failing to reach a successful conclusion because of witness or jury intimidation, David Evans and his associates were often credited with being responsible.

The young David John Evans had been born into poverty with little prospect of achieving a fulfilling and successful life. Unloved, and the product of a violent father, the boy lived every day in fear of being physically beaten. His father forced him to commit crime and punished him if he failed to deliver. David received minimal formal education and, with his family background, his prospects for advancement in legitimate society were limited.

He had grown up as a loner with no close friends. Crime, enforced by fear and violence, would be his route to a lucrative future. By early middle age, Evans had become an extremely wealthy individual. Privately, he considered his wealth exceeded one hundred million pounds, plus several expensive properties located abroad. None of it had been declared to the legitimate UK authorities.

He did not own a UK bank account and had never paid any UK income tax. He continued to operate, partly through necessity, as a reclusive individual. His use of normal telephone and Internet communication was extremely limited. He was aware his life was in danger from rival drug gangs. In addition, the UK law enforcement authorities actively targeted all aspects of his life, keen to deprive him of his freedom and his wealth, which had been gained unlawfully.

The profits to be made from importing and supplying cocaine were vast. To gain and retain control of the lucrative drug trade required ruthlessness to dominate every aspect of the process; from drug importation to supply and the ability to cultivate individuals in positions of authority to elicit their cooperation. This was achieved by violence, extortion, abduction and even murder. The payment of significant cash rewards was an added incentive. The well-oiled cogs of the organisation were kept turning by making sure it took care of its own.

The corruption of law enforcement officials, plus the aggressive disruption of the prosecution process by witness tampering and jury nobbling, was a worrying and escalating development. Whenever and wherever the police and other government institutions addressed the concerning issue of the cocaine drug trade which operated in the Home Counties, the name David Evans came to the fore as the principal target.

The critical point had been reached. A positive and immediate response was demanded.

A top-level meeting was held at the Home Office in London. Senior government officials, with responsibility for law and order, and senior police officers attended the roundtable meeting. The niceties of diplomatic language were absent. The blame game was very much in evidence. A senior government minister directed, in an off-the-record remark, that:

"People with responsibility for dealing with crime need to get off their fucking arses and sort this mess out. Sort it, or heads will roll. And I don't mean maybe."

A junior civil servant, in attendance as a note-taker, sidled up to a nervous-looking senior police officer and whispered:

"That's politics in operation. A general election is just around the corner. Certain ministers are worried about losing their seats, so the big stick comes out and the blame game begins."

To meet the challenge, a dedicated team of experienced detectives and other specialists, including forensic, technical, computer and communication experts, was formed. The team had been drawn from the various Home Counties police forces, plus from the Metropolitan Police and the National Crime Agency. The team would operate under extreme secrecy with the title Operation Goldfinger.

For reasons of confidentiality and security, the team operated from a building located within a large active military Army base situated on Salisbury Plain. It had been built and used as an army detention centre for personnel convicted by military court.

The building was isolated some distance away from other military buildings and personnel. It was surrounded by high electrified fencing, with entry via a security turnstile gate. In recent times, the centre had occasionally been used to accommodate senior military staff when undertaking and planning military manoeuvres. Now, being used by the Operation Goldfinger team, with unnamed personnel wearing civilian suits, would not raise any suspicion from army personnel working on the base. For the duration of the operation, the team members would live in hotel accommodation in nearby towns.

Chapter Two

Operation Goldfinger

The military building housing the Operation Goldfinger team had received extensive security updates both internally and externally. Prior to commencing the operation, the Major Incident Room had been equipped with heavy-duty metal drawers and filing cabinets fitted with digital keypad security locks. A complete HOLMES2 computer system had been installed.

Detective Chief Inspector Donald Ferguson, a proud Scotsman with a deep speaking voice, had been appointed the Senior Investigating Officer (SIO) to lead the Operation Goldfinger team. He was fifty-five years of age and an extremely competent and long-serving detective. Ferguson had the reputation for being a firm but fair disciplinarian. He did not waste words with long explanations. He was well qualified for his new role and came straight to the point on what he required from his staff.

Before joining the police service at the age of thirty, he had served in the British Royal Navy as a chief petty officer. In his appearance, manner and bearing, he still retained many of the attributes from his military past. When on duty, DCI Ferguson always dressed smartly in a three-piece suit with highly polished black shoes. He was slim, fit and a teetotaller. Hill-running was one of his hobbies. He possessed some mild eccentricities, on which team members quietly commented. When at a team meeting, and concentrating on an issue, he would frequently close his eyes and, with his hands clasped together, using his two index fingers, gently stroke his well-trimmed greying beard. Then, when he had reached a decision, he would open his eyes, gesticulate with his right index finger and pronounce in a few words the action he wanted to be undertaken.

The team members were also amused by the large brown leather vintage 1970s briefcase, with a brass push clasp fastening, which he would carry with him to the office. It had belonged to his late father when he was a detective with the City of Glasgow Police. He had presented it to Donald when he first joined the police. Donald had been fond of his late father and had experienced much sorrow at his early death from alcoholism. Perhaps behind the DCI's rather hard exterior lurked a more sentimental and caring individual.

When on duty, Ferguson never spoke about his personal or social life. He was a widower, but nothing further was known about his family life. It was noticeable that he never joined staff at social events, not even for coffee or at lunch breaks, preferring to remain in his office. He believed a 'healthy barrier' should always exist between officers and their staff.

Each morning, DCI Ferguson would be first to book on duty at 07:30 hours. He would spend the first thirty minutes reviewing the results of the previous day's actions and the latest intelligence received, recording his observations and thoughts in a bound A4 exercise book. The first formal briefing of the day would commence at 08:00 hours, in his office, with the three detective inspectors and the Office Manager. This was an opportunity to discuss the previous day's activities and agree on the course of future investigations.

Detective Inspector Fatima Ramiz was one of the three detective inspectors. She was in her early thirties with a master's degree in criminology and had been marked out, by her force, as a high-flyer with the potential for a much higher rank.

Detective Inspector Richard Penfold was forty-five years of age with extensive service within operational CID and on specialist units, such as counterterrorism. He had a reputation, particularly among junior officers, for his brusque 'no nonsense' manner.

John Cheeseman was the third detective inspector. He was fifty-two years of age and had spent much of his police career working in divisional CID.

Barry Bishop was the oldest of the group, approaching sixty-two years of age. He had retired from the police, at the rank of detective inspector, with over thirty years' service, and had taken up the civilian role of HOLMES2 Office Manager. He was considered an expert in the field of criminal intelligence.

At 09:00 hours, the five would adjourn to the main briefing room, where the DCI would chair the team meeting. From day one, he emphasised the need for absolute discretion, confidentiality and loyalty in dealing with Operation Goldfinger investigations. This extended to ensuring the highest professional standards were always maintained: reports submitted must be 100% accurate and complete, with no paperwork left unattended on desks but kept in secure cabinets. Staff were forbidden to discuss any aspect of the investigation with colleagues outside the investigation team, or with family or partners.

The principal target for Operation Goldfinger was David Evans, plus his extended web of associates. Significant evidence was sought to establish their involvement in the importation of the Class A drug cocaine, together with the murder and disappearance of individuals connected to the drug trade within the Home Counties, and the attempt to 'recruit' officials in positions of influence. In the investigation list of priorities, Evans sat at the pinnacle of the triangle, along with the identification of his associates. Targeting potential informants and convincing them to cooperate would be vital for the investigation to succeed.

In the initial two weeks of the operation, extensive research had been undertaken to gather and collate intelligence from the national criminal database at New Scotland Yard and from local police forces. Previously identified low-level street drug dealers and registered informants had also been visited by members of the team, often with promises of payment. Minimal relevant intelligence had yet to be forthcoming from informants. There was a clear indication that those who had had any contact with Evans and his associates feared for their own safety if found to be speaking with the police.

With the appropriate signed legal authorities and warrants in place, technical surveillance equipment and miniature cameras had been discreetly installed in the approach to Evans' house, with details recorded of all vehicles and people coming and going. In addition, all communication to and from the house, including telephone and Internet, had been subject to monitoring 24 hours per day. This included mobile phones used by close family members, suspected of working for him, and known associates.

For some time, Evans had been aware of police interest in his activities. Recent feedback to him from people who had recently been interviewed by the police also made him realise that police involvement had significantly increased. Therefore, he took extra precautions to ensure no 'business' associate visited his home, nor did any communication emanate from within the house which even hinted at his criminal activity.

He had been made aware that with recent developments in technology, even when a mobile telephone in the owner's possession had been switched off, the person could still be tracked by law enforcement agencies. For this reason, Evans rarely carried a mobile phone.

Fortunately, brother Terry Evans wasn't quite so meticulous or cautious when talking on his own mobile phone. He never directly spoke on his mobile about any criminal activity, however, he enjoyed gossiping with his friends and would often comment that he was driving David 'in the Merc' to wherever he was going. This useful information, thus, gave the Operation Goldfinger team advanced knowledge to facilitate surveillance cover to track Evans when he left his home.

Located within the walled estate, Evans had a stable block which had been converted to house his collection of classic sports cars. A recent acquisition from the Bonhams classic car auction was a 1989 Ferrari Testarossa grand tourer sports car; colour - Rosa Corsa red with beige leather seats and a V12 mid-engine. It had a top speed of over 186 miles per hour and had been purchased by Evans for £210,000: a car too valuable and delicate to drive on the open public roads.

To buy into respectability, he had purchased membership of the Goodwood Road Racing Club. The Goodwood motor racing circuit was located within the Goodwood Estate of 11,000 acres, nestled at the foot of the Sussex Downs in the heart of West Sussex.

Early on a Friday morning, the Ferrari was loaded onto his motorised vehicle transporter and driven out of the main gates, heading towards Goodwood. His twin brother Terry drove the vehicle, with David Evans seated on the front passenger seat. The previous day, Terry, whilst gossiping to a friend on his mobile telephone, had mentioned that early the next day he was taking David to Goodwood in the vehicle transporter. Monitoring his telephone communications had enabled Operation Goldfinger to arrange surveillance cover.

Whenever Evans left his house, he would be discreetly followed by two of his 'boys.' In effect, they were his bodyguards and 'spotters' who would constantly, and at a distance, look out for any signs of trouble. Evans was aware he had enemies. Given the opportunity, they could be as ruthless as him. The 'boys', driving in a Land Rover

Discovery, picked up the vehicle transporter a couple of miles away from the house and followed it, always keeping five hundred yards or more behind, travelling south en route to Goodwood.

About an hour into the journey, the vehicle transporter, travelling down the M4 motorway, turned onto a service station forecourt for petrol. Evans alighted from the vehicle and, with the pump nozzle in his hand, began filling the fuel tank. The Land Rover Discovery pulled in and stopped on the opposite side of the fuel pump. One of the 'boys' got out and, without acknowledging Evans, began to fill the Discovery with fuel. As he moved closer to the pump to replace the fuel-line nozzle, and without looking at Evans, he whispered:

"You're being followed. Two men in dark blue Focus. Looks like the law."

Evans and the 'boy' got back into their respective vehicles and drove off without exchanging a word or knowing glance. As the transporter exited the petrol station forecourt, he noted the dark blue Ford Focus, with two men in the front seats, parked on the service road.

Arriving at Goodwood Racing Circuit, the vehicle transporter was driven into the 'member owners' paddock. The Ferrari was carefully unloaded and, under guidance from the paddock Marshalls, parked alongside other classic sports cars. In all, over thirty cars had been registered to participate in the organised Track Day. David Evans appeared relaxed, shaking hands and speaking with many of the fellow entrants.

With a hot mug of coffee in his hand, he continued to slowly walk around the paddock stopping to look admiringly at other classic sports cars and gossip with their owners. His brother, Terry, remained in the background caring for the parked Ferrari. He was not a club member. His presence was only permitted as Evans' assistant and mechanic.

The Clerk of the Course called the owners together in the paddock yard to brief them on the Track Day's schedule, including the various technical and health and safety regulations. Each car was examined by a technical inspector to ensure the appropriate requirements were met. Then each owner had to show their official owners membership badge to confirm they were qualified to drive on the race circuit.

With the formalities completed, Evans slipped into his regulation red fire-resistant racing suit and put on his red full-face safety helmet. He climbed into his Ferrari and clipped closed the full body harness. He was ready to proceed. He pushed the starter button. The powerful V-12 engine exploded into life with the roar of a jet engine. The barrier to the pit lane was lifted.

With all the car engines fired into life, they moved in formation and snaked slowly towards the race circuit. A large noticeboard situated at the entrance to the pit lane listed details of each car, with the names of the respective drivers and scheduled times they were permitted to use the track.

Track Days were designed to give owners the opportunity to test and enjoy themselves and their classic race cars in safety on a genuine racetrack. Racing between individual cars was not permitted.

The Goodwood racetrack was a two-and-a-half-mile circuit dating back to 1948. It began life as the perimeter track for ex-military airfield RAF Westhampnett, which was constructed during World War ll. It had served as a Battle of Britain base for Spitfire and Hurricane aircraft. From 1948 to 1966, the circuit frequently held major British motor races. Over the years, the circuit played host to many famous drivers including Stirling Moss,

Mike Hawthorn and Graham Hill. The circuit was now noted for its annual Festival of Speed, Goodwood Revival events and private functions for classic owners' clubs.

Only club members were permitted access to the paddock, the pit and the racetrack, and various other restricted areas. However, on certain occasions, motor racing enthusiasts were permitted limited access to spectator areas overlooking the owners' paddock and sections of the circuit. Particularly on Track Days, many fans attended, clasping expensive cameras with telephoto lenses.

The presence of two undercover detectives from Operation Goldfinger, mingling with the many enthusiasts and taking numerous photographs of the cars and owners in the paddock, would not raise any suspicion. Naturally, the officers' photographs included many of Evans talking with other owners. Were the owners simply men enjoying a day out playing with their expensive toys, or were some using the opportunity to meet fellow criminals to make drug deals?

After an exhilarating morning driving his Ferrari, Evans parked his car back at the members' paddock. He stepped from his Ferrari, met with his brother Terry and together they walked the short distance to the restaurant. They shared a table and ordered a fish and chip lunch.

The restaurant was busy with classic car owners and enthusiasts. Terry whispered something which clearly interested his brother but he made no immediate response. At the conclusion of their meal, Evans ordered coffee and, rather strangely, a bottle of champagne which he insisted should be delivered unopened to his table.

On completion of their coffee, the twins stood up and walked slowly towards the exit, with Evans placing the bottle of champagne under his left arm. Before he reached the door, he stopped at a nearby table and turned and looked down to address the two seated men. Gaining eye contact with the nearest of the two, he spoke calmly:

"Hope you both enjoyed your morning on the racetrack. What car were you driving?"

The two looked at each other with puzzled expressions. The first eventually answered:

"No, we were just fans watching."

Evans gave a wry smile.

"Shame. It would have been interesting to see how your Ford Focus car would have performed on the racetrack."

Neither of the two seated detectives replied nor
showed any facial expression.

Evans placed the bottle of champagne firmly on the
table directly in front of them.

"My gift to DCI Ferguson. Suggest you tell him he
needs to improve the quality of his undercover team.
Good day, officers."

He turned and walked from the building.

Out of embarrassment, the two young detectives
sat motionless looking at the bottle. Then, a little police
humour kicked in, with one of the officers commenting:

"Do you think it would be a disciplinary matter to
accept this gift from a suspected villain we were investigating?"

His colleague, smiled and said:

"Definitely a no-no. Can't see the DCI giving his
approval. Best to leave the bottle on the table."

The two officers sheepishly left the restaurant and
drove back to the Operation Goldfinger Office.

Back at the operation's HQ, the two detectives briefed
DCI Ferguson and the team on the events of their visit
to Goodwood Race Circuit and the lunchtime encounter
with Evans. To their relief, the DCI didn't appear

annoyed. He listened in silence to their report, with his customary position of eyes closed and gently stroking his beard. He then looked around at the team:

"Pure bravado. Evans is clearly rattled. He now knows he is the subject of intensive police investigation. He is worried. Worried people make mistakes and undertake impulsive actions. That's good. We must keep up the pressure and identify his mistakes. He is an arrogant, powerful and violent villain. We must be prepared for the unexpected. All our actions and procedures must be 100% correct. He will employ top-ranking lawyers to challenge and discredit our actions."

The DCI paused, consulted his notebook and then continued:

"In the short time we have been running Operation Goldfinger, Evans has been at the top of our targeting pyramid. We have endeavoured to build a case against him by technical means and by personal intelligence from interviewing low-level street drug dealers. Neither method has produced much valued intelligence. He and his associates are extremely wary in their use of telephone and Internet communication, and the street drug dealers are too fearful to speak to us."

The DCI took a further pause, considered his next response and continued:

"I believe we must develop a much larger short-term operation covering the Home Counties and involving all the respective police forces. We need to spread the police net much wider to gather the evidence needed to mount a successful prosecution against Evans and his gang. I will urgently seek a top-level meeting at ACPO level (Association of Chief Police Officers) to recommend a major joint-forces operation. I will then discuss further the outcome with you."

With the incident room meeting continuing, the Office Manager then ran through the results of various other actions undertaken that day and issued instructions for the following day's investigations.

He also undertook his 'daily welfare check' with team members by asking each, in turn, if they had any concerns or matters requiring discussion. Staff welfare is especially important when officers are working long hours and away from their normal place of employment. From the outset, members had been assured that if they had any personal or professional issues, which they may wish to discuss in private, their respective detective inspectors were always available to listen and give guidance.

Before adjourning the staff meeting, DCI Ferguson made a final comment:

"The episode this afternoon with the champagne bottle has potentially serious implications. My appointment as SIO for Operation Goldfinger has never been made public. So, how come Evans knows? Possibly, from some careless talk picked up by one of his associates or, and more sinisterly, has he received inside information from a member of the police service? Going forward, additional caution must be employed. Remember, nothing from this investigation should be discussed with, nor mentioned to, anyone not authorised to share the information."

Several days following on from his visit to Goodwood, Evans left home early with Terry driving a silver-coloured Mercedes coupe. They headed towards Liverpool. The Operation Goldfinger team had knowledge of this car.

During the previous week, a small magnetic GPS tracking device had successfully been attached to the underside of the vehicle's subframe. Throughout the journey, at a discreet distance, the Mercedes was tracked.

The brothers' intention had been to spend the afternoon watching Liverpool Football Club, their home and favourite Premier League team. The team were playing at home at their Anfield stadium. Joining the long queue of cars slowly entering the large car park, the surveillance team lost sight of the Mercedes. This did not cause concern as, using the GPS tracker, they easily found the parked car. In the distance, the two detectives observed the brothers walking towards the turnstiles and quickly joined the slowly moving queue.

Once in the stadium, and without any apparent conversation, the twins parted, walking in opposite directions towards the main stands. Both quickly disappeared into the vast crowd of singing and cheering supporters. The two detectives had lost their target somewhere in the maximum capacity crowd of 53,000.

Evans continued to venture further into the crowd. Several times, he circulated back on himself to ensure he wasn't being followed. At what was clearly a previously identified location, he stopped and held a brief conversation with two men. The three then parted and walked away in different directions. The arranged meeting had been held to discuss and agree the final arrangements for a forthcoming major importation of cocaine from Columbia.

The two detectives never found Evans in the stadium nor realised a 'drugs meeting' had taken place. At the conclusion of the football match, the detectives decided to return to the car park to observe the Mercedes, and there they waited. Neither Evans nor Terry returned to the parked Mercedes. After two hours, the detectives abandoned the mission and drove back to Operation Goldfinger base to report on their fruitless day.

Seated around the incident room's main table, the two detectives gave an update on their trip to Liverpool. DCI Ferguson looked across at the Incident Room Manager and asked him to check the computer to ascertain, via GPS tracking, the current location of the Mercedes. Barry Bishop keyed into the system and immediately shook his head and looked in disbelief towards the DCI.

"What's the problem, Barry? You look like you've seen a ghost," queried the DCI.

The Incident Room Manager looked across to the SIO and replied:

"Worse than that, Sir. The system says the Mercedes is stationary in our secure, locked and bolted car park at the rear of this building. Or, more correctly, I would suggest that at the Liverpool stadium car park, the GPS tracker device was removed from the Mercedes and attached to our CID car."

There was total silence in the incident room.

The DCI broke the silence and said:

"This is not the time to be angry. Once again, this has demonstrated what a brazen, arrogant and confident man we are dealing with. First, he identifies me by rank and name as being the SIO. Now, no doubt, he has identified the location of our base. We must work on the assumption that he has access to technical equipment able to monitor progress of the GPS tracker."

Early the following day, DCI Ferguson travelled to London to attend the Home Office to brief ACPO on the current state of Operation Goldfinger. He did not hold back in his assessment, explaining the difficulties being encountered in trying to gain inside intelligence on Evans and his associates.

Senior government ministers, with responsibility for policing, were also present. They neither asked questions nor identified themselves. The importance of their presence was not lost on DCI Ferguson. It was plainly evident that government ministers expected significant results; the police must take swift, decisive and positive action.

Because of the Home Office briefing, a high-level meeting was called with the police forces covering the Home Counties. Agreement was sought for a coordinated and swift wide-ranging police operation. When required, such operations could be undertaken at short notice. This was achieved. No press briefing was given until after the event.

Once completed, a joint press release was issued. DCI Ferguson acted as a member of the senior police briefing team. His role as the SIO for Operation Goldfinger was not mentioned. The press release stated:

'More than 150 arrests have been made during a crackdown on serious and violent crime. Property seized includes fifty vehicles, thirty firearms, sixty-five knives, a quantity of drugs (mainly cannabis and cocaine) and £152,000 in cash. It was a joint operation involving police forces from the Home Counties and the Metropolitan Police. More than

1000 officers participated in the three days of action. The operation primarily focused on arterial roads and motorways in and around Greater London. The operation used automatic number plate recognition (ANRP) and intelligence to target vehicles linked to violent crime. Private and business premises were also searched with stolen property recovered.'

The operation had been undertaken partly as cover for the more sensitive and complex investigation to target street-level drug dealers and, thus, gain intelligence for Operation Goldfinger. The agreement was that each police force would process and prosecute suspects arrested within their own county. The intelligence gained would be available for research by the Operation Goldfinger team.

Intelligence gathered during the joint county police operation suggested that an increasing confidence existed among drug gang bosses, such as Evans, that they were 'untouchable' and beyond the reach of law enforcement agencies. Their secretive criminal networks were proving difficult and dangerous to penetrate.

It has been said that Evans' ambition was to become the most powerful and wealthiest drug baron in the UK. In a few short years, he had already acquired great wealth. His recent actions had demonstrated that the violence and extortion employed by him would increase to satisfy his ambitions. The massive demand for cocaine in Europe and beyond was escalating at a frightening speed, which would increase the opportunity to give him more wealth and power.

The frightening consequences of the illegal drug trade in Colombia, with the possibility that it could be repeated elsewhere, was a worrying prospect for democratic governments. Colombia, and other neighbouring countries, had witnessed heavily armed drug cartels fighting each other and killing, by assassination, countless police officers, judges and witnesses. Their massive wealth and power had also enabled them to bribe government and legal officials. Evans' ambitions must be thwarted by positive government direction and commitment.

Chapter Three

The Cruise

The escalating paranoia displayed by David Evans was having a detrimental effect on his home life and that of his loyal wife Fiona. For some time, she had felt uneasy about leaving the house to visit friends or to spend time at the shops. Most days, she remained unseen at home in their large, luxurious but isolated house behind high walls.

In their twenty-year marriage, she had mainly enjoyed the luxury life her husband's increasing wealth had given her. Yes, she had appreciated that the vast wealth had been gained through illegal business activities, and the main product was the importation of the Class A drug cocaine.

She had never taken an active interest in his business dealings, but, with an increased degree of nervousness, was aware that he always used her name as the principal director of all the companies he had incorporated and located in the various offshore tax havens and UK bank accounts he handled. He would hand her official documents to sign, which she did without question, but never understood the significance of any of them.

To the outside world, she appeared confident and fulfilled. In reality, she was frightened, insecure and unhappy. One of her few interests, known by her friends, was her compulsion to enter the competitions advertised in women's magazines. The excitement in winning was more important than the actual, often mundane, prize. No doubt, because she was a regular subscriber to such magazines, she received an introductory copy of a new publication entitled 'Insight', a lifestyle and fashion magazine.

To launch the magazine, the publishers had run a major value competition, the prize being an all-expenses-paid eight-day cruise on the Cunard liner Queen Elizabeth on a round trip from Southampton to Madeira. There would be two joint prize winners. The prize had been sponsored jointly by the publishers, along with various cosmetic companies who were to advertise in the new magazine.

Fiona was pleasantly surprised to receive a telephone call to say she had won the main prize. The telephone call was followed up by the delivery of a bouquet of flowers and an official invitation giving details of the cruise and what would be required of her. The two joint winners would be required to participate in photoshoots and promotions undertaken during the cruise with photographs used in future editions of the magazine.

In her younger years, Fiona had been a fashion model and was still attractive, making her perfect for the role. Her husband, David, had paid little attention to her forthcoming adventure. No doubt, he believed it would give him the opportunity to pursue one of his extramarital affairs.

Fiona was collected from her home and driven in a black limousine to Southampton cruise terminal on the south coast of England. There, she was met by Helen Harrison-Forbes, the magazine representative, and Pippa Williams, the other joint winner. The three ladies were about the same age and, so Fiona thought, were of similar appearance and character. She instantly felt at ease in their company and looked forward to spending their week together.

The three were welcomed aboard ship and escorted to a small private area for a glass of champagne and the opportunity to get to know each other. They were then escorted to their separate cabins, referred to as state-rooms, on the fourth deck, each with a balcony. Fiona was impressed. She continued to be so when she joined the other two ladies at a reserved dining table in the Britannia Restaurant for their evening dinner, with more champagne.

The next morning, the three continued their escorted tour of the massive luxury cruise liner, which accommodated 2000 passengers and 950 crew. Helen Harrison-Forbes, who had previous knowledge of the ship, possessed all the necessary passes to restricted areas which required pre-booking and payment.

The ladies spent their days together enjoying the facilities, including being pampered with cosmetics in the beauty salons, plus massages, saunas and much more in the Well-being gymnasium. Helen took the necessary photographs and said she would write up and prepare the articles for publication in the magazine.

Their friendship developed and deepened as the week progressed. Throughout the cruise, especially during the evening over meals and evening drinks, they spoke about their lives, their hopes and fears. Fiona felt particularly safe and comfortable in Helen's presence. She disclosed more about her life, hopes and fears than she had ever confided in another woman.

She confided that she had always wanted children, but it didn't fit in with her husband's aspirations. Helen gently probed, offering sympathy, support and advice where relevant, but never appearing intrusive. Fiona welcomed the opportunity to talk so openly.

Slowly, and perhaps without really appreciating what she was divulging, Fiona indicated that she was uneasy, even unhappy, with her life and with her husband's business lifestyle. To further gentle probing from Helen, she indicated that he made a vast amount of money but said she didn't ask where it came from. Yes, probably from illegal activities. And no, her husband's name did not appear on any official UK document. Why was this? She didn't know.

Her husband, David, controlled everything, but he had put everything in her name. Yes, in name, she was the principal director of his many offshore registered companies, but she didn't understand them and was increasingly becoming concerned with the growing interest being shown by the UK authorities. Official letters would arrive addressed to her with forms to be completed, or difficult questions to be answered, and even requests for her to attend government offices for interview. Her husband would take them from her and, apparently, give them to his 'tame' solicitors to deal with.

Day Five of the cruise: The weather was warm and sunny. The Queen Elizabeth was anchored a mile offshore from the island of Madeira. The three ladies were sunbathing on sun-loungers around the swimming pool and sipping the occasional glass of Martini. Life appeared good. Could it last? Her isolated life at home in England seemed a million miles away. Their days had been spent being pampered; their evenings fine-dining with more champagne.

Helen sat up, raised her sunglasses and positioned them on the top of her head. She turned and leaned forward towards Fiona and gently whispered:

"Fiona, are you happy?"

Fiona smiled, frowned, and after a slight pause, replied:

"Yes, for the present."

Helen continued:

"Forgive me for asking, but are you worried about the future?"

"Yes."

"May I help?"

Fiona paused for thought:

"Not sure how." Then added: "You'd make a good agony aunt for your magazine."

"I feel you have genuine reason to fear the future."

"Why do you say that?" responded Fiona.

Helen placed her hand gently over Fiona's shaking hand.

"May I be frank with you?"

"Yes."

"This is not easy. It is not straightforward. Please trust me and hear me out to the end."

"I promise," said a perplexed Fiona.

"Let's consider what you have already inferred about your current life. Your husband makes vast amounts of money, and you don't know how. He controls many dubious offshore companies and bank accounts, but nothing is in his name. He has registered everything in

GEORGE A SMITH: *CLIMATE OF FEAR*

your name, with you obeying his instructions to sign
official and legal documents."

"That's about right."

Helen leaned a little closer and whispered:

"And the authorities are pursuing you with difficult questions. I would suggest that the authorities will
continue in an ever-aggressive manner until they receive
answers."

Fiona looked worried but did not reply.

Helen continued:

"Fiona, you are an intelligent lady. Are you in denial
about your husband's activities?"

"Perhaps."

"Are you in fear of your husband?"

"Yes, very much so."

"Let's remove any ambiguity and get straight to the
facts. Are you prepared for this?"

"Yes."

"Your husband is a major international drug dealer,
importing vast quantities of cocaine."

"I didn't say that," responded Fiona.

Helen, still gently holding Fiona by her hand, asked:

"He is. Is he not?"

"Yes."

Helen, looking directly into Fiona's eyes, questioned:

"And, responsible for inflicting violence and, possibly, murdering others?"

"That's what I believe."

Helen adjusted her sitting position and held Fiona's shaking right hand between both her hands.

"On paper, all the responsibility for his dubious companies and activities are in your name."

Fiona nodded in agreement and replied:

"I assume so."

Helen responded slowly in a very serious voice:

"When he gets arrested, then convicted and sentenced to life in prison, the authorities will come knocking at your door looking for you. Difficult questions will be asked. Even more difficult answers will be required. What's your future? Likely, you will end up financially broke followed by many wasted years in prison."

Fiona sat in silence looking unwell. Her perfect summer cruise had suddenly come to a halt. Pippa knelt by her side and handed Fiona a glass of cold water. Leaning forward, Pippa gave her a reassuring hug.

Helen continued: "We can help you through this diffi-cult time, but in return, we need your full cooperation."

Fiona first looked at Helen and then turned to look at Pippa. She asked: "Are you the police?"

Fiona, speaking slowly in a reassuring voice, replied:

"No. We are from a similar government agency with the necessary legal authority to offer you immunity from criminal prosecution in exchange for your cooperation."

Fiona, still holding a shaking glass of water, queried: "MI5 then?"

Helen just nodded.

Fiona then turned to face Pippa and asked:

"And are you also MI5?"

Pippa also nodded.

Calmly and precisely, Helen explained what would be required from Fiona, and, in exchange, how she would be placed on the Witness Protection Programme and given a new identity to live anywhere in the world with a generous pension.

Later in the day, they adjourned to Helen's state-room. With a tape recorder placed before them, Helen commenced the first of several long sessions questioning

Fiona in detail about her knowledge of her husband's affairs.

When the Cunard cruise liner Queen Elizabeth docked back at Southampton port, Fiona, with her consent, was taken to a secure and secret address in London. Arrangements were made for a London firm of solicitors to deliver a letter to the solicitors for David Evans to advise him that his wife was to seek a separation order and, in due course, would apply for a divorce. Her involvement with MI5 would not be disclosed. He would not be permitted to communicate directly with her.

By now, Fiona had been made aware that there never had been a magazine entitled Inspire. She had not won a competition. The copy of the magazine sent to her was the only one that had ever existed. It had been an operation planned and executed by MI5 to get her into an isolated and secure environment for eight days to persuade her to cooperate. The operation was successful. Vital intelligence had been obtained which would assist in pursuing a criminal prosecution against David Evans.

The MI5 team had considered whether, following the cruise, Fiona should be asked to return home and continue as before having been tasked to gather further specific information about her husband. However, her mental condition was considered too fragile. Placing her in such a situation would have made her vulnerable and could have put her in danger. An operation of this nature, to target and to gain the cooperation of individuals to infiltrate the 'enemy', was a valuable tool in the armoury of the security services.

DCI Ferguson had been asked to attend MI5 HQ, London. He wasn't given advance notice of the reason for the meeting. He was informed, for the first time, that MI5 had been successful in interviewing Fiona Evans. They had obtained her cooperation, with a detailed account of life with her husband. Fiona had been made the subject of the UK Witness Protection Programme and would remain under the care of MI5 at a secret, secure and safe location.

He was handed a typed transcript of the interview sessions with her, which had been recorded. The interviews provided a lot of important information. The DCI was not told the circumstances of the operation. The eight-day cruise was not mentioned. As an experienced detective, with detailed knowledge of intelligence operations and methods, he appreciated the intricacies and sensibilities of such matters. He was just grateful that MI5 had been able to achieve the much-needed breakthrough. It was agreed that Detective Inspector Fatima Ramiz would liaise with Helen Harrison-Forbes to convert the transcript into a written witness statement to meet the legal requirements necessary for a criminal court of law.

The disclosures given by Fiona opened many new and important lines of investigation. Of value were details of the methods her husband employed to maintain contact with criminal associates, plus, details of his illegal business interests in the UK and foreign tax havens. She had explained that the weekly visits of two gardeners to the house was 'cover' for the delivery and collection of messages. When Evans left the house, she confirmed, he would always be 'shadowed' by two of his 'boys' to protect him and to act as 'Spotters.'

Their Georgian house had been built, as was the custom of the time, with a deep wine cellar. In the 1960s, the previous owner had the cellar deepened, with extensive alterations and at great expense, to convert it into a fully functioning family nuclear fallout shelter. Planning permission had not been sought and the shelter did not appear in the deeds of the house lodged at the UK Land Registry.

Entry to the shelter was achieved via a small, locked door, hidden from view behind a large washing machine (on wheels) located in the kitchen. Fiona said her husband kept at least one million pounds in cash secreted there. He referred to it as an emergency war chest.

From the previous wine cellar, a brick-lined tunnel ran for about a hundred yards to what was then a Victorian icehouse. [These were used to store blocks of ice throughout the year and were commonly used prior to the invention of the refrigerator. The underground brick-lined chamber would have been well-insulated with straw]. Access through the tunnel was still possible. The construction was underground with entry through a small hatch at ground level. It was located within the nearby woodland copse, with the hatch hidden underneath a movable beehive. Evans had used the tunnel as a means of escape when unsavoury characters had visited his home.

The information supplied by Fiona Evans, together with recent intelligence gathered by MI5, gave encouragement to the Operation Goldfinger team.

In discussion with the Crown Prosecution Service, the time was approaching when the evidence would be sufficient to support a criminal prosecution against David Evans, and, later down the line, other associates. The team was instructed to prepare plans and an arrest strategy.

It began as a normal working day for Operation Goldfinger. The 'outside' operations team, under the leadership of DI Richard Penfold, were undertaking enquiries within the Home Counties and taking witness statements from street drug dealers and customers. DI Fatima Ramiz was back at MI5 HQ working with Helen Harrison-Forbes, and the HOLMES2 incident room team were busy researching and analysing the latest intelligence.

It was late afternoon, about 16:30 hours, when DCI Ferguson received an urgent message from the communications monitoring staff. He called an immediate meeting with the staff, who were currently in the incident room, including the Incident Room Manager:

"Terry Evans has just been on his mobile phone telling a friend he is about to drive David to London Gatwick Airport to catch an evening flight to Panama.

I've spoken to the Border Force team at Gatwick. The only evening flight is to Panama City International Airport with British Airways departing at 20:45 hours, with one stop at Madrid Airport. The Border Force have his details, with his photograph, but say there is no passenger named David Evans booked on the flight. It's likely he will attempt to use a false passport. If this is the case, he'll be arrested for an immigration offence. However, if his details are correct, he will be arrested on our behalf on suspicion of importation of Class A drugs. We'll arrange to have an arrest team on standby and I'll remain at my desk to await a telephone update from the Border Force."

CHAPTER FOUR

Detained

19:05 hours: London Gatwick Airport, South Terminal, Border Force Passport Control.

The man had been waiting patiently in the queue and gave the appearance of a confident individual who was familiar with the surroundings; a frequent traveller. He was in his mid-forties, thick set, with a suntanned shaven head and a distinctive broken nose. The man was dressed smartly but casually, wearing a tailored well-fitting sports jacket and a white open neck shirt. He was carrying a large beige leather holdall.

He was called forward to the passport control desk. He nonchalantly walked forward, placed his dark blue British passport on the raised counter and waited. The passport was taken and opened by the seated uniformed official. He held the passport in both hands to check the content, then looked up at the standing man to compare his features with the photograph.

The official replaced the passport on his desk and took a further look at its content. Eventually, and without a display of any facial expression, he looked up at the man and requested and was handed his flight ticket.

The official examined the flight ticket and asked:

"Mr Cheshire, is your trip for business or pleasure?"

"Pleasure."

The official responded:

"I note your ticket to Panama is business class."

The man appeared annoyed with the question and replied:

"Yes, I always prefer to fly business class."

The official persisted:

"I also note it is a one-way ticket: Gatwick to Panama City."

The man immediately responded:

"Yes. I'm going for a break to see the sights with no special plans. I will probably stay for a couple of weeks then fly back home. I may also have a look around to see if there are any interesting business ventures."

The official gave a slight smile and queried:

"Where will you be staying in Panama?"

The man appeared even more annoyed and snapped back:

"A hotel. Haven't booked anywhere, but I know the city well."

"So, you have visited there before?"

"Many times."

"That's interesting," commented the official.

He discreetly placed the open passport under the scanner and continued:

"The computer screen is telling me there is no record of you travelling to Panama. In fact, the only country you seem to have visited is Spain for summer holidays."

The man, slightly flustered, stood facing the official but made no further comment.

The official pressed a small button concealed under the lip of his desk. Two uniformed Border Force guards came into view and positioned themselves three paces behind the standing man.

The man quickly became aware of the two burly guards observing him. He commented:

"The computer must be malfunctioning. My passport is genuine."

The official held the passport open in his hands and continued:

"And please confirm that you are James Robert Cheshire, and that this is your passport?"

The man just nodded in agreement.

"Yes, the passport is genuine," said the official looking intently at the man and then back to the open passport. He continued:

"The photograph is a good likeness but is not of you."

The man seemed nervous. He did not respond to the question.

The official engaged direct eye contact with the man and said:

"I am aware of your correct identity. Mr David Evans, you have attempted to depart the UK using someone else's passport. This constitutes a serious criminal offence. On indictment and conviction, you may be liable to serve a term of imprisonment not exceeding ten years. I am, therefore, arresting you on suspicion of committing a criminal offence and you will be escorted to a secure interview room for further investigation."

In response to this formal accusation, Evans chose not to give a reply.

The two Border guards stepped forward and took a firm hold of Evans by his arms. He did not resist and was escorted to a vacant interview room.

Once seated in the interview room, David Evans quickly regained his confidence and arrogant manner. With his arms tightly folded over his chest, he sat motionless and glared directly, and in a threatening pose, at the officer asking him questions. He declined the offer to have a duty solicitor present and declined to answer any questions.

The large beige leather holdall he had with him at the time of his arrest was placed on the table. The interviewing officer asked:

"Before your holdall is searched, is there anything in here you wish to tell us about?"

Evans did not comment. He remained, with arms folded, glaring menacingly at the officer.

The second officer emptied the contents of the holdall onto the table. He then held the holdall with both hands and shook it. He frowned, then placed the holdall near to his ear and continued to shake it. There was a faint sound. He smiled. From the pocket of his uniform, he took out a small penknife. Delving inside the bag, which had appeared to be empty, he removed several staples and then turned the open bag upside down. The thick inner cardboard base fell onto the table, followed by bundles of wrapped new US dollars. In total, there were fifty thousand dollars.

Evans was asked to give an explanation for the presence of the money, which had been deliberately hidden in the bottom of the holdall. He showed no outward expression, just continued with his deviant glare, and refused to speak.

Earlier that evening, Border Force officials at the airport had been put on alert to expect David Evans' arrival at Passport Control. Following the arrest and recovery of the fifty thousand US dollar bills, DCI Ferguson, the SIO for Operation Goldfinger, had been telephoned with an update.

On completion of the required legal procedures, Evans was escorted by the two officers to a small holding cell within the complex. He was issued with a bedroll and the amenities were briefly explained to him. His mood had not improved. The cell door was slammed and locked. He remained alone in the dimly lit holding cell, which was basic, with just a double bunk bed, a table and two wooden chairs. There he would spend the night. Arrangements were made for him to appear before the local magistrate's court in the morning.

Just before 02:00 hours, the cell door was unlocked from the outside and opened. The cell had continued to be dimly lit by a single lightbulb suspended from the ceiling. A Border Force guard stood in the doorway:

"Mr Evans, you have a guest to share your cell. In the morning, you will both be going to the local magistrate's court. I'll leave you to introduce yourselves."

The guard closed and locked the door behind him.

Evans was sitting on one of the wooden chairs, his legs stretched out before him, and grasping a mug of coffee with both hands. His mood remained aggressive and defiant. He made no attempt to look at or acknowledge the presence of the other man. Neither man spoke.

The visitor remained in half-shadow, standing just inside the cell. He was in his mid-forties, six feet in height, slim and fit-looking. His appearance was that of a self-confident individual, who enjoyed the outside country life, and was not intimidated by the situation he found himself in. He was casually dressed, wearing a three-quarter length khaki jacket with dark blue Levi jeans and well-worn desert boots. A burgundy patterned silk neckerchief, in cowboy style, was loosely tied around his neck.

It was evident his shaggy hair had recently been bleached by the sun, which matched his tanned complexion and several days of facial growth. His forehead and cheeks were noticeably bruised with minor cuts and abrasions. He was holding a bedroll in his right hand, given to him by Border Force personnel. After standing in silence for a couple of minutes, he confidently walked across to the metal-framed bunk beds and placed his bedroll on the top bunk.

The atmosphere in the room suddenly became explosive. An extremely angry and animated Evans leaped to his feet. He lunged the short distance towards the top bunk and grabbed the stranger's bedroll, which he threw with force across the room. He had, obviously, claimed prior ownership of the top bunk.

The visitor remained standing in the same position. He was not intimidated by the behaviour of Evans, and actually gave a brief smile and shook his head. He slowly turned to make direct eye contact with Evans. In a calm confident voice, he asked:

"Are you in a bad mood or were you just born a little shit?"

Evans looked shocked by the provocative comment and snapped:

"What?"

The visitor appeared totally unfazed by the aggressive behaviour of Evans and responded:

"Also deaf, are you?! I'll repeat myself. Are you in a bad mood or were you just born a little shit?"

Evans squared up to the man, almost nose to nose, with his fists clenched in the stance of a boxer. The visitor was not intimidated and held his ground. He smiled, quietly pushed the raging Evans aside then walked across and deposited himself on one of the wooden chairs. He leaned back in the chair in a relaxed position and looked up at Evans. After a pause, he spoke:

"If you want a fight, I'm up for it but we will both lose."

To emphasise his previous comment, he pointed towards the door and continued:

"The enemy is the other side of that door. We are in this together. Let's be united."

He smiled, holding his right hand out in an offer of friendship.

"I'm Guy Hamilton; just flown in from the good old US of A."

Hamilton spoke with a Southern English accent tinged with a hint of American.

Evans looked bewildered. In his world, he was the feared 'boss' and no one ever dared to speak to him in that manner. The standoff continued for a couple of minutes. Would a violent fistfight ensue between them? If so, it would be bloody.

Eventually, Evans nodded his head and slowly walked across to the seated Hamilton. They shook hands. The tension had eased. However, the pressure of the handshake caused Hamilton to wince. With his left hand, he gently rubbed his upper right arm.

Evans had noticed the man wince and asked:

"Are you injured?"

"Nothing serious; just a minor war wound. The other guy got it worse than me."

The dim cell light was switched off and the two men retreated in silence to their respective bunks. There, they would remain until early morning, when they would be transferred, under escort, to the local magistrates' court.

The North Sussex Magistrates' Court had been convened early. Before hearing the day's scheduled cases, they were asked to adjudicate on two late applications for remand-in-custody in respect of two prisoners arrested at nearby London Gatwick Airport.

The prisoners were detained in the holding cell situated in the basement of the court. The first prisoner was escorted up the stone steps to the enclosed dock. He was instructed to remain standing and to face the three presiding magistrates. David Evans was asked to confirm his details. The Clerk to the Court then read out the charge.

The prosecuting solicitor from the Crown Prosecution Service addressed the magistrates and outlined the facts:

"Late last evening, David Evans, a UK citizen, was arrested at London Gatwick Airport Passport Control. He had attempted to fly out of the country to Panama using another man's passport. It was a genuine passport but had been doctored to contain the photograph of the defendant. Fifty thousand US dollars were found concealed in his holdall. He declined to explain his actions. He is currently the subject of UK police investigations. Further charges relating to serious criminal matters are anticipated. For the present, the defendant has chosen not to be legally represented and has not made an application for bail."

The magistrates remanded him in custody and he was returned to the holding cell. Next, Guy Hamilton stood in the dock. The Clerk to the Court read out the charge. The prosecuting solicitor outlined the facts:

"During the early hours of this morning, Guy Hamilton, a UK National, arrived at London Gatwick Airport having flown in on a direct flight from Florida. He was arrested on behalf of the US authorities. A few hours earlier, the US authorities had issued an international arrest warrant for him. Two weeks ago, the FBI detained a then unknown Englishman suspected of fraud and money laundering. A violent altercation ensued. Two FBI agents received gunshot wounds and the suspect escaped. The assailant received a bullet wound in his right arm. Two days ago, Hamilton was identified as that man. The US authorities will be applying to the UK for extradition proceedings to begin. A remand-in-custody is sought to facilitate liaison between the two countries. He has not made an application for bail."

The magistrates remanded him in custody.

The two prisoners, David Evans and Guy Hamilton, were remanded in custody together to await transportation to the local prison.

CHAPTER FIVE

The Journey

The prison van, with a total of six prisoners on board, drove up the steep slope to the main gates and stopped. They had arrived at HM Lockwood Prison, a Victorian prison of brick and flint construction that had been built in 1853. The category B prison was located within the county of East Sussex, England. It held people on remand from the local courts, as well as convicted prisoners who had been sentenced to a term of imprisonment. The prison accommodation consisted mainly of shared cells.

Stationary at the closed and locked main prison gates, the exterior of the prison van was inspected by two prison officers. The officer in the passenger seat handed over the documentation relating to the prisoners who had been collected from three local magistrates' courts. Satisfied that all was in order, the main gates were opened and the prison van drove into the enclosed yard and parked. The six prisoners were escorted into the reception area and instructed to stand in a single line.

A uniformed prison officer addressed the group. From a typed list, he read out the rules and regulations of the prison. Remand prisoners were entitled to additional privileges. They were permitted to wear their own clothes, rather than prison uniform, and were not required to undertake regulation daily work or participate in education sessions. He listed what was forbidden in prison, including drugs and mobile telephones.

On completion of the formal briefing, the prison officer consulted his note pad and shouted:

"Guy Hamilton. Step forward."

Hamilton did as was directed.

The prison officer continued:

"Hamilton, my record says you have an arm wound that requires daily medical treatment and a fresh bandage. Each morning, after ablutions, report to the medical room. Understand?"

"Yes, Sir. Thank you."

Hamilton then stepped back into the line of other prisoners. On completion of the briefing, Evans and Hamilton were escorted to a double cell on the second floor of the Remand Wing, where they would spend their time on remand until their next scheduled court appearance.

Next morning, prison life began at 06:00 hours. The two men were required to clean their cell in accordance with the set prison regulations. They were then directed to walk together to the kitchen to join the queue for breakfast. Breakfast was served on a single metal tray. Evans was more amenable than Hamilton had experienced a few hours earlier. The two men sat opposite each other, on bench seats, at a long wooden table. Both agreed the food wasn't very appetising.

Their conversation was limited and they were still cautious of each other. Both acknowledged that, in their youth, they had each spent time in prison. The prospect of Evans spending a few weeks in prison didn't concern him. He 'knew how things worked' and, with a 'few backhanders', he was confident prison life would be comfortable. Without giving an explanation, he indicated that he didn't intend on being incarcerated for too long. Hamilton said very little.

Following breakfast, the two men were directed to the communal shower block. Whilst under the shower, Hamilton removed the bandage from his upper right arm and placed it in the nearby waste bin. Evans looked across and observed the bloody but healing and stitched wound. He said nothing. On completing his shower, Hamilton told Evans he would visit the medical centre to have his wound freshly dressed and then visit the prison library.

Hamilton returned to their cell just before lunchtime and lay on the lower bunk. He told Evans he was feeling unwell and wanted to rest on his bunk and not bother about having lunch.

Later in the afternoon, Evans returned to their cell. Hamilton was almost asleep on his bunk. Evans was in a relaxed and confident mood and appeared to want to talk. With humour in his voice, he nudged Hamilton and challenged him to say more about himself and his activities in America and elsewhere in the world.

Hamilton responded:

"I prefer my own company: I walk alone in the world. I don't trust many people. The only person I truly cared for was my wife, and she died from cancer."

Evans turned to face Hamilton directly and, speaking in a slow deliberate voice, said:

"Fraud, money laundering and shooting two FBI agents. The UK will willingly agree to your extradition. Then, when the Yanks get their hands on you, they'll lock you away for life. Are you prepared to remain in prison for most of your life? Then there's your previous UK convictions. I bet the English cops will also be taking a closer look at you."

Hamilton showed annoyance in his voice and questioned:

"How the hell did you get that information about me?"

Evans gave a knowing smile, tapping his nose with his index finger, but did not immediately reply. He did not give a direct answer to the question. After a pause, he commented:

"Are you prepared to do twenty years?"

Hamilton responded:

"Is there an alternative? Why were you attempting to leave the UK using a false passport?"

Evans gave a cynical smile and said:

"I've acquired much wealth in my business life, but lots of people are trying to take it from me. Now, my wife of twenty years, and with knowledge of most of my secrets, has left me. I feel she could be assisting my enemies to bring me down. Fortunately, over the years, I've squirrelled away many millions in far-off countries without extradition treaties. I intend to be able to spend my money."

Hamilton responded:

"So, that's why you were hoping to fly off to Panama. Well, that plan has gone pear-shaped. So, the future is now your retirement in HM Prison."

Evans snapped back:

"No, I'll be in Panama, but just a few weeks later than I'd planned."

Hamilton, with a degree of humour, probed further and asked:

"That leaves the minor problem of walking out of HM Prison."

Evans replied with an air of confidence:

"I always have a Plan A, a Plan B and a Plan C. My exit Plan A failed. Stay close, my friend, and watch Plan B develop."

Hamilton was intrigued to know how Evans had obtained information about his problems with the FBI, as Evans hadn't been in court when the details, and those of his previous convictions, had been given.

Evans looked directly at Hamilton and replied:

"Money; everyone has a price. I've had you checked out. Had your New Scotland Yard criminal record examined."

Hamilton shook his head and replied:

"Christ. You obviously have an informant in the police. But how have you had recent contact?"

From his jacket pocket, Evans produced a miniature mobile phone called a Zanco Tiny and handed it to Hamilton. It's dimensions were the height and thickness of two ten-pence coins and containing so little metal that it cannot be detected by metal detectors. It is small enough to evade prison body scanners when smuggled in via body cavities, care packages or even by bribed prison staff.

Evans took back the mobile phone from Hamilton, smiled and added:

"The only recommendation is, wash your hands after you've used it."

Later that day, Evans attended Reception to take the telephone call he had arranged earlier, to speak with his solicitor. Both parties were aware that such calls were monitored by the prison authorities, so, the conversation would be guarded and to the point. Evans had asked his solicitor to make an application before a Crown Court judge for him to be released on bail pending his trial. His solicitor was not optimistic and advised him against making the application.

The solicitor recounted the facts to him: He had been arrested attempting to depart the UK, using another person's passport, on a one-way ticket to Panama and with fifty thousand US dollars concealed in his hand luggage. The prosecution had stated that he was attempting to flee the jurisdiction of the UK authorities, having become aware that he was under police investigation and was likely to be arrested and charged with serious criminal offences. She had spoken with a representative from the

Crown Prosecution Service and the indication was that positive police action was imminent.

Evans insisted that his solicitor make the bail application. Reluctantly, she had acknowledged the 'client-solicitor relationship' and, acting in accordance with his instructions, she would prepare to represent him at the bail application, which she would expedite.

Evans returned to his cell and told Hamilton about the conversation he'd had with his solicitor. He appeared in a good mood and was not concerned about her gloomy assessment. Hamilton commented, with a laugh, that he wasn't even going to consider applying for bail.

Evans continued in his jovial mood:

"Remember. Stay close and watch for Plan B."

The two men had been on remand in prison for six days. Their relationship and trust in each other had grown. Evans had taken the lead in their conversations. Hamilton had been happy for this to occur and continued to reveal little information about himself.

Late that afternoon, both men were summoned to attend Reception. They were instructed to report back to Reception at 08:00 hours the next day to be transported to court. Evans would be delivered to Mid-Sussex

Crown Court to appear before a judge in respect of his application for bail. His solicitor would be in attendance to represent him. The prison van would then continue with Hamilton to Westminster Magistrates' Court. He would be brought before a judge who would, in the first instance, review the international arrest warrant issued by the USA to ensure compliance with UK legislation. The judge would then direct the defendant to be granted bail or to be remanded in custody. This would be the beginning of the formal process for extradition.

Evans appeared jubilant on being told the news. He whispered to Hamilton that he had some final touches to make to his Plan B. He then walked off without saying where he was going. He resurfaced two hours later. He just smiled at Hamilton but didn't mention where he had been or what he had been doing.

Next morning, just before 08:00 hours, Evans and Hamilton reported to Reception and were directed to walk together across the prison yard to the parked prison van. Evans smiled and muttered out loud:

"A meat wagon! It has been some years since I last rode in one of those."

The accompanying prison officers put handcuffs on both men and guided them into the

individual metal cages in the rear of the prison van. Once seated in their segregated compartments, the doors were locked.

For additional security, during the journey, a prison officer remained seated in the rear of the vehicle. The main rear door was closed and locked from the outside. Prison vans were fitted with all-round bulletproof glass, strong metal bars and reinforced metal bodywork. GPS units and radios were also fitted.

At 08:00 hours, the prison van departed HM Lockwood Prison, with a uniformed officer driving and a colleague in the front passenger seat. The route had been preplanned. To avoid the rush-hour morning traffic, the journey to their first stop (Mid-Sussex Crown Court) would be on the quieter country roads.

About twelve miles into the journey, which had been on an A-designated road, the vehicle turned onto a short winding stretch of B-road. The single-lane rural road was heavily wooded on either side. Traffic was light. A large lorry followed immediately behind the prison van.

As the prison van came out of a sharp bend, fifty yards in front of them and blocking the road in both directions, two cars had collided. It appeared the crash had happened only moments earlier. Both cars were on fire and engulfed in flames. The prison van came to an abrupt stop.

Near to the crash, a motorcycle rested on its side in the centre of the road. A man in full motorcycle clothing, complete with safety helmet, ran towards the stationary prison van shouting:

"There's a lady with children trapped in the burning car. Quick, quick, we need your fire extinguisher. For fuck's sake, hurry!"

Instinctively, without considering rules on prisoner-handling, the officer in the front passenger seat grabbed the vehicle's fire extinguisher. He was in the process of opening the van door when it was wrenched fully open by the 'motorcyclist.' The barrel of a sawn-off shotgun was thrust against the officer's left cheek. The attacker screamed:

"Get out! Face down on the road. Now! Be quick or you're dead."

The attack on the prison van was choreographed with brutal precision. The operation was completed within a matter of seconds by about six men. They had arrived on the scene in three Range Rovers and appeared to have driven out of the wooded area. The attackers were dressed identically in full blue disposal forensic suits, overshoes, latex gloves and black balaclavas.

Within a split second, the windows on all four sides of the vehicle shattered under the force of wielded sledgehammers. A large angle-grinder made easy work of opening the reinforced rear door. The noise was deafening and disorientating. The barrel of a shotgun was thrust through the driver's smashed window. The officer was threatened with death if he didn't rapidly get out and lie face down on the road.

The third officer was forcefully pulled from the back of the vehicle and dragged to lie alongside his two colleagues. Their wrists were secured with plastic ties and black bags were forced over their heads. Their mobile phones were wrenched from them and smashed. Sledgehammers were also used to smash all communications equipment in the vehicle.

Within the same timeframe, two attackers equipped with sub-machine guns were deployed at the front and rear of the prison van to guard against any 'outside' interference. The large lorry that had stopped behind the prison van had blocked the road and deliberately prevented vehicular access to the scene of the attack. It was part of the plan; the driver had abandoned the lorry.

The angle-grinder was also deployed to free Evans from his 'cage'. He was clearly aware the attack was to take place. The door to Hamilton's cage was then forced open. The jubilant Evans looked towards him and shouted:

"Plan B! Tick that off as successful. Are you with me?"

The two men jumped from the back of the van, briefly shaking hands, then ran to a waiting Range Rover and were immediately driven away at speed along a woodland track. The team of attackers climbed aboard the two other Range Rovers and disappeared back into the woodlands. In the three Range Rovers, the attackers quickly removed their outer clothing, which was bagged up for disposal.

In the Range Rover containing Evans and Hamilton, the radio was tuned to the police wavelength. They listened. A member of the public had reported two cars on fire, with people possibly trapped. Fire, Police and Ambulance had been sent. No mention of the 'hit' on the prison van!

It was a further eight minutes before emergency services arrived at the scene to find the prison van had been attacked and two prisoners had escaped. The sound of many emergency service sirens could be heard in the distance. The police control room were now broadcasting details of the incident over the radio. Instructions were given for roadblocks to be set up at specific locations. The prison officers had given the police a description of the vehicles and assailants and a police helicopter had been dispatched to circle the area.

Repeated police broadcasts updated officers to be on lookout for the three Range Rovers. Warnings were given that the attackers were armed and should be regarded as dangerous. Police firearms response teams were deployed to the surrounding area and to static points to assist, and protect, unarmed officers.

Within a few miles, the three Range Rovers drove off in different directions keeping to quiet country lanes. Separately, in secluded locations, the cars were then doused with petrol and set on fire. Fresh getaway cars had previously been left in situ for the men. The operation to free Evans had been well-financed and planned in detail. The presence of Hamilton hadn't been included in the original plan, but Evans was pleased to have him onboard.

Having abandoned and set fire to their getaway Range Rover, Evans, followed by Hamilton, trekked several hundred yards through woodland to a clearing. Waiting for them was a modern motorised horsebox, with the driver leaning up against the cab smoking a cigarette.

The man was dressed in clothing and jodhpurs befitting that of a smart stable groom. He opened the side door, having discreetly passed a handgun to Evans, and ushered the two men in. He pointed them to a concealed and covered section at the rear. Two standing horses, with nose bags fitted, were tethered within the box. The side door was then locked from the outside and the vehicle was driven away.

In the dark and cramped conditions, the two men rested, with eyes closed, seated on straw floor covering. During their journey, there was no conversation. After a couple of hours, the vehicle stopped and the door to the horsebox was unlocked. The driver lifted the hatch on the confined space and, in a light-hearted manner, welcomed the two guests to his home.

They had arrived at a farm and horse-riding stables, located several miles from Stow-on-the-Wold, in the rural Cotswold countryside. The complex was run as a riding school, with facilities to also hire out horses for trekking over the Cotswold Downs.

The property was owned by John Flint, the driver of the horsebox, along with his wife, Doreen, who managed the riding school and trekking element of the business. John referred to himself as 'semi-retired', and managed four holiday lets, converted farm labourer's cottages, situated in splendid isolation up on the hills.

John was a 'retired' drug dealer. He had made his fortune, walked away from villainy, and purchased a piece of the quiet life. He had met and wed Doreen after his retirement. She was not aware of his criminal past.

Evans and Hamilton, with false names, had been booked to stay in one of the holiday cottages. The registration book had them listed as keen hillwalkers from Southampton. John walked both men straight up to their holiday cottage without first introducing them to his wife.

Why would John, who had retired from his dubious past, risk his freedom and future to engage in such a dangerous activity? Assisting escaped prisoners would be regarded as a serious criminal offence, and conviction would likely result in an immediate prison sentence. Perhaps he had a dark secret from his past and owed Evans one last favour to ensure it remained hidden? Blackmail was a weapon Evans was never afraid to deploy!

The cottage was snug and cosy. The wood-burner was alight and sending out a pleasant warmth. An ample supply of cut logs was stacked next to it. Evans and Hamilton slumped down in the two easy chairs and, with his first words for several hours, David commented:

"Well, Guy, how is Plan B looking?"

Hamilton laughed and replied:

"When we left HM Lockwood this morning, I certainly didn't imagine I'd be free and spending the evening here. You obviously did! Good on your part; this must have taken some organising!"

"No. Just money and knowing the right contact to sort it out."

He then mimicked, holding a pretend mobile phone to his ear:

"The prison food is terrible. I need to get out of here. Please expedite. On your success, a bloody large payday awaits."

Evans was in a relaxed and playful mood.

Hamilton asked:

"Really; that simple?"

"That's the modern world. Everything is subcontracted out. I don't have my own team on standby: I just issue the instructions to a trusted contractor," said Evans. He then nonchalantly took the handgun from his jacket pocket and placed it on the coffee table.

Hamilton identified the gun as a Colt 45, the pistol of choice for the US Army.

Hamilton leaned forward to the low coffee table. He picked up a litre bottle of single malt whisky and poured out two tumblers of the liquor, pushing one across to Evans.

"So, David, are you saying you don't actually know the guys who carried out today's rescue?"

Evans, took a sip from his tumbler of whisky and said:

"Don't have a clue who they were. Likely recruited from our 'Romanian friends.' By now, they are probably on their way home. We can always get them at short notice and at a very reasonable price. The Romanian Mafia also operate in our European countries and in South American countries. It's almost a one-stop shop."

He stretched back in his chair, laughed, and continued:

"They are very reliable. I've often called on them to punish 'naughty boys' who have not settled their debts. By the time the cops get to know about the attacks, they have left the UK."

More whisky and laughter flowed. The kitchen had been well stocked with food, including readymade meals for heating in the microwave. A new iPad and a new cheap 'no contract' mobile phone had been left on the table for Evans, together with a brown envelope containing £5000 in cash. Finally, laid out on the sofa, a selection of new men's clothing had been left for the two men.

They continued talking late into the evening. Evans turned on the television to watch the ten o'clock news; there was no mention on the national news about the attack on the prison van. More whisky flowed. Evans was keen to talk about the future, which he had worked out in his mind. His intention was to depart the UK within two weeks. That, he joked, was his Plan E.

He confided that Plan C was to acquire his 'final big payday' in the UK. He explained that a large drug importation operation he was involved with was due within the week. Then his Plan D involved revenge against the police. He grimaced and spat out the word 'Bastards.' He was reluctant to explain further about Plan D. Evans said he had arranged new fake passports for both, which would be ready in two days.

Hamilton raised his tumbler of whisky and said: "David, cheers and thank you. Why are you doing so much for me, and telling me so much? I'm not used to such friendship."

Evans recounted: "Remember our first meeting when you suggested I was 'a little shit'? I was ready to knock you for six, but you stood up to me. Clearly not intimidated. I respected that and thought 'I could work with him.' Then, when I found out what you'd done to the FBI blokes and talked about your UK criminal record, I thought 'definitely, I like this guy.' So, after I've packed my bags and said goodbye to the UK, what do you intend to do?"

Hamilton paused for thought, then replied: "That's a difficult one. I'm now a wanted fugitive in the UK *and* the US. Unlike you, I don't have money, nor a 'Plan C, D or E' and I haven't been in the UK for over ten years. I'm a survivor but will need a few days to figure out the next step."

The next morning, the two men had a late breakfast whilst seated at the kitchen table. Evans opened the iPad and clicked onto the BBC national television news. There was no mention of the prison van attack. He then checked the local regional news for the Southeast. There was a brief item reporting from the scene, with film of forensic personnel examining the prison van and surrounding area. Neither names nor photographs of the escaped prisoners were included in the report. Evans next tuned in to regional news stations covering the Midlands; the attack had not been reported. This gave him encouragement.

On the instructions of Evans, Hamilton left the cottage with him and headed on foot uphill along an overgrown and little-used path. Evans obviously knew their destination. They were both wearing anoraks, with beanie hats, and each carried a hiking pole. They portrayed the image of typical hillwalkers.

After about half a mile, the path began winding downhill for another mile before reaching a roadside café. A dark blue Ford Focus was stationary in the car park. Evans turned to Hamilton and quietly asked him to:

"Go for a short walk."

He then got into the front seat of the Ford, closed the door, and held a conversation with the driver, which lasted about two minutes.

Evans rejoined Hamilton. They commenced walking back up the track. Evans turned to Hamilton, smiled and said: "All agreed and arranged. The drug shipment is on its way."

Back at the cottage, the two men selected a couple of ready meals and heated them in the microwave. Over lunch and a beer, Hamilton, with a degree of puzzlement, asked: "We've only been here since yesterday. How the hell have you made these contacts and arrangements?"

Evans opened the iPad, which was on the kitchen table, and turned the screen towards Hamilton.

"Simple. See this advert for window-cleaning services? Just type in a couple of innocent-looking enquiries and press send. In code, I've made a drug deal. There are thousands of such false sites."

For his more detailed and complex importation drug deals, he used the dark web, but he wasn't prepared to reveal this to Hamilton. The dark web is only accessible by means of special software allowing the user to remain anonymous or untraceable.

Next morning, on the instructions of Evans, the two men had risen early and were seated for breakfast. Evans opened his laptop computer to check the BBC TV national and regional news channels. With a smile of reassurance, he commented that none of the news channels had given an update on the prison van attack, and, more importantly, no photographs of the two men had been issued.

"Guy, it's safe to leave the cottage and go on a journey to visit friends. Let's get ready for some hillwalking."

Hamilton nodded in agreement. He made no further comment. Both men put on their outdoor clothing - walking boots, anorak and beanie hat. Evans also put on a backpack. Hamilton noted, but did not make comment, that Evans took the Colt 45 handgun from the tabletop and placed it in the outer pocket of the backpack.

They walked up the hill, along the track they had taken the previous day. On reaching the roadside café, Hamilton noticed a dark blue Ford Focus parked on the forecourt. It was the same car that had been there the previous day. However, on this occasion, there was no driver. Hamilton followed as Evans took a set of keys from his pocket, unlocked the car door, then both entered. There was a distinct lack of information emanating from Evans, who was undertaking the driving.

They were several miles into the journey, driving north on the A44, before Evans spoke:

"We're off to war. Let's hope it's not a full-scale nuclear attack. No fear, we'll be protected."

Hamilton frowned, laughed and sought an explanation for the obviously cryptic comment. Evans just laughed and replied:

"Wait and see. We'll be there in two hours."

The drive was uneventful. Evans appeared deep in thought. Conversation was non-existent. Hamilton closed his eyes and relaxed. Eventually, he opened his eyes and, from road signs, was aware they were travelling on the A49 through the Shropshire Hills. Evans stopped and parked the car at a Shropshire Wildlife Trust Nature Reserve car park.

"OK, a little more trekking."

Evans picked up his backpack and, without further comment, headed towards a woodland track.

Hamilton was puzzled, annoyed and a little concerned at the absence of communication. The atmosphere between the two men had changed. Hamilton sensed Evans was displaying his true persona of an arrogant drugs boss. Not only that, but Hamilton would be walking through an ancient oak woodland, to an unknown destination, with a man in possession of a powerful Colt 45 handgun.

After about fifteen minutes of walking, they turned left onto a smaller unused track and up to a locked five-bar wooden gate. A large sign stated 'Private. Strictly No Entry. Trespassers will be Prosecuted.'

Evans unlocked the gate, and they walked two hundred yards to a small metal container-type construction. The single door was secured with a significant internal lock, which Evans unlocked with a key. Stepping inside the container, Hamilton noted a closed metal hatch parallel to the ground.

Evans took another large key from his pocket, then unlocked and lifted open the heavy metal hatch, which exposed a deep brick-lined shaft with a metal ladder fixed to the wall. Without speaking, he gestured with his right hand for Hamilton to descend the ladder.

Hamilton stood his ground. He expressed concern and annoyance.

"What the fuck is this about?"

He stood well back from the shaft and remained close to the backpack Evans was holding, acutely aware that it contained the Colt 45. If Evans suddenly took out the gun, Hamilton was prepared to tackle him and lay the first blow.

Evans finally sensed Hamilton's concern and offered reassurance:

"Ease up, Guy. You could call this part of my Plan D. This is an old decommissioned nuclear bunker. It's mine. Three years ago, I bought it at auction."

In the 1950s, throughout the country, the UK government commissioned the construction of more than 1,500 nuclear bunkers built to the same blueprint. It was at the height of the Cold War with the former Soviet Union. They were designed as Royal Observer Corps monitoring posts to shelter observers in the event of a nuclear attack. The observers would have communicated the locations of bombs and radiation levels to the military. The bunkers provided, for the team, enough food and water for fourteen days. The sites were decommissioned and sold off in 1993.

Evans explained that the bunker had been refurbished and was habitable.

"Two of my 'boys' are down there now."

He pressed the intercom fixed by the top of the ladder and announced,

"I'm on my way down with a friend."

Still feeling puzzled, but with some reassurance, Hamilton descended the fourteen-foot shaft, followed by Evans. The shaft opened into a small room with artificial lighting. To some extent, the original dials and equipment from the nuclear era were still fitted to the walls.

Two middle-aged Eastern European-looking men were seated around a wall-mounted desk drinking coffee. Hamilton noticed two Uzi sub-machine guns resting on the desk. Both were fitted with ammunition magazines, with two further loaded magazines lying on the desk next to the guns. The men were clearly ready and prepared to defend their position, thought Hamilton. It was evident the men had been living in the bunker. What were they guarding and why?

Evans moved across to a gurgling coffeemaker, poured out two cups and handed one to Hamilton. The situation seemed surreal. No personal introductions were attempted. Evans simply asked the two men:

"Are they OK?"

Without waiting for a response, he walked across the room to a metal door with, at eye level, a small sliding hatch. He opened the hatch, briefly looked in, then closed it. He turned to face the two seated men. In response to his question, one nodded. Evans then said:

"Another two days and it should be sorted."

He moved across the room to a substantial metal safe with a combination lock, which had been built into the wall. It had probably been installed when the bunker was originally constructed and used to house government instructions required if a nuclear attack was considered imminent. Evans unlocked the safe and removed three wrapped and sealed packages which he placed in his backpack. Hamilton surmised that the packages contained banknotes.

Evans turned and began to climb the ladder, indicating, with the nod of his head, for Hamilton to follow. He made no attempt to say goodbye to the two seated men; he was the 'Boss', and they were merely his servants.

Who was incarcerated behind the locked door? What did Evans' previous comment about 'it should be sorted' mean? Hamilton had concerns. He had become involved with an unpredictable and dangerous group of people. He would need to be extra cautious about his own safety. The journey back to the cottage was undertaken in almost total silence. Evans had retreated into his own world to plan his future.

CHAPTER SIX

Allegations

The red light on DCI Ferguson's office telephone flashed. He immediately picked up the handset and listened intently as DI Penfold updated him. The DI and his team of detectives had spent the morning executing a search warrant at the gated estate of the escaped and wanted David Evans. In the converted wine cellar, the team had discovered Evans' locked war chest. From inside, they recovered over one million pounds in new Bank of England notes, together with over one hundred thousand US dollars. The notes were still in the original wrappers as issued by the respective banks.

Three handguns and a sawn-off double-barrelled shotgun were recovered from underneath floorboards. Two laptop computers, CCTV equipment and three mobile telephones had also been seized for forensic and technical examination. The DI noted an absence of any incriminating paperwork, details of property ownership or bank accounts. He suggested the cabinets and drawers were 'so clean' someone had probably, and recently, removed any relevant paperwork.

The DI had also decided to seize the collection of classic sports cars. They would be taken to a secure and covered police compound for detailed examination and held pending likely restitution claims made following criminal court convictions. Initial comparisons on several of the cars' engine and chassis numbers with the Police National Computer indicated some may have been stolen. The twin brother, Terry Evans, had not been seen at his home for several days. His current whereabouts were not known. He was not answering his mobile phone.

DCI Ferguson chaired a mid-afternoon Operation Goldfinger team meeting. He announced that since the previous meeting, significant progress had been achieved. He asked Barry Bishop, Incident Room Manager, to update the team on the main points:

1. Firstly, with the news from DI Richard Penfold concerning the work his team had been undertaking at the home of Evans. He commented that the information given by Fiona Evans had proved correct; the war chest had been found to contain a large quantity of money. The bank wrappings would be subjected to forensic examination. Finding the finger impressions of Evans on the wrappings would support evidence that he had handled the cash, and thus, knew of its existence.

2. Regarding the recovered guns, checks had been completed with the local police: Evans did not hold any firearms certificates. The weapons had been illegally held.

3. The local police force was undertaking the investigation into the prison van 'hijack.' It would include detailed analysis to establish whether any inside help or information had been given. Close liaison would be maintained between the Operation Goldfinger team and the local police team investigating the hijacking.

4.   Reference the three Range Rovers used during the prison van hijack: Although each had been abandoned and set on fire, details of their number plates were still recognisable. The vehicles could also be identified by their engine and chassis number plates. Enquiries had established that the three cars had been stolen some days earlier from different locations in the Birmingham area and fitted with false cloned number plates.

5.   Two days prior to the attack, the three vehicles were recorded by Automatic Number Plate Recognition cameras (ANPR), travelling south on the M40 motorway. All three vehicles had stopped at the Oxford Service Station. Each was being driven by one man. They met up for a meal break in the restaurant. Their movements were captured on CCTV.

6.   The three vehicles next stopped at Clacket Lane Service Station on the M25 motorway. Again, the movement of vehicles and men were captured on ANPR and CCTV. The three Range Rovers

remained parked in the overnight parking area. Early next morning, three different men drove the cars away. They looked to be of Eastern European appearance. All relevant CCTV footage was recovered by the police for further analysis to identify the individuals.

7. Prior to the escape of Evans, nothing had been recorded on any police database to suggest a connection with Guy Hamilton. The DCI suggested it had been pure coincidence that Hamilton happened to be in the prison van. Would Hamilton remain with Evans or, now free, would he go his own way? A printed copy of Hamilton's UK police criminal record was placed on the table for the team to inspect.

8. Fiona Evans had stated that the two gardeners, who visited the estate each week, acted as couriers to deliver and collect messages for her husband in connection with his drug dealings. She did not know their names, but said they

arrived at 10:00 hours each Monday. Again, her information had proved correct.

9. A small team of detectives, with backup from uniformed officers, had secreted themselves in the woods opposite the house. At the time Fiona had said, an open-back truck pulled up at the locked gates and stopped. The driver went to the intercom, pressed the button, and waited. The police team swooped. The two gardeners were arrested on suspicion of being involved, with others, in the supply of Class A drugs.

10. The two gardeners had been taken to the local police station. A small quantity of cannabis and cocaine had been found in the possession of both men. Interviewed separately under caution, and with a solicitor present, both admitted their guilt. For their service, Evans paid them in cocaine. They acted as middlemen collecting messages from, and delivering messages to, a man only known to them as 'John' who frequented the local Stag's Head public house.

11.   Detectives had visited the Stag's Head, and having identified the gardeners' contact, arrested Jonathan North. He had admitted being involved in 'small-time drug dealing' and was willing to cooperate with the police. Clearly in fear of Evans, he was a man who was keen to distance himself from the prospect of being seen as a major player in his drug empire.

12.   The two gardeners and North had supplied the Operation Goldfinger team with the names of their drug dealing contacts. Enquiries were in hand to trace and interview these people.

13.   When David Evans had presented himself at London Gatwick Airport Border Control to catch a flight to Panama, he had falsely stated that he was James Robert Cheshire. He had produced a genuine passport, but he wasn't Cheshire. Two detectives from the Operation Goldfinger team had traced the real James Robert Cheshire to a bedsit in the city of Brighton. He was a drug addict and a friend of the late Barry West known

as Digger. He was aware of the rumour that Digger had crossed David Evans and, consequently, he had been murdered, with his body fed to pigs. Cheshire was a very frightened man. Eventually, after much reassurance, he admitted to the detectives that he had sold his passport to Terry Evans for £1000 in cash and a bag of cannabis. He was not told, and had not asked, why it was required.

DCI Ferguson stated there was still much to do. However, intelligence being gained on the network of drug contacts was expanding. Each was a further step in building evidence to support a criminal case against Evans. He was feeling a degree of satisfaction with the progress of the information; people were now beginning to talk. Within hours, the DCI's world would implode.

He had received a telephone call and, although it was late afternoon, he had been 'directed' to attend a meeting at the Police Department in the Home Office. It was classed as urgent. No reason was given. He, quite naturally, thought it related to Operation Goldfinger.

At Reception, he had been directed to Conference Room number 3 and asked to take a seat. He remained seated on his own for over ten minutes. Two people then entered. They remained standing. The normal pleasantries were absent. The first introduced herself as Deputy Chief Constable Julia Lock and said nothing further. The DCI had not previously met her, but he was aware she had recently taken up her appointment within his home force.

The second officer introduced himself as Detective Chief Superintendent Joe Reece. There followed a moment of silence, and awkwardness, with no attempt at a handshake.

The DCS then spoke:

"This is an unpleasant situation for us and for you. There is no easy way to say this. A criminal complaint has been made against you. The allegation is of rape. I have been appointed to lead the criminal investigation into the allegation."

DCI Ferguson looked shocked.

"No. Is this for real?"

The DCS explained, and ensured, the correct procedures were administered, and that DCI Ferguson was
made aware of his legal rights.

The DCS outlined that two days before, Mary Jean
Butterfield had attended a police station in London,
in company with her solicitor, and alleged that about
five years ago, she had met Ferguson in a night club.
He had told her he was a detective inspector attending
a CID course and showed her his police warrant card.
She remembered his name - Donald Ferguson. They had
gone, in his car, back to her apartment where he physically forced himself on her and raped her. Through fear,
she had not reported it at the time as he was a senior
police officer. Recently, she had seen him on a TV news
item and decided she must report the matter.

The DCI remained seated, constantly shaking his
head. He readily acknowledged that five years earlier,
as a detective inspector, he had attended a CID course
in London. He also acknowledged that at the time, he
owned, and still owned, a silver-coloured Volvo, which
was the colour and make of car the complainant said her
attacker owned.

"I don't even need to know the lady's name because I've never been to a London nightclub, and I've certainly never been back to any lady's apartment."

The DCS explained that the criminal investigation into the allegation of rape was at an early stage. In due course, and after caution, Ferguson would be subject to formal interview.

The Deputy Chief Constable then spoke. In her role, she was the discipline authority within their police force and, thus, responsible for deciding whether an officer should be suspended from duty. The DCC had been informed that the female complainant had given her story to the Sun newspaper who were about to publish. The force's Professional Standards Department would monitor the progress of the criminal investigation. Under these circumstances, the DCI would be suspended from duty with immediate effect.

Before leaving the Home Office building, he would be required to hand over his warrant card, police-issued mobile phone and laptop computer, together with his pocketbook and all other police-related items and documentation. He would not be permitted to enter any police establishment without first gaining permission from the

DCC, nor could he contact any serving member of the police service. He was served the necessary forms.

He could no longer use his police rank. Mr Donald Ferguson was left to return, alone, to his home; a detached house situated in a small village west of Guildford. Since his divorce, he had lived there alone. He was a confused and broken man. No police support had been offered to him. He was not even permitted to contact the Operation Goldfinger management team to inform them of the situation.

The following morning, when a close friend and retired police colleague visited his home, there was no answer. His car was missing from the driveway. The curtains in the house were closed and it seemed no one had stayed there overnight. His mobile phone went unanswered.

The solicitor for the woman had stated that their 'victim' was a vulnerable person: interviews by police would only take place in the presence of her legal representative.

The suspension of DCI Ferguson had been upsetting news for the Operation Goldfinger team. However, the investigation would continue under the temporary leadership of DI Penfold.

The team's daily briefings were held each morning at 09:00 hours and, usually, about sixteen members would be present.

At about 08:50 hours on this particular morning, an unknown individual parked their Triumph Bonneville T120 modern classic motorcycle in the parking bay next to the main entrance of the Operation Goldfinger building. The individual was dressed in a one-piece grey textile motorcycle suit and wearing a full-face helmet. The helmet was removed, and he carried it with him as he entered the briefing room. Several team members were already seated around the oblong conference table, and they paid little attention to the motorcyclist.

He walked across to a small side table next to the coat stand and placed his helmet and gloves on the table. He had just unzipped the front of his motorcycle suit and was in the process of stepping out of it when DI Richard Penfold walked up to him. The visitor acknowledged him with a smile and said:

"Good morning. HQ have posted me here as a new member of your team."

DI Penfold was wearing a lanyard with his police identification badge on which was printed 'Richard Penfold, Detective Inspector.' The visitor looked at the badge and, in a friendly manner, asked:

"Do I call you Richard or Dick?"

The DI responded:

"This is a disciplined organisation and I expect respect of rank."

He tapped his badge and continued:

"You will address me as Detective Inspector."

The visitor nodded but made no verbal comment.

The DI added in a stern voice:

"I will be chairing the team briefing in a couple of minutes. Make yourself useful and make me a coffee; white with one sugar."

He pointed across the room to the small canteen. DI Penfold was known by the team for his brisk formal attitude.

The coffee was delivered to the DI, who was now seated at the head of the conference table. The visitor then took a seat along with other members of the team.

The DI opened the morning briefing and said:

"Today we have a new member joining the team and I would ask him to introduce himself."

He nodded in the direction of the new team member.

The new member, a man of slim build and of smart appearance, was dressed in a dark navy-blue business-style suit. He was wearing a police lanyard with his identity badge tucked into the top pocket of his jacket. He stood up, looked around the table to make eye contact with each member and responded:

"Good morning. I'm very pleased to be joining the team. I am Graham Durham. I have been a police officer for fifteen years, mostly as a detective. I have seen operational experience in Divisional CID, the Counter-Terrorism Department, Serious and Major Crime Investigation and the Home Office. I have a Law degree. You may have observed from the 'fancy dress' I was wearing when I entered the building, I'm a keen motorcyclist."

The DI interjected with a hint of indignation:

"Thank you, D.C. Durham. There's no need to stand up. We must now get on with the briefing."

Graham Durham remained standing. With a gentle but confident glance, he responded to the DI:

"Thank you. I prefer to stand when speaking. Detective Inspector Penfold, I hadn't quite finished. I was about to tell the team my rank. May I correct your assumption. For the last three years, I have held the rank of Detective Chief Inspector. I am here as your new Boss. There's much to do. I need to quickly get up to speed on the investigation."

DCI Durham gave the appearance of an intelligent, courteous and pleasant person. There was more than a hint in his voice, and facial expressions, that he possessed a healthy sense of humour, yet wasn't someone to underestimate; he was the Boss.

For his benefit, going around the table, he asked each team member to identify themselves and to give a brief update on their current actions. He made written notes as each member spoke. He thanked DI Penfold and asked him to continue chairing the morning briefing, adding, with a mischievous smile, that they would then change seats.

The Incident Room Manager then gave an overview of the investigation to date. At the request of DCI

Durham, he handed him the Policy Book, which also contained written comments to support why decisions had been made.

Tapping the open Policy Book, which was on the desk in front of him, the DCI commented:

"This is a very important book. It records the policy and direction of our investigation along with written explanation, and justification, for making the policy decisions. I set the policy and I take responsibility for the decisions, so, the buck stops with me. However, irrespective of rank, when we have our morning briefings, I give each of you permission to challenge any of my policy decisions. However, I will expect you to explain why you feel a particular decision is incorrect and put forward your reasoned alternative."

With a smile, he continued:

"I don't like people who always agree with the Boss. That is dangerous. Imagine me taking a case to Crown Court smugly thinking it's a strong case and then the judge pulls it apart and says I've been an 'idiot' and taken the investigation in the wrong direction. No! I'd rather be challenged by you, within the safety and privacy of these four walls, and told: 'No, Sir, that's an idiotic policy decision', and have you put forward a more appropriate one. If it's a good one, I'll claim it as my own and write it up in the Policy Book."

He added, with a further mischievous smile:

"Don't forget, I'm the Boss. So, if you suggest it's an idiot decision, please say it with respect."

Before the briefing was concluded, and in respect of the suspension of his predecessor, DCI Durham commented:

"We are all members of a disciplined organisation and here to serve the public. We react to the unexpected and deal with it with professionalism, loyalty and to the best of our ability. I do not want you speculating or discussing rumours about one of our colleagues".

Much activity had taken place elsewhere in the country. Early in the evening, Evans and Hamilton had left the holiday cottage in the Shropshire Hills and were travelling south on the M40 motorway in the dark blue Ford Focus car they had used the previous day. Evans was driving. He continued to act in a mysterious and quiet manner and hadn't told Hamilton their intended destination. He clearly had much on his mind. The indication was that they would not be returning to the cottage.

Just north of Oxford, after a one-hundred-and-fifteen-mile journey, they stopped at an M40 motorway service station and, at the restaurant, purchased a coffee. On the way out, Evans purchased a copy of the Sun newspaper and placed the folded copy under his arm. Back in the car, he quickly flicked through the pages, folded the paper at a certain page and handed it to Hamilton:

"Plan D almost accomplished." His laugh was chilling.

Hamilton took hold of the newspaper. The page contained a story about a police detective chief inspector who been suspended from duty following an allegation that he had raped a vulnerable woman. The story stated that the newspaper knew the identity of the suspended senior officer but would not be printing it at this time. It mentioned that the officer, before his suspension, had been heading an elite team of detectives investigating allegations of drug dealing.

"Does this refer to the team investigating you?" asked Hamilton.

"Yes, it bloody well does. He's been set up right and proper," said Evans.

Hamilton didn't verbally respond but was inwardly digesting the comment. Had Evans engineered a false allegation of rape? The next comment was even more disturbing.

Evans added:

"Just wait until DCI Ferguson is suspected of murdering the lady."

Again, Hamilton did not verbally respond, but inwardly thought:

'He is saying he is going to have the woman murdered and, by devious means, shift the blame on the innocent police officer?'

Hamilton was in the presence of a very brutal, dangerous and unpredictable man. Developments in the case were moving at a fast pace.

Evans had still not given details of their eventual destination, although it was evident he knew where they were going. Driving away from the service station, Evans turned off the M40 and continued east on the A43 for about twenty-five miles. He then turned onto the forecourt of a service station and slowly, with the car in second gear, drove around the entire parking area for both cars and lorries.

Having completed one circuit, he reversed the car into the far end of the lorry park and stopped. He switched the car lights off and, for a couple of minutes, sat silently in the darkness, leaning forward on the steering wheel surveying the car park. He then turned to Hamilton and said:

"I'm happy with that. It's almost payday time."

Hamilton was annoyed, almost to the point of showing anger, and responded:

"David, you might be happy but I'm not. I thought I was in this with you, but I haven't a clue where we are going or what we are doing. For most of the journey, you've remained in your own world, not saying what's going on. For fuck's sake, give me a clue."

Having released his frustration, Hamilton let out a smile and delivered a gentle and friendly punch onto Evans' forearm.

Evans, surprisingly, responded in a similar friendly manner:

"Sorry, mate. Have a lot to think about. I just needed to check this place out. Let's now get out of here and I'll treat you to a meal and tell you what you need to know."

He then drove them back the twenty-five miles to the same service station they had previously visited on the M40 motorway and parked. Evans said it would be safer to have their talk in the car before they entered the restaurant. He then outlined that the shipping container, with the hidden cocaine, had been delivered to the port of Southampton and, late in the evening, was scheduled to commence the road journey en route to Northampton. The trailer driver was on the 'payroll' and would stop at the service station on the A43 that Evans and Hamilton had recently 'checked out.'

Evans further explained that after they'd had their evening meal in the restaurant, they would then wait in their car to be collected in a Ford Transit van. This would be the vehicle used to 'recover' the cocaine from the shipping container, and it would have four 'helpers' on board. In answer to a question posed by Hamilton, he confirmed that firearms would be available 'if required.'

With a smile, Evans concluded by saying:

"Once we have collected the cocaine and driven away, the shipping container will continue the journey to the wholesalers in Northampton. Since they didn't know it was there, it won't be missed. After a short journey, the 'helpers' will be paid off and sent on their way. I'll drop you back off here to collect this car. Then I will take the van to a secret and secure lockup, where the cocaine will remain until I arrange the supply chain."

Hamilton interrupted:

"I wasn't born yesterday! So, you intend to drive off with all the 'goodies' and leave me sitting in a service station car park without so much as a forwarding address."

Evans turned, grabbed Hamilton tightly by the scruff of his shirt and said:

"And I wasn't born yesterday. I've lasted this long because I've always played a cautious game. If you want to run with me, and benefit from my knowledge, then you play by my rules. Once I've secured the cocaine, I'll be back for you. Then we'll travel back to our Shropshire cottage to sort out distribution of the cocaine and, if you help, I guarantee you will also get a good payday."

As quickly as Evans' anger exploded, it subsided. Hamilton agreed to the arrangement, and they entered the restaurant for a meal of steak and chips.

Arrangements had been made for Detective Chief Superintendent Joe Reece to undertake a further interview with the victim at the offices of her solicitor. However, she failed to keep the appointment and the solicitor was unable to contact her by telephone. Later in the day, the solicitor visited his client's home address but did not receive a reply. Neighbours said she had not been seen for the past two days, which was considered unusual. DCS Reece was informed of this development. More disturbing news was forthcoming.

An anonymous and brief telephone call had been made to a national news agency which stated, using his name and rank in full, that Detective Chief Inspector Donald Ferguson had kidnapped and murdered the lady who had made the allegation of rape. The information was immediately telephoned through to DCS Reece's office.

Following a case conference with the Crown Prosecution Service, direction was given for Ferguson to be visited at his home to be formally interviewed regarding any knowledge he may have about the missing woman. The conduct of the interview would be no different to any investigation into an alleged abduction; if there was evidence to indicate a crime had been committed, the suspect would be arrested.

Ferguson was not at home. Discreet enquiries with neighbours established that he had not been seen for a couple of days. Ferguson's details, and that of his car, were circulated on the Police National Computer (PNC) database.

With details of Donald Ferguson being circulated on the PNC, members of the Operation Goldfinger team quickly became aware of the allegations that had been made against him. As far as the team were concerned, since the attack on the prison van, they had not had any update on the likely whereabouts of the two escapees, Evans and Hamilton. Were they still in the UK or had they managed to escape abroad?

Chapter Seven

The Long Night

It would be a long and eventful night. Much activity would take place in different areas of the United Kingdom.

The port of Southampton, situated on the south coast of England, is the second largest deep-sea container port in the UK, with 210 acres of land for port operations. It handles more than two million containers a year. Loading and unloading operations can be performed simultaneously on four large deep-sea container ships, each capable of holding over 20,000 containers. A ship would be unloaded and returned to sea within three days.

The port has a dedicated terminal for fresh fruits and vegetables, which handles over 80,000 tons of such produce each year. This dedicated terminal ensures perishable produce is unloaded and transported to the required distribution centres with the minimum of delay.

It was mid-afternoon when the large container ship from Colombia docked. Unloading containers which contained perishable produce commenced immediately, and this included bananas. Colombia is a major exporter of bananas to the UK. Unripe bananas are first placed in ethylene-permeable containers within a shipping box arranged onto shipping pallets, which are then placed into shipping containers. This method ensures the bananas ripen en route.

Each shipping container has an identification code and various other markings in large print on all four sides. From the port's central control room, one shipping container received special attention. It was under constant police surveillance on CCTV. The joint police operation involved officers from the Border Force, National Crime Agency, firearms and selected officers from Operation Goldfinger.

Details of the operation to track the shipping container, with its cargo of cocaine, had been closely guarded and restricted as there was evidence to indicate Evans had an unknown informant within the police.

A small tracking device had been discreetly attached to the container. Highly sensitive intelligence had established the twenty-foot-long container contained over a tonne (1000 kg) of cocaine hydrochloride, hidden within some pallets. The cocaine had an estimated street value of one hundred million pounds.

Less than 2% of containers receive inspection by Customs and the container under surveillance had not been opened for inspection. The accompanying paperwork had been examined by Customs and approved as correct. The container of bananas was destined for a legitimate vegetable and fruits wholesalers' warehouse in Oxfordshire.

The container remained stacked on the dock, alongside hundreds of other containers, awaiting transport. The police operational plan would be to allow the container to clear customs on a truck-trailer. Surreptitiously, members of the team would then follow it to its destination.

Five hundred and sixty miles from Southampton, near to the village of Fort Augustus in the Scottish Highlands, Donald Ferguson's empty silver-coloured Volvo car was parked on the forecourt of a public house. The village was located just off the A82 road, fifty-six kilometres north of Inverness, in a mountainous and sparsely populated part of the United Kingdom.

It was late evening. The suspended detective chief inspector was seated alone in the small dimly lit saloon bar sipping a double whisky, his second of the evening. This was the first alcoholic drink he had consumed in over twenty-five years, throughout his entire police service and since leaving the Navy.

He walked to the bar and ordered a third double whisky. He looked fatigued and unwell.

The barman asked:

"I haven't seen you before. Are you on holiday?"

"No. Just passing through. I was born a couple of miles from Fort Augustus but haven't been back for over forty years. It's still a beautiful place."

He finished his drink, nodded to the barman and silently mouthed "thank you" before he quietly departed the pub. He turned left, in the opposite direction of his parked car, and walked along a footpath towards Loch Ness.

It was a still, warm and dark night. The only light was from the reflection of the almost full moon on the water.

He was very alone. This proud innocent man was confused and his spirit broken. Calmly and slowly, he walked deeper and deeper into the water and disappeared.

Loch Ness extended thirty-six kilometres in length and was two hundred and thirty metres at its deepest. It was the second-largest loch in Scotland. Donald Ferguson had returned home to his place of birth and happy childhood. His body would never be found. Next morning, in his parked unlocked Volvo car, his neatly folded coat was found on the front passenger seat. It contained his wallet, passport and birth certificate. There was an absence of a goodbye message.

It was after midnight when the shipping container, loaded on its truck-trailer, left the port of Southampton and commenced the journey to its destination in Northampton. The container was scheduled to arrive at the warehouse before sunrise to be unloaded of the bananas which would be available for distribution to customers when the early morning market opened. The legitimate wholesalers had not been aware that, when the container was shipped from Colombia to the UK, it had contained cocaine hidden under some pallets.

Two hours into the journey, heading north on the M40 motorway, the container-trailer turned off onto the slip road to a service station and into the large lorry park. The vehicle drove to the far end of the park and reversed alongside a row of stationary lorries, almost up against a wooded area, before parking. The area was beyond the lit lampposts situated at the entrance of the car park. The driver then casually walked the hundred metres to the single-storey restaurant for an early coffee and breakfast.

A dark blue Ford Transit van drove into the lorry park, reversed and stopped alongside the rear end of the container-truck. The van parked very close to the side of the container, leaving just enough room for a person to squeeze between the two. The area was unlit and the rear of the two vehicles could not be seen by anyone walking across the lorry park. The driver of the Ford Transit van remained in his seat to keep watch.

The rear doors of the Ford Transit van were opened from the inside. Four men, wearing dark clothing and balaclavas, climbed from the back of the van. Two remained standing near to the opened doors. The other two went to the rear of the container, with one using a key to unlock and open the large metal door. He climbed into the rear of the container and, in the darkness, switched on a head torch.

Immediately, he commenced to remove wrapped bricks of cocaine from under pallets, on which cases of bananas were packed. In a continuous chain movement, each 10 kg brick of cocaine was handed from one man to the next and stacked into the back of the van.

Within two minutes, all one hundred and ten cocaine bricks had been packed into the van. The container door had been re-locked. All five men were securely back in the Ford van, with their valuable cargo, and about to depart the lorry park. The retail street value of their 1000 kg cocaine haul was an estimated £100 million.

The last thing they wanted to do was raise any suspicion by driving recklessly away at speed; they just needed to remain calm and take time to drive away.

A lorry, which had been stationary in one of the nearby rows of parked lorries, began to manoeuvre out of its bay and towards the illuminated exit sign in the distance. The fact that it stopped momentarily in front of the Ford Transit van caused no alarm.

Suddenly, the entire canvas-curtained side of the stationary lorry dropped down onto the road. Blindingly bright search lights were beaming towards the Ford van. A loudspeaker blasted out:

"Armed Police. Freeze. Don't move."

Four Specialist Firearms Officers (SFO), wearing full tactical gear (body armour, Kevlar helmet and goggles) were standing in a line on the lorry pointing Heckler and Koch MP5SF 9mm carbine rifles at the Ford van. From either side of the standing line, three similarly equipped SFO's jumped from the lorry and ran forward to surround the van.

At gunpoint, the five men were ordered out of the van and instructed to lie face down on the road. Each was handcuffed. Several guns and mobile phones were recovered from the van. Three more marked police cars, with uniformed officers, then roared into view and stopped near the arrested men.

The Ford van was immediately sealed to ensure security of the valuable cargo. It was then fully covered in plastic sheeting to preserve its integrity for a detailed forensic examination before being lifted by crane onto a police vehicle transporter.

The five arrested and handcuffed men were quickly taken away in separate police cars to different custody suites. Evans and Hamilton were among the five men arrested. The police operation had been so unexpected, and swift, that the two men had not had time to communicate with each other.

The whole operation had been videoed by the police team. As he was having breakfast in the restaurant, the driver of the banana lorry consignment was visited and arrested. Under interview, he admitted he had received £10,000 to 'ask no questions and just turn a blind eye' and go for breakfast. The shipping container subsequently underwent further detailed examination to ensure no further illegal substances remained and to undertake forensic tests to connect the arrested men with the scene.

The sun had yet to rise above the Shropshire Hills on a slightly chilly and misty early morning. A team of soldiers from UK Special Forces had encamped in an isolated area there overnight. They were preparing to undertake a rescue mission. Several days earlier, Evans and Hamilton had trekked over the hills to visit the former Royal Observer Corps Nuclear bunker, located a mile from where the soldiers were camped.

The shaft entrance to the bunker was covered by, and hidden within, a locked metal shipping container positioned within an isolated and gated private woodland. On the occasion when Hamilton and Evans had visited, it had been occupied by two armed thugs and it appeared other people were being held captive in the bunker in a separate locked room at the end of a long underground corridor.

The door to the shipping container remained locked. There was no sign of occupants, although sensitive intelligence indicated that the two armed men and their captives were still resident in the bunker. It was of concern to the police that the captives' lives were in immediate danger. The two men guarding them possessed powerful firearms and were prepared to use them. Extracting the captives safely from the underground bunker would be difficult and dangerous. This was to be the mission the team from UK Special Forces would undertake.

During the night, two members from the Special Forces team had undertaken reconnaissance in the woodland and surrounding area, when they came across a freshly dug pit. The top layer of the vegetation had been carefully cut into squares and placed on one side. The pit measured about two metres deep, two metres long and one metre wide. The obvious deduction was that something or someone was to be buried in the pit, with the vegetation then carefully replaced to conceal disturbance. Was this to be the burial place for the murdered captives?

The discovery of the pit had been reported back to the other four members of the Special Forces team, located a mile away in a heavily wooded area. They had earlier received communication that the raid on the cocaine shipment had been successful with the main targets arrested. There was concern that the two men would likely be preparing to now murder their captives.

The Special Forces team, therefore, made final preparations to complete their mission. A small military-grade drone, fitted with a video camera, was deployed to fly over the wooded area where the metal container was located. It was flown at sufficient height so as not to alert anyone on the ground to its presence. A clear view of the area was transmitted back to the military team. All appeared clear, with no sign of any people.

Quietly, the rescue team returned to the area and stationed themselves around the shipping container. They were dressed in full combat gear with Kevlar helmets and night vision goggles, and each wore a body camera. One soldier crept forward and carefully examined the lock on the door of the container. Using a lock-pick, he successfully released the mechanism and removed the lock. Four soldiers then entered the metal container. The first soldier endeavoured to pick the lock on the hatch covering the shaft entrance. The lock would not budge. The decision was taken to force entry.

The first soldier pressed a small ball of plastic explosive, with fuse, into the lock. Soldiers numbered two and three stood on either side of the closed hatch, each holding a Heckler and Koch 9mm carbine rifle. They readied themselves for action the moment the hatch was opened. Soldier four stood, legs astride, facing the hatch and holding two stun grenades.

On the given order, the fuse was ignited. There was an immediate small, muffled explosion. The hatch lifted. The two stun grenades were pitched down the fourteen-foot shaft. They exploded with an extremely loud bang. The noise and accompanying blinding flash of light temporarily disoriented the two guards.

Two armed soldiers rapidly descended the metal ladder and were able to detain both guards without a shot being fired. Very effectively, and without subtlety, the two guards were forced to the ground and rolled onto their fronts. Their wrists were secured together with plastic ties. Two loaded Uzi sub-machine guns were recovered from on top of the table and immediately unloaded to ensure safety.

Two soldiers unlocked the inner metal door, then, with head torches switched on, cautiously made their way along the dark corridor. At the far end of the corridor, they unlocked another metal door, which revealed dark, cramped and squalid conditions with the figures of three individuals crouched in the corner. It had served as an improvised prison for the three captives.

Two men and a woman were released from their jail. It was evident that the two men had been physically tortured, and the woman had facial injuries. Each required medical attention at the scene. They were then evacuated to a local hospital in a military helicopter which had landed nearby.

The two guards were searched, then hooded and escorted to another military helicopter which was stationed nearby. The men were not cooperative and, by their actions, indicated that they did not speak or understand English.

Once the bunker and area were deemed safe, a specialist team of forensic personnel moved in and took charge of the scene. Although located in an isolated area, the local press soon became aware of the military action, no doubt, reported by early morning walkers. The brief response was that it had been a military training exercise.

It was subsequently established that the two 'captive' men were British nationals, both with criminal records for violence and drug dealing. They insisted they had been kidnapped at the instigation of Evans. He had regarded them as serious and dangerous rivals in his quest to be the dominant 'Boss' in the criminal importation of cocaine. He had believed that if he didn't 'remove' them, they, in time, would have him eliminated.

The woman was Mary Jean Butterfield, forty-five years of age. She was a vulnerable divorcee and reliant on a steady supply of illicit drugs. Mary was the lady who had made an allegation of rape against Detective Chief Inspector Donald Ferguson. It had been a totally false allegation.

She had been sought out by an associate of David Evans and paid £10,000 in cash, plus a continued supply of cocaine, to make the false allegation. He had supplied her with the content of her witness statement about the alleged rape which she gave to the Sun newspaper. It was likely that the action had been undertaken whilst in her vulnerable state and high on drugs.

Mary Butterfield had soon realised the seriousness of her action and wanted to withdraw the allegation. She had even mentioned telling the police, and this was when she had been kidnapped. Evans had planned to have her killed and arrange for the murder to be blamed on the suspended DCI Ferguson.

When the Army undertake an armed operation in a civilian environment, a formal written transfer of authority is handed over from the civil authorities, usually the police, to the Army commander. Once the danger at the old nuclear bunker had been neutralised, the Special Forces team withdrew, with the Army Captain in charge of the mission formally handing authority back to the senior police commander.

Once the three former captives had received medical treatment, DI Fatima Ramiz was put in charge of a small team of detectives to debrief them, ensure their cooperation and obtain their witness statements to be used in the case being built against David Evans and associates.

Meanwhile, Guy Hamilton was escorted into the secure Custody Suite of a Metropolitan police station. His wrists were handcuffed in front of his chest as he was dragged backwards, somewhat roughly, by Detective Inspector Richard Penfold and a detective constable. His body and arms were feeling bruised. The arrest team had certainly been swift and effective, but without much finesse.

The Custody Sergeant informed him of his rights and explained, in view of the early hour, that he would be placed in a cell to sleep, with a formal interview under caution being arranged for later in the morning with a solicitor present.

Hamilton stated that he was permitted to make a telephone call. The Custody Sergeant agreed to the request. Hamilton took the handset, dialled a number and simply spoke into the mouthpiece: "CODE 446."

He then handed the handset to the Custody Sergeant telling him to listen. The Custody Sergeant listened and, having been given a specific instruction, he replaced the handset. As requested, he then telephoned the police control centre Duty Desk to confirm authentication of the instruction he had been given. He did so and listened, before answering:

"Certainly. I understand. Thank you, Sir."

The Custody Sergeant replaced the handset, turned to the two detectives restraining Hamilton and said:

"That was a detective chief superintendent from Special Branch. He has instructed me that Mr Hamilton operates under the authority of HM Government. He is not to be interviewed or searched. He is not required to give you any information about himself or about his actions. He is to be released forthwith."

The Custody Sergeant paused and, with a puzzled expression, continued:

"This arrest and detention did not take place. A government official will call here soon to collect Mr Hamilton."

The escorting DI Penfold looked equally bemused. He quietly whispered:

"What the fuck is this all about?"

Mr Hamilton turned to the incredulous-looking detective inspector, held his handcuffed wrists forward and politely asked the officer to unlock them. DI Penfold continued to look puzzled as he unlocked and removed the handcuffs.

Hamilton leaned towards the DI and, with a slight smile, whispered in his ear:

"Should we meet in the future, please remember to address me as Sir."

It had been a busy few hours for Detective Chief Inspector Graham Durham. He'd had very little sleep having received telephone calls updating him on the night's events, so decided to leave home early for his office. He parked his car at the rear of the Operation Goldfinger major incident room building at 05:30 hours.

The DCI remained seated in his car mulling over the night's events. He was pleased with the successful arrest of the gang, including Evans and Hamilton, and the seizure of the cocaine; and he was particularly relieved that the Special Forces operation had recovered the three captives. However, the apparent death of Donald Ferguson was a tragedy.

As the DCI prepared to leave his car, he looked up and noticed a dim light on in his second-floor office. He unlocked the rear security door and walked up the back stairs. The corridor was in darkness except for a light source reflecting under his closed office door.

Slowly, he opened the door, keeping hold of the handle. He stood motionless and silent in the doorway, casting a shadowy figure. A man was seated at the DCI's desk with the desk lamp switched on. A file in front of him was open.

There was eye contact, but no words. Maintaining direct eye contact, the DCI walked into his office and sat down on one of the two visitor's chairs positioned in front of the desk. He held out his right hand. The man closed the file and handed it to him.

The DCI spoke quietly, but with authority:

"Detective Constable Roger Adams, explanation, please."

DC Adams hesitated. He attempted to speak, but nothing came out. The DCI allowed a long pause then repeated his question.

The DC offered the pathetic explanation that he thought he'd heard the DCI's telephone ringing but acknowledged he had been mistaken. In response to further questions, he admitted he did not have a legitimate reason to be in the office.

Why was he in the building at 05:30 hours when his scheduled duty for that day was 09:00 to 17:00 hours? He had no convincing answer, except to shrug his shoulders and say he felt 'restless' so thought he'd begin his working day early.

The DCI added he was disappointed in the young officer and asked him about his family.

"I'm married, with two young children; a girl and a boy."

The DCI interrupted:

"Charlotte aged five years and James aged two years. When I take charge of a department, I pride myself on quickly getting to know about my staff. I understand you have six years police service, with the last two years in the regional drug unit?"

"Yes, Sir."

"And you have a large mortgage on your home. With that, and a young family, finances are probably tight?"

"Yes, they are, Sir."

The DCI nodded and smiled, as if in acknowledgment. DC Adams began to feel more relaxed. He thought, perhaps the 'Boss' would allow this indiscretion to pass.

In his apparently more conciliatory mood, the DCI casually commented:

"Excellent news about the arrest of Evans and his gang caught red-handed with a shipping container full of cocaine."

D.C. Adams smiled and replied:

"Yes, excellent news, Sir."

Silence followed. The DCI retained eye contact with DC Adams and maintained the stare. Neither a facial movement, nor a flicker of an eyelid. DC Adams instantly realised the significance of his comment. Nervously, he looked down at the desktop, then slowly raised his eyes. The DCI was still motionless with his knowing stare towards the hapless DC.

The DCI allowed the silence to continue for a full painful minute, then continuing with his stare, he said:

"That was your mistake and you know it. News of the arrest of Evans and his gang has not been released, yet you already knew the facts."

The DCI paused then continued:

"I'm disappointed in you. We have been aware that someone within the police service has been supplying confidential information to Evans. Let's not beat around the bush. That person is you. Why?"

DC Adams did not reply.

"Why, DC Adams?" The DCI repeated: "Why, DC Adams?"

He continued:

"We will be seizing your mobile phones, laptops, everything, which will be subjected to detailed forensic and technical examination. We are aware of your unauthorised checks on the PNC."

DC Adams became visibly upset. He did not deny the allegations. The DCI explained that members of the Professional Standards Department would attend to formally deal with the matter.

After regaining his composure, DC Adams said he wished to explain himself to DCI Durham.

He said it had begun about a year earlier, when he was assigned to a road policing operation to stop and search vehicles owned by known drug dealers. One such vehicle was a Range Rover owned by David Evans. It was driven by his twin brother, Terry Evans. David was in the front passenger seat at the time of the stop. Both brothers were asked to step out of the car whilst the interior was checked.

On the front passenger seat, which David Evans had just vacated, DC Adams had picked up an unsealed brown envelope. It contained a large wad of £20 notes. He questioned Evans about it, and he had replied:

"Looks like ten thousand quid to me. It's not mine. Probably slipped out of your pocket as you bent over. Would help pay your mortgage. You must take more care of your money."

Evans had taken hold of the envelope and pushed it into the inside pocket of the jacket the DC was wearing. He had patted the pocket and added:

"Your lucky day, officer."

The DCI looked stern and asked:

"Did you keep the money?"

Adams replied:

"Yes, I did. I tried to push his hand back, but not very forcefully. I hesitated for a moment and have regretted it ever since."

The DCI asked:

"Did you find any drugs in the car?"

"No."

"Did you try to find drugs?"

"No."

The DCI asked:

"Was that because, once you pocketed the money, you stopped the search?"

DC nodded and replied:

"Yes."

The DCI leaned forward.

"From that date forward, did you supply Evans with confidential police information?"

The distraught DC replied:

"Yes, but I hated myself every time I did. I was in his trap. I'm glad I've been caught."

The DCI continued:

"And am I correct in saying that you undertook unauthorised PNC checks on Guy Hamilton and gave the details to David Evans?"

DC Adams replied:

"Yes."

DCI Durham said he would end the conversation and allow the matter to be continued with the Professional Standards Department.

Within a couple of hours, DCI Durham would be chairing the first Operation Goldfinger team meeting of the day. There would be much to report on the night's police activities and arrests, with much work still to do.

Prior to the DCI's morning briefing, the staff had not previously been made aware of the planned police raid on the shipping container, nor of the existence of the former nuclear bunker with the captives. The intelligence on the two issues had been ascertained from a highly sensitive source and, for reasons of security and personal safety, its circulation had been restricted to a limited few.

The overall results could now be disclosed although, for operational reasons, certain elements would remain classified. The team members were professional, experienced police officers and accepted that such limitations were sometimes necessary.

The cocaine drug bust had been a major success and freeing the three 'captives' unharmed had saved lives. However, the detailed work had just begun. The arrests, and recently acquired collaborative evidence, would widen the police investigation and, thus, enable further arrests and convictions for major drug trafficking. The scale of Evans' drug empire would finally be exposed and dismantled.

DCI Durham would brief the team on the sad news regarding their former 'Boss' and colleague, Donald Ferguson. It would also be his unpleasant duty to report that one of their own team had been arrested on suspicion of being an informant to Evans.

With the morning team meeting concluded, DCI Durham called a senior-team meeting in his office with DI Richard Penfold, DI Fatima Ramiz and Barry Bishop (Incident Room Manager). He acknowledged that the events and arrests of the past day had been somewhat unusual and 'secretive', but that the clandestine nature of the operation had been necessary. He would endeavour to be as transparent as possible, whilst accepting that his own knowledge was limited.

He recapped on the prime reason why Operation Goldfinger had been established. It had been to undertake a coordinated and detailed investigation into the criminal drug dealing and violent activities of David Evans and his associates. He was a shrewd operator who employed extreme violence, blackmail and bribery to persuade potential witnesses to give evidence to police.

He was suspected of personally killing rivals, and there was credible intelligence to indicate two further rivals had been kidnapped and their lives were in danger.

Immediate and positive action needed to be taken. Additional technical resources were deployed, but ultimate success would depend on physical infiltration into the heart of the organisation, which depended on getting direct access to Evans. This would be difficult and dangerous and had been successfully achieved.

The DCI continued to explain that when Operation Goldfinger was established, there was intelligence to indicate that Evans had one, or possibly more, police officers on his payroll. The issue was discussed at senior police and government level. The police were directed to proceed with the criminal investigation under Operation Goldfinger, while other government agencies would address the issue of acquiring highly sensitive intelligence.

The Operation Goldfinger senior management meeting continued to discuss the recent updates on David Evans and the other members of his gang who had been arrested during the raid on the shipping container.

The Incident Room Manager commented:

"The last information we had on Guy Hamilton was when he escaped with Evans at the time of the prison van attack. I was wondering whether the two men had remained together, or had they parted shortly after and gone their separate ways?"

He looked across the table to DCI Durham and continued:

"Just before the team meeting, I checked the PNC database and was surprised there was no longer a record for Guy Hamilton, the man wanted for extradition to the United States of America and for escaping from the hijacked prison van with Evans. It appears a button has been pressed and all mention of the man has disappeared!"

Before his retirement from the police service, Barry Bishop, the Incident Room Manager, had been an experienced and extremely competent detective inspector. When he raised the query about Guy Hamilton, he had a glint in his eye, and had deliberately not mentioned it at the general team meeting.

DI Penfold, who, earlier that morning had been involved in the 'arrest' of the man known as Hamilton, nodded in approval.

DCI Durham simply commented:

"We were grateful to receive this highly sensitive and accurate intelligence, which has resulted in the successful outcome of Operation Goldfinger. I do not intend to enlarge. We are governed by the Official Secrets Act. May I instruct - no further discussion on Guy Hamilton. The man doesn't exist."

Chapter Eight
Back to the Office

Greenwood Park was a five-star country house hotel and health spa set amidst ten acres of well-manicured grounds, with far-reaching views over the Surrey countryside, located between Ascot and Sunningdale. It was a glorious early spring morning, with a clear blue sky and a light refreshing breeze, when a grey metallic Land Rover Discovery drove slowly up the driveway and parked by the main hotel entrance.

The driver walked into the foyer carrying a large leather travel bag and presented himself at the reception desk. A tall slim man, with a suit bag slung over his shoulder, slowly exited from the car's rear passenger seat. He was in his early forties, with a tanned complexion, an unkempt beard and shaggy blonde hair. The individual was casually dressed in well-worn clothing and looked out of place in the luxurious surroundings of the hotel. In a momentary indiscretion, the expression on the receptionist's face indicated that he shared the same opinion.

The driver addressed the suited male receptionist:

"Good morning. This gentleman is Mr Julian Lawson. A suite has been reserved for him by my company."

The receptionist nodded and replied:

"Yes, Sir. For three nights with all meals included. And the bill has been settled in advance."

Mr Lawson nodded in response and simply said:

"Thank you."

A porter was summoned. He took the luggage bag from the driver and escorted Mr Lawson to a suite situated on the ground floor at the rear of the hotel. He unlocked the door with a security swipe card, entered the room and placed the bag on the luggage rack positioned just inside the hallway. The porter ensured Lawson was familiar with the layout of the suite, then handed him the swipe card and wished him a good day. Lawson was keen to refresh himself with a hot bath, followed by several hours' sleep on the king-size bed.

At midday, he strolled to the reception desk and spoke to the receptionist:

"Having had some hours sleep and a relaxing bath, I'm now feeling a little more human than when I was 'delivered' here earlier this morning. I couldn't help noticing your reaction to my dishevelled appearance. Yes, I acknowledge it was out of keeping with the high standards of your hotel."

The receptionist interrupted and was apologetic in his response:

"Forgive me, Sir; no disrespect intended."

Lawson smiled and responded:

"No offence taken. I've just returned to the UK from an expedition abroad. I'm booked in here for three days to relax and de-stress, hopefully including a massage, and to use the spa and swimming pool. Please book me an appointment with your in-house barber for a haircut and wet shave to remove my beard."

During the next few days, Lawson was able to relax and indulge in the services of the hotel and the health spa.

On the day of departure, Lawson was up at the break of dawn for a long and slow walk around the extensive and secluded grounds of the hotel. He returned refreshed to the ground-floor restaurant and ordered a full English breakfast, commencing with two hot croissants and fresh black coffee.

He returned to his room, looked at himself in the bathroom mirror and considered himself almost unrecognisable from his appearance of three days earlier. He was now clean shaven with a fresh short haircut. The bleached streaks were gone, and his hair was back to its normal hazel brown colour. Lawson had spent several previous weeks portraying a scruffy appearance. Now, he wanted to return to the civilised world and respectability.

Lawson unzipped the garment bag and took from it a new well-tailored navy-blue pinstriped suit which he put on, together with a crisp designer white shirt and a dark burgundy silk tie. He removed the cheap £20 Sekonda wristwatch he had been wearing for the past number of weeks and placed it in the waste bin. From his holdall, he took out his normal watch - an Omega Seamaster - and a pair of silver cufflinks. He was now ready to return to his office in the City.

He walked to the reception desk, handed in his swipe card, and thanked the staff for a pleasant stay. The Land

Rover Discovery car was parked outside waiting to drive him into the City of London to his place of employment.

The journey would take about forty-five minutes. He relaxed in the rear seat of the Discovery. There was little communication with the driver. Lawson was deep in thought. He reflected on the recent, and often dangerous, situations in which he had been involved, all on behalf of HM Government! During the next few days, he would, no doubt, be engaged in staff debriefs on his activities, and writing detailed reports and assessments.

Julian Lawson was a senior member of the British Security Service, more commonly known by the public as MI5. The service was responsible for protecting the United Kingdom, its citizens and interests at home and overseas against threats to national security. Such threats may emanate from terrorism, espionage and sabotage intended to overthrow or undermine parliamentary democracy.

MI5 officers operate under Ministry of Defence 'cover' but, in reality, the service is responsible to the UK Home Office. The service does not have powers of arrest or prosecution. This authority rests with the police.

The Secret Intelligence Service (MI6) is MI5's sister organisation. Its remit is the collection of secret intelligence, to mount operations overseas to prevent and detect serious crime and to promote and defend the national security and economic well-being of the United Kingdom. MI6 is responsible to the Foreign Office. The two organisations often work together.

The London Headquarters of MI5 is Thames House in Millbank on the north side of the river Thames. It was an imposing Portland stone and granite-built eight-storey Neoclassical Grade 11 listed building, opened as the HQ for MI5 in 1994. The considerable physical and electronic defences for the building were not immediately apparent.

There was no signage on the outside of the MI5 building to identify its function. The main entrance was for use by visitors. Attendance was by appointment only, which explained the lack of external door handles. The façade of the building was the public perception of MI5, as often pictured in media news reports and photographs.

Prior to 1990, the UK government did not publicly acknowledge the existence of its security services. In recent years, MI5 has slightly come out of the shadows.

The location of its HQ and function are now in the public arena. However, for operational and safety reasons, the identities of members of the service remain strictly guarded.

Staff working in the building enter via one of several doors located along the rear of the building accessed from a side street. The road is under twenty-four hour camera surveillance and monitored by security personnel.

Lawson entered the complex via a rear secure door. He proceeded to the ground-floor Reception, which was a secure isolated area, where staff acknowledged his arrival. He clipped his security pass onto his breast pocket in preparation for entering the main restricted area of the building.

Security passes display a colour photograph of the recipient and incorporate proximity-card technology, which enable access to secure areas without the need to physically use a swipe card. The system records arrival and departure times of the holder. An airport-style full-body scanner is incorporated within the security system, which can also detect non-metal objects. Selected staff are permitted to take previously approved and examined electronic items into the building. Visitors are required to leave electronic items, including iPads, mobile phones and cameras, at Reception.

Each floor of the eight-storey building was occupied by a different department within the organisation. Throughout, the requirement for maximum security remained paramount. The handling and movement of sensitive and secret intelligence at every level was scrupulously managed. Access to each level of the building, and to each section, was strictly limited to authorised personnel with an operational requirement to be there.

Lawson's office was situated on the second floor and was identified simply by a number on the door. Corridors on each floor were identical, with a line of closed and locked doors on either side. Staff only visited another office or section by prior appointment. A casual walk around the building for an informal chat with a colleague was not only prohibited but also impractical.

He unlocked his small single-occupancy office and entered. The office furniture was modern and functional. On the polished wooden desktop sat a computer, a mainline telephone, a table mat and a small desk lamp. Nothing else. He sat down on the brown leather swivel chair and switched on the lamp. The room was devoid of personality, and deliberately so. No photographs or any personal items which might identify the occupant were permitted. The policy dictated that whenever an office was vacated, all files and other material must be placed in the locked office safe.

Lawson still had some difficulty adhering to the restrictions imposed on operational officers, or agents, working within the service. For good logical and practical reasons, members operated under a covert identity.

MI5 is a secret organisation. Officers depend on the trust and professionalism of their colleagues, often whilst on sensitive and dangerous operations, yet they do not know their colleagues' true identities, nor anything about their family background or recreational interests. Therefore, Lawson's colleagues did not know his true identity. The reason behind the policy is to maintain the integrity of the service and safety of staff. One potential defector, operating within the organisation, would not be in a position to betray the true identity of its members to a foreign enemy intelligence agency. Hence, only a very few people within the top management of MI5 were aware of Lawson's true identity.

He logged on to his computer, registered that he was on duty, and checked the electronic diary for his department, noting that Director Jane Rigby was on duty and working in her office. Therefore, he made an appointment to visit her at 10:00 hours to give her a personal one-to-one debrief on his recent operational activities. For the previous four years, as Director of Special Operations, she had been his immediate 'Boss.'

In a professional capacity, he was fond of her. She was an extremely knowledgeable and competent Operations Director who demanded high standards but possessed a genuinely caring attitude towards the welfare of her team. As with other members of the organisation, he did not know her true identity. He assessed that she was in her mid-forties, with a public-school education and likely from a middle-class family background.

She was elegant in manner and dress, always had well-manicured fingernails, and usually wore tortoise-shell-framed spectacles on a thin, gold-linked chain around her neck. Was she married? He didn't know - she used the title 'Ms' In nearly four years of working together in the same department, the only information he had gleaned about her private life was that she enjoyed summer evening visits to watch opera at Glyndebourne and owned a horse.

Jane Rigby's office was larger than Lawson's with the addition of two comfy armchairs and a low coffee table positioned at the far end. She greeted Lawson with a gentle embrace as he entered her office:

"Julian, I was genuinely worried for your well-being and felt guilty for sending you on this dangerous assignment, especially as it was shortly after you had been shot in the arm."

Lawson smiled and responded:

"Goodness. I'm grateful to have received my first hug from an MI5 Director. You were kind enough to visit me whilst I was recovering from the wound to explain the situation and I readily agreed. I'd never been in prison before. It was an adventure, but the food was grim."

They both laughed and Rigby, with a smile, added:

"Getting wounded, then to be asked to spend time in prison and forced to eat grim food… a hug from an MI5 Director is the least 'reward' I can offer."

Rigby served up fresh coffee and placed the two cups on the table, along with a plate of chocolate biscuits. She suggested that they settle themselves in the two comfy armchairs. Her manner reminded him of the late Margaret Thatcher, the former Conservative Prime Minister of the United Kingdom, a positive lady, confident in her own ability and with an uncompromising leadership style. Men would underestimate her at their peril. However, she also possessed a feminine side and was never too proud to be the perfect host.

Rigby continued:

"The situation required urgent action. Police intelligence strongly indicated that the David Evans gang had kidnapped two drug rivals, *and* the missing Mary Jean Butterfield, and were planning to murder them. However, there was no indication of where they were being held. The infiltration of an undercover officer was risky but offered the best option for saving their lives. Placing you alongside Evans, with your wounded and false narrative, added authenticity to the sting. You, as a fugitive from the FBI with a genuine gunshot wound and a criminal record, end up sharing a prison cell with him."

To successfully infiltrate into a criminal gang to fit in with their illegal activities, an operative will often need to commit crime. However, the individual would be protected from being prosecuted provided prior approval had been authorised at a senior management level. Such approval had been given, and Lawson had been briefed on the restrictions under which he would operate. He would not be permitted to sample or participate in taking drugs. If drugs were offered, his response was to have been that he could not take drugs because he had been a drug addict in the past.

In addition to the priority to save the lives of the three kidnapped individuals, the increase in killings and intimidation attributed to Evans had intensified the urgency to collect incriminating evidence against him and his associates to support a successful criminal prosecution.

When Lawson, in the guise of Guy Hamilton, was in prison with Evans, he had been able to use the excuse of the daily visit to the prison doctor as an opportunity to make telephone contact and update MI5. He had been able to inform them that Evans had the use of a Zanco Tiny miniature mobile phone. Thus, the 'technical team' had been able to monitor telephone conversations, which included plans to hijack the prison van. From the telephone interception, Lawson had been made aware of the plan, and had confirmed with MI5 that he was happy to run with it.

Since there was strong intelligence that Evans had an unknown informer within the police, the operation involving the infiltration of Lawson had not been shared with the police, except at the senior level.

The infiltration of Lawson into Evans' organisation had been a success. Evans was now in custody having been caught red-handed involved with the illegal importation of a large amount of cocaine; the three kidnapped victims had been safely recovered; his wife was now cooperating. With Evans' arrest and remand in custody, previously frightened associates and witnesses were now beginning to cooperate and supply evidence towards his prosecution.

Rigby confirmed that following the late evening raid by police on the lorry carrying the imported cocaine, each of the arrested attackers, including Evans, had been quickly handcuffed and placed in separate police cars. Subsequently, in the Custody Suite, Evans had been formally interviewed, after caution, in the presence of his solicitor. As had been expected, he had responded to each question:

"On the advice of my lawyer, no comment."

After several 'no comment' interviews, Evans had been charged in connection with the importation of cocaine. He was also charged in connection with the earlier hijack of the prison van and his escape from lawful custody. At the local magistrate's court, he had been remanded in custody to HM Prison Belmarsh, a category A prison. Such institutions are of the highest security level and are reserved for prisoners deemed a high risk to the public or of escape.

The prosecutor stressed that further charges relating to allegations involving serious crime would be laid at a later date. In due course, the case would be sent for trial to the Crown Court.

The arrests had taken place at night, in darkness, and with powerful blinding spotlights. The police interviewers indicated to Evans that, in the confusion, one or more of the attackers may have escaped arrest. Evans had declined to give the identity of the other attackers in his gang or how many were involved. The interviewers had made no mention of Guy Hamilton, leaving Evans to assume he must have escaped arrest.

Following discussion with Jane Rigby, it was provisionally agreed that within the next couple of weeks,

Lawson should contact senior police officers involved with Operation Goldfinger to disclose limited but relevant information to assist the investigation into Evans. The proposal would require approval from top management.

For the present, only senior members of the Police Department within the Home Office had been aware of Lawson's involvement in the infiltration operation against David Evans. The police, in conjunction with the Crown Prosecution Service, would be responsible for preparing the many case files.

The involvement of Lawson, using his cover identity of Guy Hamilton, would be included in the case files, and would be subject to disclosure. However, where disclosure could cause real damage to the public interest in the protection of national security, the prosecutor may apply to the trial judge for authority to withhold the material, in the form of a claim for 'public interest immunity', made based on a certificate signed by the Home Secretary. The court, not MI5 or the government, ultimately decided what must be disclosed in a particular case.

Lawson discussed with Rigby his future safety. It was agreed, for the immediate future, that he would take up the offer of living in a staff apartment within the MI5 building. He was keen to return to living in his cottage on the outskirts of Petworth, West Sussex, this being the location where he had been attacked and shot in the arm.

Military grade security had been installed in the cottage, with miniature cameras and intruder detection sensors located in the surrounding woodland. Before concluding the meeting, Jane Rigby was keen to ensure that Lawson underwent a full medical checkup conducted by the in-house medical team.

Lawson returned to his office and would spend several days typing up his report and assessment. For the present, he sat and reflected quietly on the strange existence he was now living. Did he wish to continue with MI5 or return to his normal life as a serving police officer?

His life had taken many unexpected turns; some extremely sad. The early and unexpected death of his beloved wife had given him a different perspective on life. Life is short and precious; it must be lived to the full without regrets.

The MI5 operative, using the cover 'Julian Lawson', was born Benjamin Swan. He joined the Police as a young and ambitious uniformed constable. Early in his career, he had been appointed a detective constable in the Criminal Investigation Department (CID). He had been in his element. Life was good and exciting. He had enjoyed the freedom that came with the role.

Early assessments had described him as 'a natural detective.' He had attended various detective courses with commitment and enthusiasm. He became an authorised firearms user and was qualified to drive high-powered police cars in pursuit and surveillance. Perhaps, with hindsight, the young officer had not appreciated the responsibilities and dangers that came with the role.

The young Ben Swan thought life was good and would go on forever. He had a beautiful wife who was a schoolteacher. They were extremely happy and had plans for their future together. They had met while students together at Canterbury Christ Church University, where he had obtained a degree in Politics and Law. They had been married for ten years when, unexpectedly, she was taken ill… extremely ill with terminal cancer.

The end came quickly. She had died within six months of being diagnosed, at the tender age of thirty-four years. That was now six years ago. His late wife remained constant in his thoughts, but he rarely spoke publicly about her.

A year before the death of his wife, they had purchased a cottage with twenty-two acres of woodland located within the South Downs National Park on the outskirts of the small historic rural town of Petworth in West Sussex. The Victorian cottage and woodland had originally been part of a much larger country estate. The cottage had been the home of the estate's gamekeeper. It had been the dream home for their future. Following her death, he had continued to live alone at the cottage.

Shortly after his wife died, he had been promoted to the rank of detective chief inspector and posted to the Counter-Terrorism Directorate, operating in the UK and Ireland. It had been an extremely busy working environment and he was acutely aware of the constant dangers.

Reality struck one cold and dark winter evening whilst on active service in Northern Ireland. He had been travelling to a cross-border intelligence conference in an unmarked police car, with a detective inspector, when the car was ambushed. Bullets rained in on the vehicle from several directions.

His fellow officer had been seriously injured. Ben shot and killed the armed attacker. A subsequent coroner's court ruled his actions had been justified. Nevertheless, in the eyes of the paramilitary organisation who carried out the ambush, they would continue to seek his identification and regard him as a legitimate target for revenge.

In the circumstances, he received authorisation to always carry a concealed handgun in the UK. However, he had chosen not to carry it unless there was a specific threat to his life. For most of the time, the firearm would remain in his locked wall safe in the study of his Petworth cottage.

Shortly after the shooting incident, on the recommendation of his chief constable, he attended for interview in London. He had been advised that the interview and selection process was for a two-year secondment to the Home Office. Although he had reservations and thought it might be a 'boring job', it would look good on his CV and be an advantage for his future career.

At the end of the selection process, he had been pleasantly surprised to find that the chairman of the interview board was the Deputy Director General of the UK Security Service (MI5).

Swan was recruited to operate as a full member of MI5, for an initial two-year attachment, with his police rank suspended for the duration. His appointment, with the suspension of his police rank, required written dispensation, which was authorised and signed by the Home Secretary.

Ben's new cover identity was Julian Lawson. Before he was able to take up operational employment with MI5, he had been the subject of vigorous and in-depth vetting procedures.

There then followed attendance on a two-month familiarisation and training course. At the conclusion of the initial two-year secondment, Lawson had accepted the invitation to extend his involvement with MI5 for a further two years.

During his four years with MI5, he had seen active service throughout the UK, working on cases involving tracking terrorists, foreign spies and international criminal organisations. He had also operated in the USA with colleagues from the Federal Investigation Bureau (FBI). Now, Lawson was nearing the end of his deployment and, shortly, would need to consider his future.

Sadly, the tranquillity of his private retreat in Petworth had recently been tarnished when he had been attacked and shot by an intruder, resulting in a wound to his arm.

The identity of the attacker, who, in self-defence, Lawson had shot and killed, remained unknown. Initial DNA tests suggested the man had originated from one of the former Soviet Union republics and was likely to have been a professional contract killer. Had Lawson been deliberately targeted? The consensus was 'yes', he had been.

Without much room for doubt, he had been targeted as a direct consequence of his MI5 involvement in dealing with international organised crime syndicates emanating from former Eastern Bloc countries. On this occasion, the mission to assassinate him had failed, but he would remain a target and would be required to maintain extra vigilance at all times.

The electronic diary on his computer flashed. An appointment had been booked for him to attend the Silver Conference Room at 14:00 hours. The subject: To review the assassination attempt on his life. In addition to Lawson, Jane Rigby and Randolph Beaumont would be in attendance.

The Silver Conference Room was located on the top floor of the MI5 building. There were three main conference rooms, named Gold, Silver and Bronze. As with all other rooms within the complex, when unoccupied, they remained locked, with strict security procedures in place. Before each meeting, a member of the internal security team would undertake an in-depth sweep of the room to ensure no electronic 'bugs' had been secretly installed. Major top-secret meetings would be held in the rooms, so it was paramount the discussions were not compromised by unauthorised recordings being made at the instigation of an enemy security service.

Lawson arrived at the conference room a few minutes before 14:00 hours. Rigby and Beaumont were already present and in discussion. He had previously had dealings with Randolph Beaumont. The three shook hands and exchanged polite greetings.

Beaumont was a man in his mid-fifties, thick set, with a slightly ruddy complexion and a neatly trimmed ginger beard. He spoke with an upper-class English accent. He was wearing a light-pink tailored shirt with dark grey pinstripe trousers, bright red braces and expensive, highly polished, black brogue shoes. His suit jacket was placed over the back of one of the chairs.

Lawson surmised that 'Randolph Beaumont' would have been the man's cover identity but, no doubt, would have chosen the name to reflect his true status and family background. Within the organisation, he was known for his sartorial elegance and bright red braces and considered extremely intelligent but slightly eccentric in manner and speech. He would often 'sprinkle' Latin quotes into his conversations.

Beaumont possessed an apparent encyclopaedic knowledge of Russia and of the former Soviet Union. Lawson thought Beaumont had probably, at one time, worked at the British Embassy in Moscow for MI6 but, no doubt, using Foreign Office cover. Within the UK security services, it was an accepted practice for officers to transfer between organisations.

Rigby looked at her wristwatch.

"Gentleman, it's almost 14:00 hours. Let's press on. I've allocated just one hour for this meeting. My next meeting is scheduled for 15:15 hours."

Rigby gestured for Lawson and Beaumont to take their seats at the conference table and then she turned to a small side table which held a coffee machine. She returned with three cups of coffee, which she placed on the conference table, then added three side plates, each with a paper napkin and some chocolate biscuits. Lawson gave an inward smile with the thought:

'Yes, just like Mrs Thatcher.'

Randolph Beaumont chaired the meeting. Together with a small team, he had been tasked to examine the background and circumstances surrounding the shooting of the intruder who had unlawfully gained entry to Lawson's cottage. He was also the MI5 representative who would take the case forward to liaise with the other official agencies such as the Police, Crown Prosecution Service and the Coroner. Beaumont stressed that today, he would give a preliminary update; there was still much work to do and further meetings would follow.

He sat very upright in his chair, displaying a serious and professional posture, as he opened his leather-covered notebook and carefully unscrewed the top of his Montblanc fountain pen. Looking over the top of his gold half-frame spectacles, he momentarily engaged with his two colleagues, before consulting the detailed notes he had prepared.

Lawson thought to himself: 'Randolph must be one of the few people still to use a notebook and fountain pen', but it emphasised his character. In comparison, Rigby and Lawson used iPads to type up their notes.

Beaumont chaired the meeting very much as a 'run through' of his prepared list of the known facts. As he began, Rigby raised her hand to stop him in mid-sentence and, with annoyance in her voice, asked:

"Randolph, for such an important meeting, I would have expected to have in front of me a document detailing the facts you are about to give us. Following this meeting, please ensure Julian and I are each sent an electronic copy. For the present, please continue."

The Boss had spoken! Beaumont nodded and appeared contrite. He continued to read from his handwritten notes. After the completion of each 'bullet point', he would pause and look up to check if either Rigby or Lawson had a question. Few questions were raised. Rigby commented that detailed discussion would be reserved for further meetings once outstanding issues had been addressed. Beaumont continued:

- From the outset, the local police had taken charge of the scene: i.e., the cottage and surrounding area. The investigation would be conducted under the leadership of the Head of the Major Crime Investigation Department. The team of experienced detectives had been vetted to the appropriate security vetting requirements, with the stipulation that the work would not be discussed, or details disclosed, outside the confines of the team.

- In the interests of national security, the incident had not been disclosed to the press. The local residents had been aware of police activity and emergency vehicles attending the cottage and had simply been told that it was in response to a burglary.

- The local Coroner had been informed of the death and had received a personal and confidential briefing on the sensitivity of the case. She would be kept updated on the progress of the investigation. In due time, an inquest into the circumstances of the death would be held. In accordance with UK legislation, all inquests are held in public, except where, in the interests of justice or national security, certain sections would be conducted in private. The involvement with MI5 would be the subject of later discussion.

Rigby interrupted:

"Please confirm that our Legal Team have been fully briefed on this matter and will continue to participate and give legal advice as required."

Beaumont confirmed that the Legal Team were fully engaged. He then continued:

- The identity of the dead man remained unknown. He was a white male, about thirty-five years of age and of athletic build. All labels from his clothing had been deliberately cut out. He had not been carrying any documentation to identify him.

- A full postmortem examination had been undertaken on the body, conducted by a senior Home Office pathologist. Further tests were ongoing within his forensic department. Genealogical DNA analysis indicated his ancestry as being from Central Asia. The dental evidence strongly suggested he had been raised in the former Soviet Union republic of Kazakhstan. Each tooth is essentially a time capsule. Once a tooth forms, it does not change. The chemical signature of a person's childhood environment is locked into each tooth. The evidence showed that he had a rural upbringing with a diet consisting of crops and little meat. The style of dentistry that had been carried out on his teeth strongly indicated it had been undertaken in Russia.

- His fingerprints had been checked on the UK databases at New Scotland Yard and Interpol but with a negative result.

- The handgun he used with silencer, which had been recovered at the scene, was a military GSh-18 9mm semi-automatic pistol used by Russian elite special forces for close combat fighting. With the breakup of the Soviet Union, some former KGB and military personnel had become billionaire oligarchs. Others had drifted, or had been recruited, into organised crime gangs. Many such weapons were now in the hands of criminals. In recent years, there had been increasing evidence indicating that such

international crime gangs were actively operating in Europe and the UK.

- The evidence suggested that the dead man had
been a professional assassin deployed to the UK
specifically to kill Lawson. Did he act alone or
with others? To date, how, when or where he had
entered the UK had not been established.

- Extensive police searches had not found any
trace of a car he might have used to travel to
the location. CCTV checks at railway and bus
stations had failed to identify him. Had he been
driven near to the location by an accomplice? If
so, those who ordered the assassination must be
aware that their target was still alive.

- An important issue. How and when was
Lawson identified as a target for assassination?
In Lawson's initial report, he had stated that on
that fateful evening, when he returned home, he
noticed the gravel near the rear of his parked
Land Rover Defender appeared disturbed, as if
someone had crawled under it. Bearing in mind
his previous deployment in Northern Ireland, his
initial thought had been that an explosive device

may have been attached to the underside of the car. However, subsequently, when the forensic team examined the clothing of the deceased, a small magnetic tracking device had been the only item found in the man's possession. The disturbed gravel had likely been caused when the man had crawled under the vehicle to remove the device, having first been deployed to track Lawson to his cottage. How, where and when was it fitted?

Lawson added:

"On occasions, I would use my Land Rover to travel to the office and park it in our secure underground garage. The CCTV needs to be checked to see if anyone, however unlikely, had tampered with the vehicle. Likewise, as is 'company policy', when I've undertaken certain enquiries, I've travelled in my own vehicle. Perhaps, one of the 'good guys' we were cultivating was actually batting for the other side. This will need to be reviewed."

Beaumont assured Lawson that the matter would be addressed, and he continued with the last item of his presentation.

- Members of the MI5 technical security team had visited the cottage and installed upgraded sensors and CCTV cameras in the building and surrounding woodland. Any individual entering the woodland would activate the system, which would video and monitor the intruder's progress, and send an immediate alert to Lawson's mobile phone and MI5's control centre.

Jane Rigby asked that the meeting be concluded as she was scheduled to attend her next meeting. It was agreed a further meeting involving the three participants would be scheduled for a date in the coming weeks. Lawson returned to his office and continued typing up his reports.

Following the shooting at his Petworth cottage, his Land Rover, which had been parked on the driveway, had been removed and stored in a secure garage some miles away. In the circumstances, it had been decided that, for the foreseeable future, the vehicle would remain in storage, and he would seek to purchase a replacement car.

At the end of his work week, Lawson decided he wished to return to his Petworth cottage for the weekend. During the week, he had hired a VW Golf car.

He had left MI5 HQ at 17:00 hours to begin the fifty-five-mile journey to Petworth. On the journey, he travelled through the pleasant countryside of Surrey then Sussex. Lawson relaxed and made the mental switch that, now 'off duty', he would revert to his identity of Ben Swan. He had developed a fondness for the town Petworth and its inhabitants.

The small historic town of Petworth had a population of three thousand inhabitants. It was mentioned in the Domesday Book of 1086 as having forty-four households, eleven smallholders and nine slaves. The town, located within the glorious rolling South Downs National Park, was dominated by the large seventeenth-century stately Petworth House and its large country estate with its seven-hundred-acre deer park. The entire estate was enclosed behind a thick, high, local sandstone wall running for five miles. The imposing gatehouse faced the main road running through the town.

On arriving in Petworth town, he parked outside the late-night general grocery store in the high street to buy food for the weekend. The familiar smiling face of the assistant, Brenda, was behind the counter. She welcomed him as 'Ben.'

To the locals, for the six years he had resided in Petworth, he had always been known by his true identity - Ben Swan. He had never disclosed that he was a police officer. To be identified as a police officer who worked with the Counter-Terrorism Directorate in Ireland brought with it obvious dangers. When asked about his occupation, he would simply respond that he was a self-employed consultant who often worked away from home; a boring job but it paid the mortgage.

Brenda was her normal happy and talkative self. Having not seen him for many weeks, she was interested to know where he had been. He gave his normal response:

"I've been working abroad on a 'boring' consultancy project."

He purchased a bag of groceries for the weekend, which included a large bottle of his favourite tipple, Highland Park single malt scotch whisky.

Four years ago, after he had joined MI5 and taken the cover name Julian Lawson, when he arrived home for the weekend and was intending to meet up with family or friends, he would go through the ritual of placing his MI5 identification documents in his study wall safe and take out his own 'Ben Swan' documents, including his driver's licence and credit cards. For his time at home, he would revert to his own identity and be known to the locals and friends as Ben Swan.

Having bid Brenda 'Goodnight', he travelled in his car the two miles south to his cottage, which was situated in the rural outskirts of Petworth. The nearest other residential property was over a mile away.

Lawson turned off the 'B'-road onto the short unlit track to his home and stopped the car at the closed five-bar wooden gate, which led onto the gravel driveway and the front of the cottage. He unlocked the gate and began to push it open. His presence had activated the automatic motion sensors fitted to the front of the cottage, which turned on two floodlights and cast a broad penetrating beam across the previously darkened gravel driveway.

He stood almost motionless as he gripped the top of the wooden gate tightly with both hands and stared towards his home. Emotions were high and unexpected.

His thoughts were back recalling in painful detail the last time he was there.

On that occasion, it had been slightly later in the evening with a dark overcast sky when he arrived home. He had spent the day with Sally Chambers, a fellow member of MI5, with whom he had worked on a recent operation, and she had driven him home. He had walked from her car to open the wooden gate when the flood-lights had been activated. This had been a normal and expected event. However, on that occasion, his professional and operational experience had sensed danger. All was not well!

His Land Rover Defender truck had been parked all day in front of the cottage. He observed that gravel at the rear of the vehicle had been disturbed, as if someone had crawled under it. Why? His immediate thought was that an explosive device may have been attached to the underside of his truck. He had been involved in operations against paramilitary organisations in Ireland and, as a potential target, this was a possibility. He had also noticed that the side gate to the rear of the cottage was insecure and ajar, and there were signs that items of garden furniture near to the side window had been moved.

His first thought had been to ensure Sally was safely away from potential danger. Without telling her the reason for his concern, he had wished her 'goodnight' and waved her on her way.

With some trepidation, plus an element of anger, he had checked both the front and rear doors. Both were secure, but he had noted faint scratch marks around the locking mechanism of the rear kitchen door and finger-marks in the dust on the glass of the side window.

He was satisfied that an attempt had been made to gain entry. Had it been successful? It was evident that in the past few hours, an unwelcome visitor had visited the cottage. The property was situated in an isolated location, surrounded by woodland and not visible from the road. Had it been the subject of a potential burglary, or something more sinister?

During the past few years, he had been involved in operations tracking killers, assassins and spies. He was acutely aware that he remained a potential target for revenge from various criminal organisations.

On that evening, after unlocking the front door, he had quickly entered and switched on the downstairs lights. He had made his way to the ground-floor study and unlocked the wall safe. He had retrieved his Glock 19 handgun and quickly loaded it with a full magazine of fifteen rounds. In view of his experiences in Ireland, and for his personal protection, he had authority to lawfully retain the firearm.

Holding the gun with both hands in the 'prepared for action' position, he had cautiously checked all rooms on the ground and upper floor, including cupboards and other potential hiding places. He had found no evidence of an intruder, nor of any recent disturbance.

He had then returned to the ground-floor study and poured himself a large whisky but had then thought better of it. The potential threat was still present, and he may be required to take positive action. The consumption of alcohol would not be a sensible move. He placed the tumbler of whisky on the side table and sat down in his brown leather recliner armchair. The handgun remained in his possession resting on his lap.

He had switched off all the lighting and sat in darkness and in silence, as he calmly mulled over the situation and his options. He still favoured the likelihood that, during the day, someone had been under his Land Rover to attach an explosive device. Should he telephone MI5 Control Centre and request the attendance of the Army Bomb Squad (correctly known as 11 Explosive Ordnance Disposal and Search Regiment) or wait until the morning when, in daylight, it would be relatively safe to check for himself?

Explosive devices usually contain a sensitive 'rocker' which would not activate until the target vehicle was moved. Seated alone in the darkness, he decided to hold fire and not request attendance of the Bomb Disposal Squad.

On the slim evidence available, he was concerned not to overreact and be regarded as paranoid. Land Rover Defenders were regular targets for motor vehicle thieves. Therefore, had it simply been someone tampering with the truck in an unsuccessful attempt to steal it?

For over an hour, he had remained seated in darkness and deep in thought with his handgun on his lap. He was facing the open study door, which led into the sitting room. Suddenly, he heard a slight metallic grating sound. The external kitchen door lock was being tampered with and then the door slowly opened. He had sat motionless, not daring to breathe. The silhouetted figure of a slim individual slowly and gently stepped across the sitting room floor.

As the figure passed the open study door, he noticed the silhouette, including the outline of a gun. The figure walked directly to the stairs which led to his bedroom. This indicated that the intruder had prior knowledge of the layout of the cottage.

In almost total darkness, he stood up from his chair and waited. Without moving from his position, he grasped his gun with both hands and mentally prepared himself to confront the armed intruder. Without much doubt, the intruder had been sent to assassinate him. There was movement from upstairs as the intruder appeared to search but failed to find his prey.

Lawson stepped closer to the open doorway and waited for the intruder to return. The silhouette slowly stepped down the stairs with his gun held in front of him. The room remained in darkness.

As the man was about to reach the bottom step, Lawson flicked on the sitting room light, jumped into a challenging position and shouted:

"Freeze. I'm armed and prepared to shoot."

The two men stood within ten feet of each other, both pointing their weapon at the other man. The barrel of the intruder's gun was fitted with a silencer. He was dressed all in black and wearing a balaclava. Only his eyes were visible. There was no hesitation. The man had been surprised by the appearance of Lawson, but his reaction had been immediate.

The intruder had held his gun in his right hand only, and, as he stepped off the bottom step, he was slightly off-balance. In this awkward position, he had managed to fire a single shot, which wounded Lawson in his upper right arm. Instantly, on firm ground and holding his gun with both hands in the firing position, Lawson had been able to accurately fire three shots in quick succession. The intruder had fallen backwards onto the stairs. He was dead before he reached the ground.

Immediately following the shooting, Lawson had telephoned MI5 Control Centre, who took charge and dealt with all aspects of the event. His injury was initially painful but, fortunately, it was only a flesh wound which required an overnight stay at a private hospital and minor surgery.

Although the shooting had taken place over two months back, the events of that night remained very vivid in his thoughts. He had been determined to relax and enjoy his first weekend back at home. He had entered the cottage and cautiously checked that all external doors and windows had been secured. He had previously been briefed on the upgraded security system installed in the cottage and woodland following the shooting, which gave him a degree of reassurance.

The enhanced security system included miniature CCTV cameras with motion detection sensors positioned discreetly within the woodland surrounding the cottage. They were linked, via an app, to Lawson's iPhone and iPad and would send an immediate alert upon activation by an intruder.

Cooking for one was something he did not enjoy and, whenever possible, would make an excuse to avoid. When at home, he would venture out to the town to eat in a restaurant or public house. Preheating a shop-bought pizza or ready meal in his microwave was about the limit of his culinary skills. This evening, he would stay at home, having prepared himself a cheese roll, with yoghurt and a mug of fresh black coffee. He rarely watched television and preferred to have the radio on in the background.

He had looked forward to spending a relaxing weekend back home in his cottage. After a hot bath, he had poured himself a large whisky, sat back in his leather recliner armchair, closed his eyes and listened to the radio. However, the recent killing of the intruder in his home played heavily on his mind. The exact moment he had shot and killed the intruder remained so vivid. The image of the man grimacing as the three bullets exploded and entered his body constantly flashed through his mind.

This had been the second time he had shot and killed a man. The first had been in Ireland, when the police car he had been travelling in had been ambushed by an armed paramilitary group. His police colleague, the driver, had been seriously wounded. Lawson had returned fire to avoid being killed. It had been a case of kill or be killed. The terrorist had died at the scene.

Lawson recalled, with sadness, how he had walked up to the lifeless body lying by the side of the road, kicked the offending rifle away to a safe distance, then bent down and removed the man's balaclava. He had been shocked and surprised to notice the young boyish face of the deceased. The youth reminded him of his own eighteen-year-old nephew. What made a young man develop such hatred that he would equip himself with a high-powered military sniper's rifle and set out to murder men he'd never met? The conflicts arising from religion and politics had much to answer for.

When he joined the police and had been appointed a young detective, in his wildest dreams, he had never imagined he would be responsible for killing two fellow human beings. Nor had he considered he would then be the target of at least two criminal organisations who sought his death. In addition, his recent involvement with the investigation and prosecution of David Evans made him a likely target.

The two killings, and the many other operations he had been directly involved with, were beginning to take their toll on his physical and mental health. He had never been a person to show his emotions. In his professional working environment, whether as a police officer or as a member of MI5, he had displayed the attributes of a calm, positive, confident and competent individual. Introspection had not been part of his character. He had regarded that showing signs of stress and outward emotion was destructive and a sign of weakness.

Recently, he had experienced increasing and painful headaches. Inwardly, he acknowledged why this was, but preferred to deal with it personally and quietly and not seek medical help. For some time, he had been in denial and hated the prospect of seeking help and confiding in another. Throughout his life, he had never discussed or shared his emotional concerns with anyone. He had considered this a strength, but it was possibly also a weakness.

The noise pounding around inside his head had become almost unbearable. Another large whisky didn't ease the pain. He attempted to read a book, but found he was unable to concentrate and gave up after only a few pages. Through sheer fatigue and still seated in the recliner armchair, he eventually fell asleep but awoke soon after, confused and in a cold sweat. He consumed more whisky, drinking direct from the bottle, but it didn't aid sleep.

At 05:00 hours, he staggered from the armchair into the kitchen. He made himself a large mug of black coffee and sat trembling at the kitchen table. He was embarrassed and hated himself for his behaviour. After sitting in silence at the table for about half an hour, he made his way slowly to the bathroom and endured a long cold shower, which he regarded as personal punishment.

He made a determined effort to recover from his drunken night. He hadn't realised how low, and lonely, he had become. The pressure he had been working under had clearly taken its toll both physically and emotionally. Excessive consumption of alcohol wasn't the answer.

It was still early morning with a chill in the air and a light mist slowly rising from the damp ground and trees. He particularly enjoyed early mornings, especially when in his woodland. He put on his walking boots and his well-worn but much treasured fleece-lined woodman's lumberjacket and, with another mug of black coffee, went into the back garden.

In view of his recent absence from home, the vegetable patch had become overgrown. He sat down on the wooden bench and surveyed the garden to mentally assess the work he would need to undertake in the coming months. His friendly robin landed on the nearby rickety table and looked towards him with a knowing glance. Lawson smiled:

"Hello, Mr Robin. Sorry for neglecting you."

The bird was after his morning feed. Lawson leaned down to the side of the bench, flicked open the lid of a rusty old biscuit tin and retrieved a handful of bird seed, which he sprinkled on the top of the table.

With his coffee finished and Mr Robin fed, he picked up his walking stick and ventured at a brisk pace into his woodland. He first inspected the four-acre section of sweet chestnut trees, which had recently been coppiced by professional forestry contractors. He was pleased to note the developing new growth since the work had been undertaken.

He continued walking at a brisk pace onto the far side of the woodland to inspect the ten acres of tall beech trees, which grew within a magnificent carpet of native bluebells. He stopped, looked round and listened. The early morning birdsong was one of the joys of owning a woodland. Another was the enjoyment of entertaining family and friends for barbecues, both in the summer and winter. He had now reached the wooden log cabin that he had built from timber from the woodland.

He unlocked the double doors of the cabin and entered. The interior contained a table and two chairs, plus a single collapsible camp bed. On the table sat a brass oil lamp, which, when lit, gave off a pleasing warm glow. On the far wall was fixed a large white noticeboard covered with many coloured photographs of family and friends; photographs of happiness at summer barbecues and evening campfires. Several were of a beautiful young smiling lady. He stood quietly looking at the photographs:

"Good morning, my darling Lucy. I still miss you."

With his right-hand index finger, he gently caressed the main photograph of his late wife Lucy. When she had been diagnosed with terminal cancer and told she had less than six months to live, at her instigation, they had talked about his future life without her. Lucy had made him promise that he would be happy and, in time, find a new partner. Before he removed his finger, he quietly whispered:

"Thank you, darling Lucy. I'll be back soon."

Walking away from the cabin, he felt sadness but also a calm moment of contentment as he reflected on the happy times he'd been privileged to spend with Lucy. He continued to walk up the woodland track, through the section of Scots pine trees towards his cottage and was pleased to see several roe deer in the distance. In the south of England, wild deer numbers have significantly increased in recent years.

Deer do cause some damage to trees, and a neighbouring woodland owner had been encouraging him to join forces to employ a professional hunter to undertake a cull. Understandably, and particularly in view of recent events, he wasn't keen to have a 'professional' with a rifle killing in his peaceful woodland. He would rather see live deer roaming and able to enjoy the freedom and safety of his woodland.

Nearing lunchtime, he walked the two miles into town, then continued the extra mile up North Street to The Stonemasons Inn, a rustic 17th-century public house. Motor traffic through the town was light. It had turned into a warm sunny day with clear skies. En route to the pub, he had passed several of the residents and exchanged pleasantries with them.

At the pub, he had opted to sit at an outside table in the well-kept and peaceful garden. For lunch, he had fish pie, followed by a glass of lemonade and a leisurely cup of strong black coffee. He did not partake in alcohol.

Later in the afternoon, he took a leisurely stroll around the extended grounds of the Petworth Park Estate, a National Trust property. He held National Trust membership in his identity of Ben Swan. On previous visits with family or friends, he had taken a tour of the house as well as the park. On this occasion, he would spend over two hours just strolling around the lake and extensive grounds.

The celebrated artist JMW Turner had enjoyed a long and productive relationship with Petworth House and the park, drawing great inspiration from the beauty of the estate. By the 1820s, he had become somewhat of a fixture at Petworth House, as a consequence of his friendship with the 3rd Earl of Egremont. This had given him the freedom to paint without the usual constraints that would have been placed on other visitors. Many of his majestic landscapes and magnificent interior paintings remain on display in the house and available for public view.

Lawson sat and rested on a bench overlooking the lake and watched with fascination at the interplay between the various species of wildfowl, including a flock of elegant white swans. He had begun to relax and was in no rush to return to his home. On several warm summer afternoons in the past, he had sat at this location observing the wildlife and the splendour of the lake. On the wall of his study, he had a framed copy of a painting by JMW Turner of the lake, entitled Dewy Morning.

He would spend Sunday alone in his woodland undertaking repairs to the cabin and engaging in photography, recording wildlife and the changing seasons. He enjoyed the woodland environment.

As Ben Swan, he had retained a presence on the social Internet platform Facebook. However, since taking employment with MI5, his contact with friends and police colleagues had been infrequent. They believed he was on attachment at the Home Office. His absence was explained away with the excuse that he often worked away from London.

All too soon, the weekend would end. Early on Monday morning, he would put on his business suit, unlock the wall safe in his study, take out his Julian Lawson identification documents and lock away his Ben Swan documents. The empty whisky bottle had been relegated to the recycle bin and no further alcohol would be purchased. His journey back to the City would begin.

CHAPTER NINE

Investigations Continue

Shortly before the arrest of David Evans, his twin brother, Terry Evans, had disappeared from his normal haunts and had not been seen since. Terry was unmarried and lived within the estate in a small cottage owned by David. From childhood, he had been regarded as David's 'shadow.' They shared a close relationship, but his character was totally different to that of his brother. He appeared content with life and did not seek the wealth that David strove to achieve. Terry was not a violent man and David was regarded as his protector.

Terry, in view of his position, obviously knew much about this brother's criminal activities and associates but turned a blind eye to the violence and drug dealing. He was considered very loyal to David and would never challenge him on any issue. His friends would say he was dominated by and, perhaps, frightened of his powerful brother. DCI Graham Durham, the Senior Investigating Officer for Operation Goldfinger, placed the finding and interviewing of Terry Evans high on his list of priorities.

DCI Durham sought to increase the size of the Operation Goldfinger investigation team. DCs Dave Hooper and Michael Sharp were two experienced detectives recruited to join the team. DC Hooper was a man in his early thirties, physically strong, with curly black hair and a thick black beard. His most distinctive feature was the numerous tattoos covering both arms and the lower sides of his neck. DC Sharp was of a similar age, of slim build and smart appearance. He was clean shaven and didn't have any tattoos. The two had worked in divisional CID for about three years, with much of their time operating together as an effective crime-detecting team.

It had been their first morning with Operation Goldfinger, so, seated in the briefing room, they had read up on, and familiarised themselves with, the progress of the investigation. DCI Durham was in his office, which overlooked the briefing room, discussing matters with DI Penfold.

DI Penfold looked through the glass partition to the briefing room and made disparaging remarks about the unconventional appearance of DC Hooper. He further commented:

"In my younger days as a DC, that man would never have been appointed to the CID."

DCI Durham held back from making an instant reply. He frowned, then spoke slowly and deliberately:

"DC Hooper joined the police at my instigation. DC Hooper was appointed a detective in the CID on my recommendation. DC Hooper is one of the most tenacious, tough, honest and loyal police officers I have had the pleasure to know. DI Penfold, in a couple of months' time, I will appreciate receiving your revised assessment on DC Hooper."

DI Penfold was very aware that he had offended the DCI and considered it prudent to remain silent.

DCI Durham continued:

"Five years ago, a young police constable was on the forecourt of the local railway station, having been directed to attend to deal with a group of rowdy youths being abusive to a taxi driver. The group of six youths had then turned on the PC. He was punched to the ground and, as he lay helpless and almost unconscious, he was repeatedly kicked. At this point, a young man walked from the direction of the platform and onto the forecourt. He carried on his back a heavy backpack.

Without hesitation, he stepped into the melee and calmly said:

"Officer, I believe you need some help."

He placed his backpack on the ground, and, with amazing speed, raised both wrists and lashed out backwards knocking two of the youths to the ground; and they stayed there. Then he dispatched two more in a similar manner. By the time police reinforcements arrived, the six youths had 'surrendered.'"

The DCI continued his story:

"The young man ensured the injured PC was OK, picked up his backpack and was about to walk away, when the officers asked if he would make a witness statement. The very modest young man played down his role in the fracas. It only became apparent when the CCTV footage was viewed. I viewed that footage and was extremely impressed and later spoke with the young man. He had a poor start in life, didn't know the identity of his parents, and had been fostered at a young age.

By the age of sixteen, he was living on the streets and, after two years drifting around Europe, he eventually joined the French Foreign Legion. It was his first proper home and his first real family. It was hard, but he excelled. He saw active service with the Legion in West Africa and Afghanistan, as a member of the 2nd Foreign Parachute Regiment, who are considered some of the toughest men on the planet and are recognised as such among warriors for it. He had completed his six-year contract the week before we met and he had just arrived back in the UK looking for employment. That man was former Legion Corporal David Hooper."

DCI Durham called Detectives Hooper and Sharp into his office to introduce them to DI Penfold.

DC Hooper smiled at the DCI, and they shook hands as the DC said:

"Boss, it's great to see you again."

The DCI turned to DI Penfold and said:

"This team of two are as good as a team of ten. I have confidence that they will find Terry Evans, arrest and interview him, *and* obtain a full and frank confession of everything he knows about the criminal activities of his brother. They will work under your command.

Please give them the freedom to use their well-skilled initiative."

Initial police intelligence suggested that Terry was now a frightened man. David, his 'protector' and only means of regular financial support, was now locked up in prison, which left Terry vulnerable. He had been aware that the police wanted to speak to and, no doubt, arrest him. He would also have been aware that other drug barons would seek to take over David's drugs empire and to settle old scores. He would also consider his life to be in danger.

Terry had vacated his cottage and had not been in contact with friends; nor had he visited his local haunts. His mobile phone had remained switched off since David's arrest and had likely been destroyed to prevent police attempts to track him.

Detectives Hooper and Sharp commenced their enquiries by visiting the local pubs and clubs previously frequented by Terry Evans. Most were aware that his brother David had been arrested and acknowledged they knew he had been a drug dealer and a man not to be crossed. The officers purchased drinks for the men they interviewed and discreetly offered cash payment as a reward for receiving useful information. Eventually, one friend recalled that a couple of days before he disappeared, he was seen driving a fairly new grey-coloured Audi saloon. He didn't recall the registration number or model of the car.

By telephone, the detectives contacted Audi car dealerships in the area and quickly identified a showroom in the nearby cathedral city of Salisbury. They then visited the premises. They confirmed that Terry Evans had purchased a grey-coloured Audi Q5 saloon SUV with Quattro four-wheel drive. The car was three years old. He had paid in cash - £26,500.

The salesman remembered that Terry Evans specifically wanted a four-wheel drive car with a good-sized boot and he had asked about its capabilities for driving off-road. The officers viewed CCTV footage taken from inside the showroom and were able to confirm the identity of the purchaser.

Working on their hunch, the officers then visited the local camping and sporting shops. On the same afternoon that Terry Evans had purchased the Audi car, he had also purchased camping equipment including a tent, sleeping bag, torch, camping gas cooker and utensils. It was apparent that his intention had been to 'disappear' for the present and live off-road, away from civilisation, camping in the hills.

The two detectives had continued their enquiries at local petrol stations. They established that, following the purchase of camping equipment, he had called at a petrol station to top up his new car with petrol. Again, CCTV had captured footage of his car on the forecourt. The car had been filled to its maximum capacity. A quick telephone call by the officers to the Audi dealer confirmed this would have allowed the car to travel approximately 400 miles. The petrol station CCTV had also captured Terry Evans in the express shop purchasing provisions, including fresh fruit, which was further evidence to indicate he was about to leave the area and embark in a long journey to camp out at an unknown location.

Back at Operation Goldfinger HQ, the two detectives updated DI Penfold on their progress. Next, they contacted the Police Control Centre to have the Audi car's registration number checked out on the ANPR system. With CCTV cameras located on major roads and linked in with ANPR, the system automatically records car registration numbers and tracks movement.

At about 19:30 hours the same day, the Audi car had been tracked leaving the county of Wiltshire and travelling north on the M5 motorway. Two hours later, the car had stopped at a service station on the outskirts of Birmingham. It was tracked as it continued travelling north on the M6 motorway. The next stop was at a service station on the M74 motorway near Glasgow. At that stage, the car had travelled approximately 390 miles from Wiltshire. This was considered the likely stop at which Terry Evans would have filled the car with petrol.

The ANPR system had continued to track the car travelling north until it reached the area of Aviemore on the main A9 road. It appeared the car had turned off the A9 at that point as there was no further tracking of its movements. The information from ANPR was of events that had occurred six days earlier.

DI Penfold gave the two detectives permission to continue with their enquiries and follow the route taken by Terry Evans, on the assumption that he would still be hiding out somewhere in the Highlands of Scotland. Early the next morning, the two officers equipped themselves with sturdy walking boots and clothing and commenced their car journey to follow the known route taken by Terry Evans. They stopped and under-took enquiries at the service stations where it had been identified that Evans had stopped.

The service station stop on the M74 motorway, just outside of Glasgow, proved extremely useful. The officers ascertained that Evans had indeed refuelled his car with petrol but of more relevance was his purchase of a new pay-as-you-go 'no contract' mobile phone. He had paid cash for both the petrol and the mobile phone. In respect of both transactions, Evans had been captured on CCTV.

The staff had been able to supply the officers with the telephone number assigned to the mobile phone. The officers immediately contacted Operation Goldfinger HQ with the information. The correct administrative procedures were immediately put in place to enable lawful research to be undertaken on the mobile tele-phone number.

At the time of manufacture, all modern mobile phones are fitted with GPS (Global Positioning System) which enables them to function. When switched off, all functions, including wireless communication, are temporarily deactivated. However, when switched on, the police are able, by means of the GPS, to track the location of a mobile phone.

The two officers continued their journey north whilst, back at Operation Goldfinger HQ, enquiries into the use of the mobile phone were undertaken. The ANPR system had been able to track Terry Evans' car a total of 517 miles since he had departed Wiltshire. However, as he had neared Aviemore, he had turned off onto a minor road which was not covered by ANPR cameras.

Fortunately, luck had been on their side. DI Penfold had contacted them to report that within four hours of purchasing the new mobile phone, it had been activated and remained switched on for the next twelve hours. The initial activation of the mobile phone had been located within the area of the small hamlet of Struy, situated at the end of Glen Strathfarrar, in the heart of Scotland's Central Highlands. Since the initial activation, the signal had only moved several miles north-west into the local hills and back to the centre of Struy.

For the past six days, Evans had remained in the area. It appeared likely he had been camping in an isolated woodland location and frequently returned to Struy for provisions. The research had established that he frequently switched off his mobile phone for many hours at a time and, in the six days of ownership, he had not used it to make any telephone calls.

The assumption was that he had been switching off the phone to preserve the life of the battery and had not used it to contact friends or family for fear of having his present whereabouts discovered.

The evidence was that he switched the mobile phone on for the same timeframe each day. Was this to give him access to news service Internet sites to check on any news updates on the police investigation into his brother David and on himself? Mobile phones are also a very useful tool to research the weather and a multitude of other things, particularly when endeavouring to evade justice.

The two detectives arrived in Struy during the late evening and booked into a small family-run hotel. They endorsed the hotel register with their correct names and simply stated they were spending a short walking holiday exploring the Highlands. Early next morning, equipped in their hiking clothing and backpacks, the two went exploring on foot. They headed north out of the hamlet, over the bridge that crossed the River Farrar and turned west along Glenstrathfarrar Road, headed in the direction where the GPS results indicated Evans was camping.

Within three miles of the village of Struy, they turned north and began the walk up a long woodland track towards the mountain Beinn a Bhathaich Ard. After a ten-minute walk, they came across impressions of car tyres in the mud. The marks appeared fresh, all of the same tread pattern, but overlaying each other. They had likely been made by the same vehicle but at different times, which suggested the same journey had been undertaken on different days. As they continued their walk into the wooded area, and to add a touch of authenticity, Dave Hooper took from his backpack his Canon camera and hung it around his neck.

A fifteen-minute walk into the woodland, trekking through towering Scots pine trees, they came across a fast-flowing stream with a small green canvas tent pitched nearby. Sharp called out in a loud friendly voice:

"Good morning. Anyone at home? We are two hikers just passing by."

There was no response. Sharp repeated his call, but with no reply. He nodded to Hooper, who bent down and entered the tent. He made a quick check without disturbing the contents and photographed the inside and outside of the tent and surrounding area.

Hooper spoke in a quiet voice:

"The tent, sleeping bag and equipment all match the items purchased by Evans at the camping shop in Salisbury."

They departed the campsite and began their walk back through the woodland and onto the muddy track. At the end of the track, they turned right back onto the main road towards Struy. As they did so, Terry Evans' grey Audi, travelling from the direction of Struy, turned onto the track and proceeded on its journey into the woodland. They identified the driver as Evans and noted he had acquired several days' growth of stubble. He would have seen them but made no sign of acknowledgement.

The two detectives returned to their hotel and arranged lunch. Hooper checked his watch and commented:

"It's one o'clock. Have a quick errand to undertake. Won't be long."

Without further comment, he left a slightly bemused Sharp to finish his lunch.

Hooper returned to the hotel after about one hour and handed Sharp a newspaper and a single cream cake.

"Thought you might like a newspaper to read and a cake with your afternoon coffee as we discuss our next move. Do we go straight to his camp and arrest him or should we be a little more subtle? I favour the more subtle approach."

Hooper spoke about his visit into the small village and how he had taken the opportunity to talk to the local shopkeepers in his persona as a holidaymaker. He had visited the small café, located within the bakery shop, and engaged in a 'chat' with the friendly owner.

During their light-hearted conversation, Hooper mentioned that he was from the south of England and asked if this small quiet hamlet had many visitors from his part of the UK and, in particular, her bakery and café.

His 'subtle' enquiry had produced a significant result. The owner replied that each morning for the past week, at ten o'clock, a 'southerner' called Alan would call in for a full cooked breakfast. Yes, she expected him back tomorrow morning and normally he would park his grey-coloured car outside the bakery. Hooper told her that in the morning, together with his friend, they would call in to sample her delicious, cooked breakfast.

Sharp smiled and responded:

"Well done, mate. Once again, taking the time to befriend the locals and going the extra mile has produced the goods."

The two detectives would spend the afternoon at the hotel. At 18:00 hours, Hooper checked the time on his watch and commented:

"Must just pop out on another errand and see who else I can chat up."

He returned within the hour and, with a smile, said he thought the visit would hopefully produce a result. Sharp had great faith in Hooper's ability and trusted him as a working colleague. However, he was aware that on occasions, Hooper's enthusiasm and commitment to achieve a result could cause a raised eyebrow among senior management.

At 10:15 hours next morning, as Detectives Hooper and Sharp walked along the quiet high street, they were pleased to notice the grey Audi Q5 parked outside the bakery shop. They entered the shop to be greeted with a warm welcome from the friendly owner who added:

"Two full cooked breakfasts and each with a mug of coffee?"

They nodded in agreement and were handed two freshly poured mugs of coffee.

Terry Evans was seated at a table located in the corner of the small café eating his cooked breakfast. He didn't look up or appear to notice the two new customers. Holding their mugs of coffee, they walked across to the table where Evans was sitting. There were three empty chairs.

Hooper politely asked:

"May we join you at this table?"

Evans just nodded. He did not speak and appeared disinterested in their presence. His facial expression indicated that he'd rather be left alone. Sharp seated himself next to Evans. Hooper seated himself directly across the table. Hooper held his mug in both hands and slowly sipped his coffee. Their heads were no more than a metre apart. Hooper looked straight forward whereas Evans had his head lowered as he concentrated on eating his breakfast.

Hooper spoke in a quiet, non-aggressive voice:

"Struy is a beautiful place. The scenery is magnificent. It's our first time in the Highlands. Just here for a brief three days of hill walking. Are you a visitor?"

"Yes."

"Where are you staying?"

"Nearby."

Hooper placed his mug of coffee on the table, leaned slightly closer and continued:

"In a hotel, bed and breakfast or camping?"

"Camping."

Hooper continued:

"Apologies, how rude of me; we haven't introduced ourselves. I'm Dave and my friend is Mike. What's your name?"

It appeared the man did not wish to have a discussion with him. With reluctance, he simply replied:

"Alan."

Hooper looked towards Sharp and commented, ensuring Evans could hear:

"Mike, I hope we haven't upset Alan. He looks frightened. It can't be anything we said. Why do you think he is frightened? Do you think we look intimidating?"

Sharp gently tapped Evans on his shoulder and, with a smile, commented:

"Dave, it can't be anything we said. Unfortunately, in this bad and wicked world, people have secrets and concerns which others don't know about. What are you worried about, Alan? Are you on holiday or, perhaps, running away and hiding out?"

Evans looked more uncomfortable but did not speak. The café owner approached the table and served Hooper and Sharp their cooked breakfasts. Evans indicated to her that he had finished his breakfast and was ready to leave.

Hooper gently lifted his right hand, indicating to him to remain seated, and said:

"Alan, we haven't finished our nice little chat. I'll order you another coffee." He turned to the café owner and politely asked for a coffee for Alan.

Evans remained seated, still holding his knife and fork. His right hand began to shake violently. Hooper placed his large powerful right hand over the hand of Evans to reduce the shaking and just looked at him.

Following a significant pause, Hooper spoke:

"Alan, we have been looking for you. We travelled a long way to find you. Do you know who we are?"

In a trembling voice, he spoke hesitantly:

"Please, you can trust me. Please tell my brother David that his secrets are safe with me."

From his top pocket, Hooper produced his police warrant card and placed it before Evans. Sharp then placed his warrant card on the table.

Hooper continued to speak in a quiet voice, but with an injected air of serious authority:

"We are police detectives working with the team investigating your twin brother David and his criminal associates. Now let's cut the bullshit. You are Terry Evans. We require your cooperation, but I suggest you need our help and protection even more. You have good reason to fear for your safety. Your brother made many enemies and, with him locked away, you could be their target. This is the time for honesty. What is your main concern?"

Evans took some convincing that the two detectives were really police officers. However, when satisfied, he spoke about his main concern:

"My brother doesn't think I can be trusted not to talk to the law. He has put out a contract for me to be murdered. I knew he was a monster, capable of most

things, but I didn't believe he would order the assassination of his own twin brother."

Sharp asked:

"How do you know David has ordered that you be
murdered?"

Evans responded:

"As you said, with David locked up in prison, I was
aware I would be vulnerable to reprisals from former
associates and other drug gangs. Now I know that David
wanted me dead. He has promised a large cash sum to
have me assassinated."

Evans paused to compose himself. Sweat poured
down his face. He then continued:

"In the last couple of days, I've had telephone calls
on my mobile warning me to watch my back as David
has put out this contract for my assassination. They are
obviously getting close to knowing where I am."

"Why do you say that?" asked Sharp.

"Before I left the county, I destroyed my old mobile
phone and only bought the new one a few days ago. Yet,
somehow, they have found my new mobile number. It
looks like someone in the gang doesn't agree with the

order to kill me, perhaps someone I was friendly with, so they've telephoned to warm me."

Sharp asked if Evans knew or recognised the voice of the person who'd warned him.

Evans replied:

"No. He didn't say who he was and sounded as though he was disguising his voice. He sounded serious and said a large amount of cash would be paid out once the job was done. He sounded scared himself. Each time he phoned, it was from a public payphone, probably, so the caller couldn't be traced."

Sharp looked across at Hooper. There was direct eye contact with a knowing momentary hint of a smile. Sharp silently reflected to himself on his colleague's unexplained 'errands' of yesterday into the hamlet. Perhaps to visit the public telephone kiosk? No doubt, an element of subterfuge had been involved!

Hooper retrieved his warrant card, put it back into his top pocket and said:

"Terry, it's decision time. Do we treat you as a willing and active accomplice of an extremely violent major criminal who is now in custody for murders and importation of cocaine? Or do we treat you as a vulnerable and very frightened individual, who did not himself directly commit crime, but was dominated by David and turned a blind eye to the criminality being committed? I make no promises, as such decisions will be made by the prosecution authorities. However, we can put in a good word for you. If you decide to cooperate, we will protect you, with the chance of a new identity and a new life. If you don't receive police protection, even in prison the evil bastards will get you."

Hooper explained he would need to telephone his office with an update and decision. He said that at this initial stage, he would require a brief outline of Terry's working association with his brother.

Terry explained he had worked for his brother David since he was 15 years old. He had never had any other form of employment. David paid him in cash, about £2,000 each month. He lived rent-free in his cottage which was owned by David. They never discussed David's criminal activities. David had always portrayed himself as a successful businessman who made his money investing in property development and classic sports cars.

He accepted he was aware of occasional rumours that David was involved in drug dealing, but he was adamant he'd never seen evidence of it, nor had his brother ever admitted it to him. Yes, he also acknowledged that his brother undertook cash transactions, probably, Terry had assumed, to avoid paying tax. He was simply David's driver.

In addition, Terry said that he would deliver sealed packages and envelopes of cash to people and would also collect packages. Terry would never be told what was in them. He would drive David to various houses, hotels and other locations but would wait outside in the car. He never attended any of the meetings with his brother. David was very secretive and never told Terry what he was doing. In their business relationship, David was the 'Boss' and Terry the 'Servant.'

Terry said he would be willing to identify to the police the properties he'd taken David to and name many of the people he had contact with. He also told them about David's mistress and the location of the large country house she lived in, which was owned by David. Terry had seen her on a couple of occasions, when he'd driven David to her house, but didn't know her name. They had never been formally introduced. She was Italian, about fifteen years younger than David, and a very attractive and elegant lady.

Terry was aware that in David's large country house, he kept false passports and details of bank accounts in false names. In addition, he knew where David had hidden away large amounts of cash. He also believed David kept sensitive documents at the house of his mistress.

The two detectives were keen to know how Terry had been able to pay £25,500 in cash for his car and other expenses. He explained that in the sitting room of his small cottage, by the fireplace, was located a large Victorian copper box for the storage of logs. It had a false bottom in which David secretly kept wads of banknotes. David referred to it as his 'emergency fund.' Terry didn't know how much was there. However, when his brother had been arrested, Terry's source of income had stopped, so he had decided to look in the box. He had found about £200,000 in Bank of England currency, mostly in £50 and £20 notes. He had removed all the money and had been using it for his own benefit. He thought he had about £150,000 left, which he'd hidden under the boot cover of his car.

When they questioned Terry about taking the £200,000 for his own use, he replied, in a rather vague and inconclusive manner, that at the time, he hadn't regarded it as theft. It had been put there by David and, since its legitimacy was in doubt and tax had been avoided, he didn't think his brother would make a complaint that it had been stolen.

Following telephone consultation with management at Operation Goldfinger HQ and the Crown Prosecution Service, the two detectives formally arrested Terry Evans. He appeared pleased and expressed relief that he would now be in the safe custody of the police and would not have to spend another freezing night sleeping in a flimsy tent in the Highlands.

Arrangements were made for the collection of his car and equipment from the mountain, not forgetting the safe recovery of the large amount of cash in the boot of his car, and for the transportation of the prisoner Terry Evans. His ultimate fate had yet to be decided.

Would he eventually appear before the Crown Court as a defendant or as a witness for the prosecution? A defendant who wishes to give evidence against a co-accused (for example, his brother David) can only do so if he ceases to be a defendant in the case. This can be achieved by the defendant pleading guilty to obtain a reduction in sentence, or by the case against him being discontinued.

Back at Operation Goldfinger HQ, Detective Constables Hooper and Sharp briefed the senior management team, which included DCI Durham, on the outcome of their enquiries in Scotland. A senior representative from the Crown Prosecution Service was also present. Terry Evans had been escorted to the regional police custody suite, where he would be formally interviewed after caution by the two arresting officers. DC Hooper explained to the management team that Terry Evans had continued to say that he would cooperate.

At the senior management meeting, the DCI explained that he had been contacted by MI5 to be advised that a senior member of the service would visit Operation Goldfinger HQ to give a confidential update of their involvement in the David Evans investigation. The DCI stressed that details of the visit must remain confidential and not be disclosed to anyone outside those present.

CHAPTER TEN

The Killing of Max Bowman

It had been a pleasantly warm early spring morning when Max Bowman set out on his regular Sunday ten-mile circular cycle ride through the quiet country roads. He lived with his wife and two young children in their detached house in a small village two miles west of the cathedral city of Winchester, located within the county of Hampshire, England. Max was thirty-five years of age and prided himself on his fitness. He also played cricket for his local village team.

His Sunday morning ride would usually take no more than one hour. That morning, Max kissed his wife goodbye at 07:30 hours. By 09:00 hours, he had not returned. His wife had felt concerned. Perhaps he'd met a friend and stopped off for a coffee at one of the lay-by cafés?

By 09:45 hours, his wife was worried as she stood in the kitchen pondering her next move. She had called Max's mobile phone, but there was no reply. Unusually, there was no signal; the mobile appeared to have been switched off.

At that moment, a marked police car drove up the driveway and parked directly opposite the front door. Two uniformed police officers approached. As she opened the front door to meet them, the sombre expression on their faces said that they were there to deliver bad news.

In response to their respectful and quietly spoken questions, she confirmed she was Mrs Rosie Bowman, the wife of Mr Max Bowman, who, earlier that morning, had gone out on his bicycle. And, yes, it was a white and silver-coloured Cube Attain Pro road bike. There was a slight pause.

By the officer's expression, Mrs Bowman already knew the answer, but she still asked:

"Is it serious?"

Both officers nodded, and one stepped forward to offer her comfort and quietly replied:

"I'm sorry, he has been seriously injured. He has been admitted to the Intensive Care Unit at the city hospital. We need to take you there as soon as possible."

Mrs Bowman appeared composed, but tears were streaming down her cheeks. Hesitantly, she asked:

"Is Max going to die?"

One of the officers replied:

"The doctors will be doing everything possible for Max, but I understand things are not looking good."

When Mrs Bowman arrived at the hospital, she was taken to a side room and given the sad news that Max had died. In the company of a doctor and a nurse, she was taken to the ICU to see the body of her husband and was permitted to remain with him to say her goodbyes.

Sadly for Mrs Bowman, the horror of the morning had more shocks in store for her. She was driven to the local police station to be given further details on how Max had come by his injuries. Detective Chief Inspector Dawn Brooks introduced herself to Mrs Bowman. She offered her condolences and, from the outset, said hearing about the circumstances of Max's death would be distressing. The DCI stressed that she could, at that time, only give a brief outline of what appeared to have happened. Much investigation by the police still needed to be undertaken.

Max had been shot. He had received gunshot wounds to his upper body and neck. He had been unconscious when he arrived at hospital but had died before the surgeons could operate on him. Police currently had one known witness to the attack.

The fifty-year-old male witness had been driving his Ford saloon car along the particularly quiet country road and had been aware of a cyclist, about fifty yards in front of him, travelling in the same direction. Suddenly, in his rear-view mirror, he noticed a motorcycle speeding fast behind him.

Without slowing down, the motorcycle overtook him and continued at a fast pace. He noticed two people on the motorcycle, both dressed in black and wearing full-face crash helmets. The motorcycle slowed as it approached and prepared to overtake the pedal cyclist. As it did so, the pillion rider appeared to have a gun in his left hand which was pointed at the cyclist. The witness saw flashes and heard several loud bangs as the cyclist toppled and fell onto the grass verge.

The motorcycle had continued on its way and disappeared. The cyclist lay motionless on the grass embankment. There were no other vehicles travelling in either direction.

Quite understandably, the motorist said that having witnessed what he considered to be a shooting, he had stopped his car and taken a few seconds to acknowledge what had just happened. He had then run to the man, who appeared apparently lifeless, and noticed blood covering his upper clothing. He didn't feel there was anything he could do to help the injured man. He immediately dialled 999 to request attendance of the emergency services.

DCI Brooks explained to Mrs Bowman that the police would need to identify a motive for the attack. Was Max Bowman deliberately targeted, and if so, what was the motive? Was it a case of mistaken identity or a random shooting carried out by two perverted and dangerous individuals?

Mrs Rosie Bowman had assured the DCI that she wished to continue and answer questions about her husband's background, as it may disclose a motive for the shooting. The police investigation increased in pace once Mrs Bowman had spoken.

Max Bowman and his wife were both freelance journalists. He had been an investigative journalist. His current assignment had involved the investigation of organised crime gangs in the UK and the importation of Class A drugs; mainly cocaine. She said her husband rarely spoke in detail about his investigations, but he would have kept detailed records on his iPad which was locked in his home safe.

Had he previously received any threats relating to his work? She hadn't been aware of any.

Suddenly, Mrs Bowman stopped talking. She shook her head in disbelief and anger, then cried:

"What idiots we've been. It all makes sense now. Four or five weeks ago, Max went off on his usual Sunday morning bike ride and came back upset that the front wheel of his bike had been damaged. He said a car had driven past him too close and at speed and had clipped his front wheel in the process. Max had taken a tumble but was fortunate to fall on the grass verge and only received a few minor bruises. The car didn't stop, and it was all so quick he didn't notice the colour or make of the car."

"Did he report the incident to the police?" asked the DCI.

"Yes, he did, but the driver wasn't traced. It also got a mention in the local press with a request for anyone driving along that road with dashcam footage to come forward, but no one did. Max put the incident down to an 'idiot.' However, at the time, I remember him making the comment that it had been so reckless that it could almost have been deliberate."

The drive-by shooting had all the indications that it was a deliberate and planned attack on a targeted individual. The evidence suggested that the previous incident had been a failed attack to kill him, possibly by ramming him off the road to make it appear an accidental hit-and-run, where the driver had failed to stop.

Such a case would have received a lesser police response than an 'assassination' attempt and, when that failed, the option of a gun was employed. The fact that Max had been investigating UK organised crime gangs involved in the importation of drugs would have made him a likely target. Later that afternoon, following the death of Max Bowman, the UK Counter Terrorism Department, based at New Scotland Yard, became involved in the investigation.

The Ford car of the male driver who had witnessed the shooting had been fitted with a forward-facing dashcam that had captured on video the sequence of the offending motorcycle as it approached the cyclist and the shots fired. The video footage was seized by the police for detailed analysis. The motorcycle's rear numberplate had been completely obscured by a bag fitted across the back of the seat. No doubt, this had been a deliberate act on the part of the attackers.

Within hours of the attack, the police issued a press release which requested drivers with potentially useful dashcam video footage to come forward. Extensive efforts were also commenced to check the ANPR system and local CCTV for possible identification of the motorcycle.

Later the same evening, two officers from the Counter Terrorism Department visited Mrs Bowman at her home. With her permission, they seized, and took away for further detailed analysis, her late husband's files, laptop computer, mobile telephone, address book and camera.

The initial police review identified that Max Bowman's current active investigation had involved research into the alleged illegal financial activities of David Evans, the same David Evans who was the subject of investigation by Operation Goldfinger. The Counter Terrorism Department often worked closely with MI5, who were informed about the killing of Max Bowman and his known connection with David Evans.

For the past ten years, Max Bowman had been a well-respected freelance investigative journalist. He often undertook complex and protracted investigations on behalf of various national newspapers. In the main, they would be in-depth investigations concentrating on a single story and involve allegations of corruption, money laundering and extortion.

Max Bowman had been investigating the alleged criminal activities of David Evans and his property empire for the past ten months and had reached a point where he was almost ready to publish. He was also in discussion with a film production company to make a documentary exposé on the results of the investigation.

David Evans was British by birth and had always been a UK resident. However, extensive research by Bowman had failed to trace a single UK bank account in his name. Neither was there any record that Evans had ever paid any government tax on earned income. On paper, he owned no property and had no visible means of acquiring a legal income. This UK-based national lived a millionaire lifestyle, in a large luxury country house paid for with cash, yet there was a total absence of evidence of how he had achieved his wealth.

In recent years, Evans had also acquired expensive properties abroad. As with his four-million-pound English country house, they were all registered in his wife's name, and purchased with cash. The properties included: Spain – villa in Marbella valued at £8 million; Italy – villa on the shores of Lake Como valued at £8 million; Austria – chalet on the outskirts of Salzburg valued at £1.5 million; Panama – luxury family house in Panama City valued at £6 million.

Max Bowman's investigation had also established that Evans held, in different names, bank accounts in various European countries and in Panama, holding vast amounts of cash. The evidence had established that he held false UK passports, which enabled him to open the accounts. In addition, Bowman had established that Evans had also been involved, in company with other international organised crime gangs, several fictitious banks and dubious financial entities, in illegal property transactions.

In recent days, MI5, working with the Counter Terrorism Department, had established that in the days prior to Evans' arrest at London Gatwick Airport whilst attempting to catch a flight to Panama, he had become aware that Bowman's story was nearing publication. Via the dark web, Evans had 'placed an order' for the assassination of Bowman.

Following the first failed attempt, the latest intelligence indicated two assassins had illegally entered the UK to carry out the mission. By the end of the day, following the killing, it had been suggested but not confirmed that they had already been smuggled out of the UK. The fee paid was £100,000. The killing of Max Bowman continued to be the subject of extensive police investigations.

The 09:00 hours morning briefing of the Operation Goldfinger team was about to begin. At short notice,

DCI Durham had asked DI Penfold to chair the team briefing, as he had to deal with an urgent issue which had recently arisen. He asked DI Cheeseman to join him in his office and closed the door. The DCI's knowledge of the DI was limited. They had no prior knowledge of each other before the DCI had recently joined the team. Privately, he considered the DI a rather cold and selfish individual, who gave the impression that he would seek any occasion to make disparaging remarks about senior management and the police service.

DCI Durham was seated behind his desk and invited DI Cheeseman to take the seat in front of him. The DI looked glum and suspicious as to why he was there.

The DCI spoke:

"John, last week at our management team meeting, l mentioned an arrangement had been made for a senior member of MI5 to visit us to discuss their involvement with the David Evans investigation. I stressed that the information must remain confidential and not be disclosed outside our team. At that meeting, only you, the other two DIs and the Office Manager were present."

DI Cheeseman expressed agitation and stood up:

"I don't like the way this is going. I'm the only one sitting here. I hope you are not pointing the finger at me."

DCI Durham stopped the DI before he could continue. Speaking louder and in a more authoritative voice than was normal for him, he went on:

"Please sit down. John, sit down. Calm down and listen to me. Only five of us had the knowledge that we were to have a visit from an MI5 officer. From a secure and reliable source, I have been informed that David Evans, who is currently in custody in HM Prison Belmarsh, has been made aware of the proposed MI5 visit."

DI Cheeseman still standing and showing annoyance replied:

"Well, it wasn't from me, and you'd better be careful about making such allegations."

The DCI asked:

"Have you mentioned the proposed MI5 visit to anyone?"

"No, I haven't."

The DCI continued:

"I have information the disclosure came from you."

Again, the DI interrupted:

"That's enough. I'm not staying here any longer. You'll be hearing from the Police Federation."

The DI turned and stepped towards the closed office door. The DCI continued:

"DI Cheeseman, we have the evidence. It's in your best interest to listen. The information about the MI5 visit, and other pieces of evidence emanating from Operation Goldfinger, have been leaked to Evans. We have been aware of the leaks for a few weeks. The individual passing the information was identified as Bob Wilson. Do you know him?"

"No."

"He is a property developer. He regards himself as a bit of a big shot and flaunts his wealth by driving an Aston Martin car and he wears a twenty-thousand-pound watch among other things. Wilson is a member of the ABC Gymnasium and Health Spa. Does that ring any bells?"

DI Cheeseman sat back down in the chair and replied in a quiet voice:

"Yes, my wife works there."

"John, I'm sorry to have to report that close surveillance has been undertaken on Bob Wilson. He attends the gym most mornings for a workout then has breakfast in the café. Your wife joins him most mornings for a chat over coffee. We have her on record updating him with information on Operation Goldfinger, which he, in turn, relays to one of David Evans' associates."

The DI remained seated and silent for a minute, before asking:

"Is she having an affair with him?"

Lowering his voice, and showing a degree of compassion, the DCI spoke:

"John, that is something you will need to ask your wife. The surveillance operation was to identify the source of the leaks and that has been achieved. The leaks have breached the integrity of Operation Goldfinger and for that I am concerned. On a personal note, I am concerned for your welfare and that of your wife. Please be sensible. It is my duty to inform you that with immediate effect, you are removed from this investigation and will today report to the Personnel Department of your force, who are expecting your return."

DI Cheeseman acknowledged that, on occasions, he had been indiscreet and had 'mentioned' to his wife matters regarding Operation Goldfinger. He found himself embarrassed, apologetic and annoyed, and stressed he had not deliberately divulged confidential information. He had wrongly assumed his wife could be trusted not to repeat such information.

The DI explained his current role had involved working long hours and, when he returned home, his wife would ask what he had been doing; a natural response in his view. It was in that context that he had let slip the occasional indiscretion.

By prior agreement, at the same time as DCI Durham had been speaking with DI Cheeseman, officers had been deployed to interview, and, if the circumstances became relevant, arrest Mrs Cheeseman and her 'friend' Bob Wilson. It had been established that Wilson was a cocaine user and had relayed the snippets of information he had obtained on the Evans investigation to his supplier. Through the drug fraternity grapevine, the information had reached the associates of Evans.

By appointment, at 10:00 hours the same day, Julian Lawson and his MI5 colleague Mark Holloway arrived at the Operation Goldfinger HQ and were met by DCI Graham Durham. The two visitors were taken to a secure conference room and introduced to the management team consisting of DI Fatima Ramiz, DI Richard Penfold and the Officer Manager Barry Bishop.

Coffee was served as they sat down to share information, with both parties (police and MI5) requiring an update from the other. From the outset, there was agreement that much of the information would be highly sensitive, and thus, 'classified', and would not be disclosed to outside parties without prior approval.

Prior to the meeting, DCI Durham and his management team had been made aware that MI5 had been supplying Operation Goldfinger with extremely sensitive and beneficial intelligence on the activities of the main target, David Evans. However, they had not been aware of the secretive operation to embed one of their officers/agents, Julian Lawson, alongside David Evans.

DCI Durham had opened the proceedings by giving an outline of their investigation, which included background on Evans and his associates; the increasing violence and killings undertaken apparently on his orders; the hijack of the prison van; the police raid on the consignment of imported cocaine; the recent arrest of Terry Evans in Scotland and the tragic assassination of the investigative journalist Max Bowman.

Julian Lawson acknowledged that MI5 had already been made aware of much of what had taken place. Both sides asked and answered questions to clarify and enlarge on certain points.

Fresh coffee was served before Julian Lawson addressed the Operation Team. Firstly, he outlined the role of MI5 as the security service responsible for the protection of the country and its citizens.

One of the roles of the service was to gain intelligence. MI5 did not have powers of arrest: that authority remained with the police. To be effective, and for reasons of security, the identity of their operatives remained unknown to the public and the media.

Julian Lawson continued:

"When David Evans was snatched during the prison van ambush, he escaped with another prisoner called Guy Hamilton, a fugitive apparently wanted by the FBI in America. They remained together whilst on the run. Hamilton was with Evans when the lorry carrying the imported cocaine was raided by police."

DCI Durham asked:

"May I ask, what happened to Hamilton? I am given to understand he was among the attackers arrested, then he just disappeared. All records of him were also deleted from the PNC database."

Julian Lawson smiled and replied:

"Graham, I believe you have already worked out the answer."

DCI responded:

"So, he was an MI5 plant?"

Julian Lawson continued:

"On the orders of Evans, three people were kidnapped and being held against their will. There was strong evidence that he had ordered that they be killed. Intensive police activity had failed to find where they were being held. The situation was urgent. It was known that Evans would not cooperate with the police. So, at senior government level, the message went out: 'Do what needs to be done to find them and secure their safe release.' At short notice, we at MI5 devised a plan to infiltrate his organisation with one of our team. That was the introduction of Guy Hamilton."

DI Penfold gave a knowing smile at Lawson and asked:

"From our contact with the Prison Service, we know Guy Hamilton had a genuine bullet wound in his arm, which the prison doctor tended each morning. The story was that Hamilton had been wounded during a gunfight in Florida with an FBI agent. Are you able to comment?"

Julian Lawson responded:

"When the plan for the infiltration was being considered, authenticity was the key. Evans had to be 100% convinced that his new fellow prisoner was the genuine article. And this is what we were able to supply; a wanted man on the run, with serious criminal convictions and, to add authenticity to his cover story, a recent bullet wound. An MI5 officer had recently been wounded in a shooting incident, and one of our directors put forward the possibility of deploying him. He readily agreed to go undercover, so we were able to deploy an officer with a genuine wound and a false identity."

Mark Holloway smiled, looked at Julian Lawson and commented:

"A brave man."

Julian Lawson continued with his presentation:

"When involved in an undercover operation, it is imperative that the individual does not act as an agent provocateur. Throughout his time with Evans, he remained a passive sidekick. With this case, a detailed witness statement will be provided by the undercover officer known as Hamilton. Naturally, discussion will take place between our MI5 Legal Department and the Crown Prosecution Service to agree disclosure for the forthcoming trial before the Crown Court. Should one of our officers be required to give evidence before a court, with the agreement from the presiding judge, it will be given behind a screen. The officer's identity will not be disclosed. If considered relevant on the grounds of national security, parts of the MI5 evidence may be given before a closed court."

DI Penfold, with a glint in his eye, looked at Lawson and asked:

"Do I call you Sir?"

Julian Lawson smiled and then laughed:

"OK. For the benefit of our colleagues here this morning, I'd better explain your rather cryptic remark. Last time we met, I was handcuffed in a police custody suite. I had long bleached hair, a beard, and looked like a right scruff. You treated me roughly. I remember being annoyed. I whispered to you saying that should we meet in the future, you may wish to address me as Sir. Yes, I was operating undercover for MI5. I was in the guise of

Guy Hamilton. That information must remain within our restricted group."

This last comment referred to the occasion of the arrest of David Evans and others following the police raid on the lorry transporting the illegal importation of cocaine.

The meeting had then discussed future working cooperation between the two services, which they anticipated would lead to the prosecution of David Evans and his associates. Before the meeting was concluded, the two MI5 officers outlined their view about why the assassination of Max Bowman had taken place.

Julian Lawson said intelligence indicated David Evans had been worried and angry about the forthcoming Max Bowman exposé, more than he was about being prosecuted for his illegal drug activities. That was why Bowman had to be assassinated. He had ordered that the killing be undertaken without delay and before the exposé neared publication, no doubt hoping the brutal assassination of the principal author would cause fear within the publishing company and, literally, kill off the story.

Bowman's investigation had concentrated on dubious financial transactions undertaken by Evans.

This concerned the illegal movement of tens of millions of pounds from the UK to banks in Europe and elsewhere, the setting up of shell companies, and the purchase of luxury properties. The exposé would name the corrupt companies and the individuals who had received cash payments to facilitate fraud, money laundering and extortion at the instigation of Evans and to his benefit.

The Bowman investigation had established a detailed paper trail of vast sums of illegally appropriated money being deposited in foreign bank accounts using fake passports. Some of the money had been used to purchase multimillion-pound luxury villas. Evans had also set up foreign investment and property agencies. The agencies were a front to buy and then sell villas in an operation to money-launder the vast amounts of cash he had accumulated from his illegal cocaine drug dealings.

Bowman's investigation had concentrated on the financial aspects of Evans' vast wealth. His report had acknowledged that Evans' wealth had been acquired from illegal drug dealing. Bowman had not investigated the mechanics or background of the international criminal drug trade.

David Evans had believed that Bowman's exposé had the potential to trigger the downfall of his financial empire. He thought legitimate international financial institutions, investors and property agencies would refuse to deal with him and withdraw their services. He perceived that his reputation as a responsible property developer would be ruined.

However, he was confident that he possessed sufficient ruthless cunning, contacts and money to thwart the UK authorities from bringing successful criminal prosecutions against him. He had done so in the past. He had boasted about helping colleagues defeat justice by, as he called it, 'get out of jail free cards' being bought for £50,000.

In the first instance, he would be prepared to threaten, blackmail and offer large sums of money to convince witnesses not to give evidence. He would also endeavour to corrupt police officers and other members of the justice system in an attempt to halt the prosecution.

Evans considered that the current complex prosecution cases being built against him would each be scheduled for an eight-to-ten-week Crown Court trial before a jury and he intended to plead Not Guilty and fight every allegation. He would be prepared to target the judicial system by threatening and intimidating witnesses and jurors and, if that failed, buying off jurors to return Not Guilty verdicts.

The meeting held at the Operation Goldfinger HQ acknowledged that, in the recent past, it had proved difficult to successfully prosecute gangs of international drug dealers involved in long complex trials. Why? Because of the large amounts of illegal money freely available to target, threaten and corrupt every element of the judicial process.

Regarding the murder of Max Bowman, Julian Lawson spoke of the concern within government departments on drug trafficking organisations becoming increasingly bold in targeting their perceived enemies, specifically journalists. In the past twenty years, in Columbia, eight to ten journalists each year had been deliberately targeted and murdered as a direct consequence of investigating drug trafficking. Worryingly, the spread of executions had reached Europe and beyond. The violent activity of organised crime gangs had become a major threat to press freedom.

Recent years had witnessed at least one killing each year of an investigative journalist in Europe. The gangs had even been bold enough to kill one of Europe's most famous investigative journalists, Peter R de Vries, who was the victim of a Mafia-style hit when he was shot in the head outside the Amsterdam TV studio.

A Spanish journalist had also been murdered whilst investigating a gang smuggling drugs into the UK. The authorities had identified the involvement of an English man in the killing. To illustrate the growing problem, Italy currently has about twenty journalists who live under permanent police protection.

The meeting between the Operation Goldfinger management team and the two MI5 officers concluded. DI Penfold took the opportunity to shake hands with Julian Lawson and to make an apology:

"Julian, it's been good to meet with you today. I just wanted to say sorry for my rough handling of you following your 'arrest' and later at the police custody suite."

Lawson replied:

"Thank you, Richard. I found my role as Guy Hamilton very interesting on several levels and it has given me a better understanding of society and personal interactions. When I visit people smartly dressed in a suit and in my official role, I'm treated with courtesy and respect. In my persona as a scruffy individual, the opposite was true."

DI Penfold responded:

"My current colleagues here don't know much about my background. I personally find dealing with drug dealers very difficult, and I let my feelings show when I was dealing with you when I believed you to be part of Evans' gang. My late brother was a drug addict and died a slow painful death through taking cocaine. When I became aware he was addicted to cocaine, I cut off all contact with him. As a police inspector, I thought having a drug addict as a brother would damage my career. All too late, I realised what a bastard I'd been and tried to help him. Sadly, and to my eternal guilt, he died shortly after our reunion."

Lawson thanked the DI for sharing his experiences and expressed his support.

Chapter Eleven

Visit to Brighton Hotel

A thirty-year-old white male by the name of Peter Dice had booked a double room at the four-star Gladstone Hotel for a two-night stay. The Victorian-built seafront hotel, located in the city of Brighton on the south coast of England, had recently undergone extensive renovation. The booking had been made through an online agency, and a specific request had been made that the double room must be located on the top floor with a sea view.

Around mid-afternoon, Mr Peter Dice arrived at the reception desk and presented his Mastercard to confirm his identity. He said his girlfriend would be joining him a little later; she had walked into town to buy a new dress. With a smile, he commented they would be spending their first romantic weekend together. He had not booked to have any meals at the hotel, having stated they intended to 'eat out' to enjoy the atmosphere of the town.

His chosen double room was located on the 7th floor, with a small balcony and an unobstructed view of the sea.

The next morning, just before daybreak, a fellow hotel guest, who had been out for an early morning run along the seafront, rushed up to the reception desk and, in a flustered state, reported having seen the body of a man lying face down on the pavement. She had noticed a lot of blood and believed he was dead.

Two members of staff immediately rushed out to the front of the hotel and confirmed the presence of a body, which appeared lifeless. A blanket was placed over the body, with the immediate area cordoned off. A member of staff remained in situ to guide people away.

The emergency services were telephoned. Very quickly, an ambulance and police car were in attendance. The man's death was confirmed. On the instructions of the police, the body would not be removed until various enquiries had been undertaken and the man's identity confirmed.

Had the man been the subject of a brutal assault as he walked along the seafront road, or had he fallen from one of the hotel balconies? Two detectives from the local CID attended and liaised with the uniform officers and hotel staff.

A small team of hotel staff undertook to knock on the door of every guest room with a sea view. They failed to receive a reply from room number 706. The door was locked. A master key was used to unlock the door. They found the room unoccupied with the double doors to the balcony wide open.

They looked over the balcony and confirmed that the body was lying directly below on the pavement. By this time, the hotel manager was on duty and confirmed that the room had been booked in the name of Peter Dice. It was also confirmed that none of the staff had seen his girlfriend.

Without touching anything, the two detectives undertook a cursory examination of the room. The lights in the room were still switched on. They confirmed there was no female clothing in the room, or toiletries in the bathroom, to indicate Dice's girlfriend had spent time there. On the coffee table sat a litre bottle of whisky, which was almost empty. The detectives directed that the room be relocked and secured, with no staff allowed to enter.

The death of Peter Dice currently remained unexplained. The detectives requested the attendance of a Scene of Crime forensic team, with a photographer, to examine the hotel room, and for a forensic tent to be placed to shield the body. The police officer who was the first to attend the scene had reported that the body gave off a strong smell of whisky.

Where was his girlfriend? Had she ever visited the room? Had she failed to turn up for their first romantic weekend? Had Dice drowned his sadness in whisky? Had he been in an inebriated state then accidentally fallen over the balcony, or committed suicide? Many questions remained unanswered. The CID would continue with their enquiries.

Room 706 was subjected to a detailed examination, including fingerprint impressions taken, along with photographs. Likewise, following initial forensic examination and photographs, the body was secured in a body bag and taken to the local mortuary in preparation for a postmortem.

The mobile phone and wallet of the deceased were taken to the police station for further examination. Documents contained in the wallet appeared to confirm that the body was that of Peter Dice and gave an address in Guildford.

Later in the day, the two detectives travelled to Guildford and visited the apartment given as the residence of Peter Dice. The door was opened by a man who introduced himself as Thomas Knight. He said it was a rented apartment, which he shared with Peter, and they had resided there for about six months. The officers gently explained the circumstances relating to the death of a man who, according to the hotel register and documents found in the room, would appear to be Peter Dice.

What could he tell the officers about Peter Dice?

Thomas Knight explained that they had originally met as part of a larger group who drank at the King's Head public house in Guildford. By coincidence, both were looking to find better accommodation when their present apartment came on the market. He considered Peter a reserved, intelligent and caring individual. Peter was about thirty years of age and single. Thomas Knight was aware that Peter had recently met a girl in a London nightclub and he had been very excited that they had planned a romantic weekend together.

Knight had met her, very briefly, when she had called at the apartment with Peter. She had been introduced as Amelia. He said she was very attractive, about 28 years old, slim with long blonde hair, and elegantly and expensively dressed. Knight had formed the view that she hadn't realised anyone would be in the apartment and was surprised to see him there.

The girlfriend clearly didn't wish to get involved in conversation and indicated that she wanted to leave the apartment without delay. Knight hadn't decided whether she was shy or arrogant. He did notice a slight foreign accent.

Knight was aware that Amelia, he didn't know her second name, had been the one to push for them to have a romantic weekend away together. Peter said he had given Amelia his credit card to decide on the hotel and to make the booking online. Peter did not own a car, and Amelia had picked him up for the journey to the south-coast hotel.

Continuing their interview with Thomas Knight, they mentioned that it appeared Peter Dice had consumed almost a litre of whisky before the fall.

Thomas Knight shook his head vigorously:

"No way. Peter detested whisky. He only ever drank beer."

The officers explained that an almost empty whisky bottle had been found on the coffee table in the hotel room, and the body of Peter Dice had given off an extremely strong smell of whisky.

Thomas Knight continued to shake his head:

"No way. I remember him saying even the smell of whisky made him feel sick. If the body you found smelled of whisky, and that man had drunk whisky, then it's not Peter."

With the permission of Thomas Knight, they carefully examined the bedroom of Peter Dice, including his unlocked desk. One of the detectives, holding an open passport, turned to Knight and commented:

"Is this a photograph of your mate Peter Dice?"

Knight leaned forward to have a closer look.

"Definitely, but I see the name is different."

The passport had been issued by the Republic of Belarus and stated the holder as Vladimir Petrova. In response to further questions from the detectives, Knight said he had little knowledge of Peter's background, but had a vague recollection that Peter wasn't born in the UK and had 'anglicised' his name. Knight said he had never seen the passport, nor been told Peter was a Belarusian national. As far as he was aware, all his flat mate's documents were in the name Peter Dice.

Knight added that Peter worked as a freelance journalist and often undertook investigations for articles which had appeared in UK national newspapers. Perhaps, he surmised, the use of the English name was more convenient when working as a journalist. The two officers took possession of the passport and other relevant documents. They also obtained from Thomas Knight a written witness statement detailing what he knew about the man he called Peter Dice.

When the officers had returned to their police station, they had undertaken further research and checks on the deceased with the PNC database. During the day, other detective colleagues reviewed the CCTV footage taken from within the reception and ground-floor area of the Gladstone Hotel. Peter Dice had been identified as leaving and returning to the hotel on several occasions during the evening. There was no video record of him accompanying a female. Who was the mysterious Amelia?

At the County mortuary, a Home Office-appointed pathologist conducted a postmortem on the man known as Peter Dice. The deceased had been beaten prior to death. He had sustained blunt force trauma to the back of his head. There were no defensive wounds to his hands or arms. The evidence indicated he had been attacked from behind and had not fought with his attacker.

The forensic evidence indicated he had been unconscious or semiconscious before he hit the ground. There were no measurable levels of alcohol or drugs in his blood. The face and upper body clothing had been soaked in whisky. Traces of whisky were also found on the floor of the hotel room. The suggestion was that whisky had been splashed over the semiconscious man as he lay on the floor.

Fibres recovered from the top metal railing of the balcony matched those from the casual short-sleeved Polo shirt he had been wearing. Faint scuff marks on the carpet indicated that the unconscious or semiconscious body had been dragged onto the balcony. It appeared likely the body had been propped up against the balustrade railing, then lifted by the feet and pushed over.

With the description given by Thomas Knight of the girlfriend Amelia, further checks on the hotel's CCTV footage had been undertaken but with a negative result. The reception, foyer, stairs and public areas were covered by CCTV. However, for the privacy of their guests, CCTV had not been installed in the corridors leading to the bedrooms. So, unfortunately there was no video footage of who may have visited Room 706.

When the body of the deceased had been discovered on the pavement, the door to his room had been found locked. Had he answered the door to his attacker, allowed the person into the room and then locked the door? At that stage, it would appear he either knew the person or had no reason to fear for his own safety. The hotel door key issued to Dice was missing. Had the assailant used it to lock the door as they left?

The facts, including the mysterious missing girlfriend, suggested it had been a premeditated attack. At that stage, the police had still not established a firm motive. During the material times, no male or female had been captured on CCTV ascending or descending the stairs from the direction of the seventh floor.

Was it possible that the attacker or attackers had pre-booked a room on the same floor 706, and 'Amelia' was the bait in a long-term plan? If so, this would indicate a professional assassination operation.

That night, the hotel had just over two hundred guests staying. Many of those staying on the seventh floor, and on lower floors, had been coached down from nearby London Gatwick Airport for a one-night stopover stay, and all had departed the hotel at 05:30 hours to catch their onward flights. Stopover Gatwick bookings for the hotel were a frequent feature. Was it possible that the attacker or attackers were now safely out of the UK?

In view of the accumulated evidence, the death of Peter Dice had been formally recorded as a murder. The investigation would now be undertaken by the county Homicide and Serious Crime Unit.

Their checks with PNC had quickly identified links with the killing of the investigative journalist Max Bowman, subject of investigation by the Counter Terrorism Department, and with the Operation Goldfinger investigations into the criminal activities of David Evans and his associates.

Julian Lawson and Mark Holloway from MI5 made a return visit to the Operation Goldfinger HQ for a meeting with DCI Graham Durham and his management team. Lawson said that because of the killing of Peter Dice, he had met with the Senior Investigating Officer leading that murder investigation to discuss progress of the investigation and to supply him with information gleaned by MI5. In addition, he had met with the SIO at the Counter Terrorism Department, who was leading the investigation into the shooting of the investigative journalist Max Bowman.

Lawson told the Operation Goldfinger team that he would update them on the latest information available on the shooting of Max Bowman and discuss its relevance with their investigation into the activities of David Evans.

The motorcycle used in the attack had been recovered and, although burnt out, it had been established that the bike had been stolen two days before the attack, whilst parked in a residential street in West London. Police had undertaken door-to-door enquiries in that street and, from one house, had recovered video doorbell footage of the bike being pushed along the road by one man. Footage from other houses in the next street had recorded the bike being loaded into the back of an old white Ford Transit van, with the assistance of a second man.

As the van had been driven away, the police had been fortunate to find that another neighbour's video door-bell camera had recorded the van's registration number. Several hours later, using the ANPR system, the van was seen arriving at the Cricklewood Service Station. It had remained stationary for two and a half hours before departing. During that time, nothing was removed from the rear of the van.

Two men had left the van when it was parked, and it was the same two men who returned to the van. Photographs of the two men, taken from the CCTV footage, were of good quality, and, of particular interest, they showed that on their return to the van, each man was holding a motorcycle helmet, which matched the helmets worn by the two attackers, as shown on the dashcam footage belonging to the witness,

Both men were of East European appearance, which may be relevant. Intelligence obtained on previous killings which had been linked to David Evans strongly indicated that he employed the services of 'visiting' hitmen from former Soviet Bloc countries.

Shortly after driving off from the Cricklewood Service Station, the Transit van had turned onto a road not covered by CCTV. The current location of the vehicle was unknown. Police enquiries would continue. The address for the registered keeper of the vehicle was in Liverpool and the address would receive a visit from the police without delay.

The recovered bullets used to murder Max Bowman had been forensically examined. The bullets were of Russian origin. The striation marks left on the surface of the fired bullets identified they had been fired from a PB Besshumnyy semi-automatic silenced pistol, issued to special forces' personnel in the Russian army. Further enquiries were being pursued at pace.

Lawson then addressed the Operation Goldfinger team with an update on the killing of Peter Dice at the Gladstone Hotel:

"Earlier this morning, before setting out for this meeting, I received an update on research undertaken regarding Vladimir Petrova. We can confirm 100% that

Vladimir Petrova and Peter Dice were the same person. Petrova was a citizen of the Republic of Belarus. The passport in that name, seized from the apartment in Guildford, was genuine."

Lawson continued to give an outline on what had been established:

"About five years ago, as Vladimir Petrova, he successfully applied for a UK Student Visa to undertake a full-time postgraduate course at the London School of Economics. Prior to that, he had worked as a freelance journalist in his own country, Belarus, and various other capitals within Europe.

On completion of his postgraduate studies at the LSE, in his correct name, Petrova applied for asylum in the UK. He sought humanitarian protection for fear of persecution should he be required to return to Belarus. He had stated that, in his opinion, recent elections had not been free, fair or democratic.

Petrova had become extremely critical of the highly centralised authoritarian government, which had moved closer to Russia. His critical investigative reporting had concentrated on allegations of corruption by government officials, drug dealing and organised crime gangs operating throughout Europe. He was aware that he had been closely monitored by the authorities in Belarus.

Since completing his studies at the LSE, he had used the name Peter Dice. He held bank accounts and credit cards in that name. There was no suggestion that he had used the change of name for any unlawful purpose. He continued to work as a freelance investigative journalist, contributing articles to many of the national UK newspapers. He had remained critical of Belarus in his articles.

None of his friends or work colleagues were aware of his nationality or true name. Currently, there were gaps in his background. However, and very important from an evidential point of view, he had personally met with, and undertaken email correspondence with, Max Bowman. The correspondence dealt with, and shared information on, corrupt government officials and their links with drug dealing by international organised crime gangs. He had named various officials and drug dealers, which included David Evans and his associates."

The meeting at the Operation Goldfinger HQ concluded with Julian Lawson and Mark Taylor saying that they would be returning to MI5 HQ, and they would ensure DCI Graham Durham and his management team would be kept updated.

The police investigations into the two separate murders of Max Bowman and Peter Dice continued to make fast and positive progress.

Police officers had visited the address in Liverpool of the last registered keeper of the white Ford Transit van, seen transporting away the motorcycle used in the murder of Max Bowman.

The man named as the last registered keeper had been somewhat hostile to the police visit; a person with many previous criminal convictions. His response was rather vague. He insisted that he had advertised the van on eBay two months earlier and subsequently sold it to a man for £500 cash. It was an old vehicle and he thought it would be used for 'parts or scrap.'

He said he was unable to give a description of the man, other than that he was 'probably middle-aged.' He hadn't taken the telephone number or name of the man. The police were able to establish that the van had been advertised on eBay, but no further details were forthcoming.

Four hours after the Ford Transit van disappeared off the radar, ANPR cameras identified it rejoining the motorway network and travelling north on the M1 motorway. The Counter Terrorism Team investigating the killing of Max Bowman were immediately informed. Just outside Birmingham, the Transit van had stopped at a service station. The CCTV covering the parking area had identified two men leave the van and walk across to a parked silver Mercedes estate car.

They unlocked the rear door and loaded two full holdalls into the back. They then drove off and continued their journey north on the motorway. The men fitted the description of the two men seen in the previous photographs. The police checked details of the car's registration number, which produced the name and address of the registered keeper; a woman who lived in Cornwall. An immediate visit by local police identified that her silver Mercedes estate car was still parked on her driveway.

The car being driven up the M1 motorway was using cloned number plates. It was, no doubt, a stolen car. This was a common ploy. When criminals steal a car, they will often research on the Internet for an identical car and have made up a set of identical number plates.

Once the Mercedes car was a safe distance away from the service station, the Counter Terrorism team arranged for the parked Transit van to be seized and transported to the local police HQ for a detailed forensic examination. The area firearms team was put on alert to liaise with the Counter Terrorism team and prepare for an armed intervention to arrest the two occupants of the Mercedes car.

The latest report was that the Mercedes had turned off the M6 motorway and onto the forecourt of the service station just south of Manchester. The motorway police control centre monitored the car on CCTV as it pulled up at a petrol pump. The driver got out of the car and used a self-service fuel pump to fill the car with petrol. He paid for the transaction using cash.

The car was then driven across the forecourt to the nearby service station hotel and parked. The driver walked into reception and, several minutes later, returned to the car. Both men collected holdalls from the rear of the car and walked back into the hotel. Their movements had been captured on CCTV. Again, the police were able to confirm that the men matched the photographs of the suspects.

The two men were strongly suspected of being the two men responsible for the brutal killing of Max Bowman. It was reasoned that they would still be armed. They were clearly dangerous and would be prepared to use the guns to avoid arrest. Killing one or more police officers would not cause them concern. An armed police raid into the hotel to detain the two suspects would present many risks.

It was now late evening and getting dark and many people had booked into the hotel for overnight accommodation. The police deployed a covert surveillance van and parked it nearby. It had the outer appearance of a commercial delivery van. Inside, it was a fully equipped surveillance vehicle with two detectives aboard. They would remain in situ, reporting any movement to the police control centre.

During the evening, a meeting had been held at the local police HQ, which involved officers from the Tactical Firearms Unit, the Counterterrorism team and local police commanders. A decision had been agreed that a raid into the hotel presented too many risks. No attempt would be made to detain the two suspects until they had exited the complex of the hotel. Challenging them as they walked to their car would also present a potential risk to members of the public who would, no doubt, also be in the car park.

The police must plan on the basis that the suspects would be armed and a gunfight could ensue. With no police presence in evidence, the two suspects would be allowed to walk to and get into their Mercedes car. Once the car had begun to drive slowly towards the hotel car park exit, it would be intercepted in accordance with policy on armed intervention. Overnight, much police preparation continued, with armed personnel and vehicles discreetly deployed.

From the car park, overnight surveillance continued on the Mercedes car. The police were also able to monitor CCTV coverage of the hotel foyer and reception desk. This would give useful advance notice of when the two suspects were preparing to leave the hotel.

At 07:58 hours, the two suspects walked into the foyer and left their room key on the reception desk. Each was wearing an outdoor jacket and carrying a holdall. The police control centre, by radio communication, alerted the police teams to be prepared. The two suspects walked slowly out of the hotel and momentarily stopped and surveyed their surroundings.

The police control centre updated the police teams - the two suspects were being extremely cautious. Each was holding a holdall in their left hand, and both had their right hand deep in their jacket pocket. Caution; each could be holding a gun!

The two climbed into the Mercedes car, held a brief discussion with each other and slowly began to drive towards the car park exit.

"Strike, Strike, Strike!" was the loud command shouted over the radio communication system.

The hotel car park suddenly came alive, with a great deal of noise and action. A white Ford Transit van suddenly appeared in front of the moving Mercedes and blocked its path. At the same moment, a similar white Ford Transit slammed into the rear of the Mercedes, intentionally disorientating the two suspects. In coordination, two marked police cars, with blue lights flashing and horns blaring, blocked the Mercedes from either side, with the suspects unable to open the doors.

In an instant, the rear doors of the two Ford Transit vans burst open and an armed team of officers from the Tactical Firearms Unit streamed out to surround the Mercedes, with rifles pointed at the two suspects. They were dressed in full combat gear and wearing black bala-clavas. An officer shouted into a handheld Tannoy:

"Armed police. Keep both hands on the dashboard. Remain in the car."

He repeated his message, with a few added swear words, as the suspects appeared to show body movement.

With the two suspects complying, and with several rifles trained on them, the police car blocking the driver's door reversed. One officer yanked open the door. Another officer grabbed the driver and unceremoniously pulled him onto the ground, turned him onto his front and secured his hands behind his back with plastic ties. The same operation was repeated on the other suspect. Both were searched.

A handgun was recovered from the jacket pocket of each suspect and each man was placed into the back of a separate police car. An initial search of the holdalls revealed two motorcycle helmets and two black boiler-suits, together with a box of ammunition and approximately £50,000 in cash in each one. Previous intelligence had suggested the contract killers of Max Bowman had been paid £100,000. No doubt, the cash found in their possession was from that payment.

The two suspects would be escorted back to London for formal interrogation by the Counter Terrorism team, whilst full forensic examinations would be undertaken on the Mercedes car and the hotel room they had occupied.

Lawson then updated the meeting on the murder of the man known as Peter Dice. The correct name of the deceased was Vladimir Petrova. The UK Foreign and Commonwealth Office had formally made the Belarusian authorities aware of the death and that the police were investigating it as a murder. The identity of the mysterious Amelia remained unknown.

However, CCTV footage taken on Brighton seafront had identified a red Mini Cooper motorcar, on the relevant afternoon, stopping about fifty yards from the main entrance to the Gladstone Hotel. A man got out from the front passenger seat and the Mini immediately drove off eastbound. The driver appeared female, although the quality of the video was very poor. The man, carrying a small case, entered the Gladstone Hotel. The same man was picked up on the hotel's CCTV system. It was definitely the man who had booked in as Peter Dice.

Extensive research of the city's CCTV system was undertaken.

The distinctive car and the narrow timeframe enabled the car to be identified and tracked through the city's main roads. The car had taken the shortest route to reach the outskirts of the city and join the M23 heading north. The car was then tracked onto the M25 circular motorway heading east for eight miles before turning off onto a road not covered by CCTV.

The police had researched the registration number with DVLA, and the registered keeper had stated that the previous week, he had sold the car for cash to a man who said he wanted it as a surprise present for his wife. No name had been given.

Having dropped off Peter Dice, his 'girlfriend' Amelia had not wasted any time in driving straight out of Brighton and heading north on the M23 motorway. She clearly did not have any intention of visiting the town centre to buy a new dress for her 'romantic weekend' with her new boyfriend.

Without much doubt, from the outset, Peter Dice was targeted by this individual to form a relationship and lure him to the hotel; and to his brutal death. Who was she working for? Enquiries to identify and trace her continued.

Enquiries with the Internet booking agency, which took the booking for Peter Dice, established that shortly after, a further booking had been made for a one-night stay at the Gladstone Hotel. The online booking was for a double room and had been accompanied by a request for a room on the top floor. Payment was made with an international American Express card in the name of Walter E Goldman.

The hotel register had been signed by W E Goldman and he, together with a male companion, were captured at the reception desk on CCTV. They were allocated room number 715. Both were booked out the next morning at 05:30 hours and were recorded on video leaving the hotel with other guests to catch a coach to London Gatwick Airport.

Enquiries would continue to establish if Mr Goldman and his companion had flown out from Gatwick Airport. Room number 715 would be subjected to a detailed forensic examination. Enquiries were also in hand with American Express.

CHAPTER TWELVE

The Arrests

The two men, arrested in the car park at the Manchester service station as suspects in the murder of the investigative journalist Max Bowman, were formally interrogated after caution and in the presence of the duty solicitor. It was confirmed that both suspects spoke reasonable English, however, each declined to answer any of the questions put to them. They refused to communicate verbally with the officers, which included disclosure of their names.

No passports or other documentation was found in their possession. They were confident in their defiance and, with their silence, were prepared to sit it out. Neither man was fazed by his interrogation. Their manner indicated they had undergone previous military training; likely in a special forces regiment.

Both men had extensive tattoos on their arms, which indicated association with the military from former Eastern Bloc countries. The evidence suggested that they had recently arrived in the UK and were in the country illegally. Details and photographs of the two men were forwarded to Interpol for further research into their identification.

The two handguns recovered from the suspects were PB Besshumnyy semi-automatic silenced pistols. Police forensic experts confirmed that the bullets that had killed Max Bowman had been fired from one of the pistols. Each man, at of the time of their arrest, was in possession of a mobile phone. Both had refused to disclose the passwords to unlock them. The police had submitted the phones for forensic examination to gain access to the contents.

The Mercedes car the two men had in their possession had been fitted with cloned number plates. It had been stolen from Birmingham. They refused to disclose any information about the car.

Further police investigation would be undertaken to establish the identification of the two men and outstanding enquiries would continue. However, in consultation with the Crown Prosecution Service, it was agreed that there was sufficient evidence to charge the men with the murder of Max Bowman and unlawful possession of the two guns.

Later, it was anticipated that further related criminal charges would be laid against the two men. Following their appearance before a court, they would be remanded in custody to await trial at Crown Court.

The investigation into the murder of Peter Dice at the Gladstone Hotel in Brighton was nearing a successful conclusion. At the police Central Control Centre, an ANPR alert had been flashed up: a red Mini Cooper, of special interest in a murder investigation, had entered the M25 motorway at junction 18 and was travelling west. In the control centre, the duty status had identified that a Robbery Squad double-crewed car was on general patrol in the area.

Over the police secure radio system, the Robbery Squad team were given further details and directed to follow the Mini at a discreet and safe distance. They were told the car should not be stopped; further directions would be given.

The crew confirmed that the car was in their sights and was being driven by a young woman with long blonde hair. The details were telephoned through to the incident room dealing with the murder of Peter Dice. The car continued to be tracked. It joined the M4 motorway, then continued onto the A332, Royal Windsor Way, and into the small town of Windsor.

The car stopped and reversed into a parking bay. The police Control Centre directed that if the woman exited the car, one officer should follow her. The controller added that a full surveillance team was en route and would shortly be deployed. The woman left her car and walked briskly in a westerly direction. She was elegantly dressed, displaying the appearance of a confident and successful businesswoman. One officer followed her. The other officer remained in the Robbery Squad car.

The blonde-haired woman walked for a matter of minutes before entering the St. George public house and restaurant. The officer followed. He ordered a pint of beer and sat on a stool at the bar. He observed the woman walk onto the terrace of the restaurant and join a man, already seated at a table, who was wearing designer sunglasses. It was a warm sunny early summer day. They greeted each other as if they were good friends, with a kiss on the cheek.

A waiter appeared at their table and they ordered lunch with a bottle of white wine. She was observed handing the man a package. Without first checking it, he immediately placed the package into a dark brown leather shoulder bag. The indication was that he had expected to receive the package and was aware of the content.

The couple appeared relaxed talking together. He was in his mid-thirties, slim build, clean shaven with dark short hair, and formally dressed in a well-cut dark suit. During the course of the meal, on several occasions, they would clink their wine glasses as if making a toast. Perhaps in celebration of a successful business deal?

To avoid raising suspicion, the officer seated at the bar used his mobile phone to text an update to his colleague seated in the Robbery Squad car. She, in turn, radioed an update to the police control centre.

The officer seated at the bar received a text message that the Surveillance Team was now deployed and ready to follow the two targets when they left the restaurant. There would be sufficient officers available should the two walk off in different directions. If so, each 'target' would be followed. The text message added a caution: one or both targets may be armed. Therefore, an armed Surveillance Team had been deployed.

The officer remained seated at the bar, slowing drinking his single pint of beer, and continued to observe the two suspects. With a brief text message, he sent an alert that the two were preparing to leave. The man had paid the bill with a credit card.

The couple walked out of the premises together. Still talking and relaxed, they turned left towards the pathway that ran alongside the River Thames. The Surveillance Team took up their positions and followed.

The waiter who had served the couple had returned behind the bar and was tapping details on the computer screen to finalise the transaction. The officer leaned across the bar, flashed his police warrant card before the waiter and politely asked to be shown the restaurant copy of the bill. He then texted a message:

"Man paid by American Express. Card in the name Walter E Goldman. Is this relevant?"

It was very relevant. Within thirty seconds, the police control centre broadcast a message to the armed Surveillance Team:

"Authority to strike. Strike now. Caution; targets considered dangerous and may be armed. Arrest on suspicion of murder."

The team responded in a well-rehearsed and coordinated set of movements. Two members of the Surveillance Team, holding hands and appearing to be enjoying a stroll out together, walked past the targets and continued walking. Two other couples continued to walk discreetly behind the targets.

When there were no members of the public nearby to cause a potential safety hazard, the front couple suddenly stopped. They quickly spun round with guns drawn to face the two targets. One shouted in a deliberate aggressive voice:

"Freeze. Armed police. Don't move."

In that instant, the two targets were grabbed by both arms from behind and unceremoniously, but extremely effectively, pushed forward and down onto the ground with their arms held firmly behind their backs. Their hands were secured with plastic ties. Each was frisked.

A small Italian-manufactured handgun was seized from a shoulder holster worn by the man.

The gun had been loaded with a magazine holding six live rounds. A second loaded magazine holding six rounds was recovered from his inner jacket pocket. He had been carrying a dark brown leather shoulder bag. It contained a package from which the officers recovered £100,000 in new Bank of England notes. The couple were formally advised they were being arrested on suspicion of murder and cautioned. Neither made a comment.

By this time, several unmarked police cars had arrived and parked on the nearby road. Each suspect was escorted to a different police car. As they were being separated, the man shouted in Italian to the woman: " Mantenere il sillenzio" (Maintain silence).

Julian Lawson made a return visit to the Operation Goldfinger HQ to speak with DCI Graham Durham and the management team and gave an update:

"Over the past few days, I have kept you updated with developments on the Max Bowman and Peter Dice murder investigations and the arrests of the four suspects. I am now pleased to report that, in respect of both investigations, the Crown Prosecution Service has authorised that all four suspects will be charged. Also, there are further significant and welcome developments which will assist with the prosecution of your 'favourite target', David Evans."

Regarding the murder of Max Bowman, Lawson spoke about the 'excellent evidential trail' which began with the two suspects caught on camera stealing the motorcycle. They were then caught on another camera taking the motorcycle away in the Ford Transit van. Next, they were captured on dashcam when they carried out the shooting. Then they were recorded on CCTV when they parked the Transit, still carrying the motorcycle helmets, and transferred to the Mercedes, which was on cloned plates.

With the aid of ANPR and other CCTV systems, the two had been tracked to the Manchester hotel where they were arrested by members of the Tactical Firearms Unit. The motorcycle helmets and black boiler suits worn at the time of the shooting were recovered from their possession, together with almost £50,000 in cash recovered from each of their holdalls, this being the £100,000 payment the killers had purportedly received.

In addition, the forensic team had confirmed that the bullets that killed Max Bowman had been fired from one of the two pistols recovered from the two suspects. Both men had continued to refuse to supply any information about their identities. Enquiries with Interpol were ongoing. However, that issue did not preclude them from being charged with murder and other associated major crime offences. They would be remanded in custody.

Lawson smiled and added:

"Some more good news for your team. The arresting officers found, in the jacket pocket of one of the men, a screwed-up piece of paper, on which had been handwritten, 'if in urgent need, phone…' with a mobile phone number. We have made discreet enquiries. The phone is registered to a Lawrence Churchill-Butler with an address in Leeds?"

The Office Manager Barry Bishop replied:

"That's the long-lost younger brother of David Evans. He allegedly gravitated away from the villainous Evans family, changed his surname, and with a somewhat spurious CV, reinvented himself as a successful property developer in Leeds. When brother Terry Evans was interviewed, he mentioned the only contact the family had with Lawrence was a very occasional phone chat with David."

DCI Durham commented:

"We need to visit and arrest Mr Lawrence Churchill-Butler asap and ask him to explain himself. His mobile phone number was found on the man who killed a journalist investigating the criminal activities of brother David Evans! Yes, that's an important link. Mr Churchill-Butler has a lot to explain."

Lawson, with a sense of humour in his voice, continued:

"I'm enjoying this. The good news keeps on coming. May I refer to the arrest of the mysterious Amelia along with her lunchtime date in Windsor on suspicion of the murder of Peter Dice? With the seizure of the loaded handgun and the £100,000 in cash from the man, we were already on a 'good starter', although, initially, both refused to speak. Although the man was using the American Express card in the name Walter E Goldman, that wasn't his real name. However, we have identified that he possessed an Italian passport in that name and has used it to travel widely on supposed business trips."

Lawson continued to explain that from an MI5 sensitive and reliable source, his service had obtained his true identity. He had been born Emiliano Gallo in Naples. He had strong Mafia connections and was said to be a contract killer for hire. On several occasions in recent years, he had appeared before Italian courts charged with murder, but, in all cases, the trials had either collapsed or he had been found Not Guilty. Mafia involvement was suspected.

DI Penfold asked:

"What is a sensitive and reliable source?"

Lawson laughed:

"It's what it says on the tin. 'Reliable' - because we have used the source before, and the information has always been accurate. 'Sensitive' - never in a million years would we disclose how or where the information came from."

Lawson continued:

"Regarding the arrest of our blonde-haired Ms Amelia. The man had shouted across to her to remain silent. For her first police interview, she did just that. When arrested, she had in her possession her Italian passport. We have confirmed she was an Italian national, born in Naples and called Francesca Benedetti. Her family has known connections with the Mafia. In recent years, she has been a frequent visitor to the UK, apparently on business.

When she met the man in the restaurant, she was observed passing him a package, which he immediately placed into his shoulder bag. That package contained £100,000 in cash, all wrapped in bundles of new and unused £50 and £20 notes.

Now the interesting and evidentially important revelations. The wrappers have been subjected to forensic analysis. On nine wrappers, the fingerprints were those of your David Evans. Without doubt, Mr David Evans had handled the money. The prints of Ms Francesca Benedetti were on most of the bundle wraps. Obviously, she had been responsible for packaging them up and handing the package to the man who we say murdered Peter Dice."

Lawson appeared to have concluded his presentation. After a pause, and with a mischievous smile, he continued:

"Did I mention the interesting hook about Francesca Benedetti? In her second police interview, she began to appreciate the deep hole she was in, so decided to cooperate. She admitted being Amelia and that she had set up Peter Dice, but denied knowing he was to be murdered. She thought Peter was only going to be threatened and just given a 'light beating.' The interviewing officers commented that her version wasn't logical. She had paid out £100,000 in cash. A very expensive payment for a light beating? Eventually, she made a full confession. Why? Benedetti explained that she had been the mistress of David Evans."

DI Penfold responded:

"The mistress of David Evans! What a turn up. Her confession will certainly ensure we have sufficient evidence to lock David Evans away for many years."

Barry Bishop, tapped into the screen of the HOLMES2 system and responded:

"When Terry Evans was interviewed following his arrest, one of many things he disclosed was that David had an attractive young Italian girlfriend who lived in a luxury house owned by him. Terry didn't know her name but knew the address. A member of our team had visited the address on two occasions but did not receive a reply."

Lawson explained that Benedetti had endeavoured to convey to the police that she wasn't aware Dice was to be killed and she had only played a peripheral role. Subsequent checks strongly indicated she was probably the joint principal in the plot to have Peter Dice murdered. Like David Evans, she feared media revelations could do immense harm to their foreign business empire and, thus, their luxury lifestyle.

When the police searched her home, her laptop computer was seized and subjected to detailed examination. It was established that several weeks before she had met Peter Dice, she had already researched him on the Internet, which included his presence on Facebook, to see the clubs and pubs he frequented.

Her fingerprints were the only impressions found on the computer keys. Three weeks prior to the death of Dice, various Internet searches had been undertaken on the computer, which had included:

'How high from a building does a man have to fall to kill him?'

'How often do men commit suicide by jumping from buildings?'

During the same day, Benedetti had also researched hotels with 'high-rise' rooms. Extensive police research of the ANPR system subsequently identified her red mini travelling south on the M23 motorway. She had entered the city of Brighton to undertake hostile reconnaissance on the hotel. Her car was recorded as having parked on the other side of the road opposite the Gladstone Hotel. A woman, almost certainly Benedetti, was captured on the street CCTV video getting out of the car. She spent several minutes looking up at the hotel and surveying the area. Within days of that visit, the booking for Peter Dice was made via the Internet.

Lawson said that Francesca Benedetti had an interesting background, and there were parallels with the background of David Evans. She had been born in the poor suburb of Scampia, a dangerous neighbourhood in the far north of Naples, noted for its 1960s' brutalist tower blocks, and the area controlled by drug trading gangs. It had been rumoured her grandmother was the result of a one-night union with an unknown British soldier following the liberation of Naples at the end of the Second World War.

Through necessity, Benedetti's family had connections with the local Mafia. From childhood, she had been determined to rise in society. She was ambitious, intelligent and attractive, which she used to her advantage.

By her early twenties, she had reinvented herself as an elegant young lady working in the apparently glamorous world of high-end luxury Italian property development, much of which had been financed from the illegal drug trade. That was how she first became involved with David Evans.

From the outset, she had known how Evans made his money. As long as his money ensured she could lead a life of luxury in the UK, with the occasional 'business' trip abroad to help David expand his empire, she was happy to oblige. Just like David Evans, behind her elegant exterior, she was prepared to do whatever was required to continue her life of luxury, and that included arranging and paying for people who posed a threat to be 'eliminated.'

Detective constables David Hooper and Michael Sharp had been the officers who had successfully traced, interviewed and arrested Terry Evans, the brother of David Evans. DCI Durham considered them the ideal team to visit Leeds to interview the absentee brother, Lawrence Churchill-Butler. He would not receive prior notice of the officers' visit.

The two detectives travelled by car to Leeds, located in the heart of West Yorkshire. They arrived mid-afternoon at a large plush office complex in the upmarket business area of the city and entered the building by the open-plan reception foyer. Printed in large gold and black lettering on the glass backdrop to the reception desk was the name 'Churchill-Butler Property Management Company Ltd'.

DC Hooper deliberately did not mention he was a police officer. He smiled at the receptionist and politely asked:

"Good afternoon. We don't have an appointment, but as a matter of urgency, we need to have a private word with Mr Lawrence Churchill-Butler. My name is David Hooper."

The receptionist picked up the phone and delivered the message. The detectives noticed, through the glass partition, a man in the large open-plan office stand up and look towards them. He held a telephone receiver in his hand and his facial expression indicated that he was annoyed. The receptionist turned to the two visitors and explained:

"I am sorry. Mr Churchill-Butler has a very busy schedule and is unable to see you. Please leave your business card and we will be in touch."

By this time, the man behind the glass partition had sat back down. DC Hooper said:

"I'm sorry to cause you conflict with your boss; he looks annoyed, but it is urgent we speak privately with him. Please tell him we're here to discuss David Evans."

On this occasion, the receptionist opened the glass door and walked into the office to deliver the message. The door remained open. Delivery of the request was met with unpleasant shouting.

The upset-looking receptionist returned to address DC Hooper. He gently indicated with the open palm of his right hand that he understood the reply. The man was again standing and looking through the glass partition. DC Hooper looked back at him, nodded and smiled. With his thick beard and physique, the man likely thought the two visitors had been sent on behalf of his brother David.

DC Hooper said softly to the receptionist:

"Sorry, I have tried to be discreet. I'm assuming that angry man is Mr Churchill-Butler?"

She nodded. DC Hooper leaned on the desk and faced the man through the glass partition. From his top jacket pocket, the DC took out his police warrant card and held it up. In a loud deep voice, he bellowed:

"Mr Lawrence Churchill-Butler, we are police detectives investigating serious criminal allegations against your brother, David Evans, who you will be aware is currently on remand in prison. We need to speak with you now. Not tomorrow. Not next week, but now."

DC Hooper turned to the upset receptionist and, with reassurance, whispered:

"My advice? Never let a bastard like that treat you like a piece of garbage. There are plenty of good bosses out there."

Still looking towards Churchill-Butler, DC Hooper gesticulated for them to meet. The harsh tactics had worked. The two officers were directed to a small conference room. Coffee and biscuits were delivered and, within two minutes, a contrite Lawrence Churchill-Butler arrived, shook hands and had transformed into an extremely polite professional businessman.

The two officers gained the distinct impression that Churchill-Butler had been relieved to find they were police officers. Had he thought they were gang members seeking payment or, perhaps, to offer him violence? He confirmed he had been aware that both his brothers, David and Terry, had been arrested and were currently in custody. He was reluctant to say who had told him.

The detectives had deliberately decided not to disclose the fact that his telephone number had appeared on a written note found on one of two men arrested for the murder of the journalist Max Bowman.

Churchill-Butler was asked a series of questions about family background, from his youth to the present time. The questions were asked in a friendly, non-threatening manner. He was happy to emphasise he'd had very little contact with the brothers since he left home many years ago.

The officers did not challenge his answers. Slowly, and gently, they outlined the in-depth scale of the investigation and the vast amount of incriminating evidence the police had gathered on his brother David Evans.

The experienced detectives quietly noted, with an element of professional satisfaction, that Churchill-Butler was beginning to appreciate the seriousness of the situation. Since the police investigation had turned up so much evidence on his brother's criminal activities, what had they found out about him? Did they know his involvement?

Before the meeting was brought to an end, fresh coffee was served, and the two officers casually asked him about his business empire. The meeting ended.

Churchill-Butler was thanked for the time he had taken out of his busy business schedule. Their hands were shaken, and the two detectives went on their way.

Churchill-Butler sat back in his office chair, initially feeling confident and satisfied with the way the meeting had gone. However, the longer he sat quietly recalling what the detectives had said, and the answers he had given, the more uncomfortable he became. On reflection, the meeting had been a skilful gentle interrogation. He was worried.

The day and timing of the interview with Church-ill-Butler had been carefully planned to coincide with when his luxury detached home would be unoccupied. Whilst he met with the two detectives at his office complex, two members of the 'technical team' had gained entry to the house and installed miniature covert recording equipment. The appropriate signed authorities for the installation had been obtained.

The two detectives had done their job well. They had anticipated that within the next few days, Churchill-Butler would express his frustrations and concerns about the meeting to associates and, in doing so, divulge his own criminal involvement.

Later the same evening, Churchill-Butler arrived home. There was no one else in the house. Within ten minutes of him arriving home, a male visitor arrived and together, they decamped to the study. The door was firmly closed behind them. From the tone and content of their conversation, it became apparent they were close friends and shared confidences. Churchill-Butler referred to the man as 'Tom', and he, in turn, called him 'Larry'. Larry offered Tom a glass of whisky, followed by the clinking of glasses.

The man was subsequently identified as Thomas Bluewater, a practising solicitor with offices in Leeds. He had known Churchill-Butler for many years. They had originally met through their membership of the local Masonic lodge, which had developed into a personal friendship.

Bluewater also acted, in his professional capacity, as legal advisor to Churchill-Butler's group of companies.

Over the years, as their friendship and trust in each other had developed, the rich businessman Lawrence Churchill-Butler lavished gifts and treats on his friend and legal advisor Thomas Bluewater. The transformation from legitimate gifts to corrupt payments for illegal business deals was slow and deliberate. By an element of naivety and greed, the respectable solicitor had become hooked.

Tom asked Churchill-Butler:

"Larry, I was intrigued by your telephone call. You said it was urgent and it couldn't be discussed on the telephone. I hope it isn't anything too serious. Are you seeking my advice as your legal advisor or as a confidential friend?"

Churchill-Butler sounded nervous and explained:

"This is a difficult one and it could have serious implications. This afternoon, I had an unexpected visit to my company office by two police detectives. They said they were part of the team investigating my brother David and wanted family background information on him. I feigned innocence and said I'd rarely had any contact with him during our adult life."

Tom interrupted and asked:

"Did they make any suggestion that they doubted your assertion?"

Churchill-Butler replied:

"No, not once did they indicate that they doubted any of my replies. When we finished the meeting, I felt reassured the visit had been merely a 'fishing trip' to glean any additional information about David. I felt pretty pleased with my replies. Now I have doubts. The detective with the beard casually explained to me the shooting and killing of the journalist from Winchester, which I acknowledged I'd read about in the newspapers. He said David's gang had been involved in that. On reflection, the detective seemed to concentrate on the two guys they'd arrested for the shooting and the Mercedes they were driving, which had been on cloned plates."

Tom queried:

"Did they suggest you were in any way involved in that?"

Churchill-Butler answered:

"No, but in retrospect, that's my concern. The bearded detective was sitting back in his chair casually telling me what had happened. He never once asked me to comment. But, as he explained the situation, his eyes were fixed on me. I felt he was reading my mind. He wasn't asking me questions because, I felt, he already knew the answers and my involvement."

Tom rested his whisky glass on the arm of his chair and commented:

"So, you think he was playing mind games to unhinge you. That could be dangerous. Larry, if the police start digging into your recent involvement with David, it could prove explosive. Let's first deal with the issue of the Mercedes. Why and how did you get involved?"

Churchill-Butler responded:

"You are fully aware of my involvement to help David. He is on my client portfolio under the false name Frederick James Birch, with ownership of several properties in Europe, all in place as a complex web to launder his vast undeclared income, and which had involved paying corrupt politicians and bankers. Yes, figuratively speaking, my fingerprints were all over the transactions, so I was obliged to help sort the problem. That bloody investigative journalist from Winchester, together with the other one, was getting too close to the truth. David ordered their elimination. The two foreign guys imported for the Winchester shooting didn't speak much English, so I got involved in arranging their vehicles. Much against my better judgement."

Tom shook his head and simply asked:

"Why? For Christ's sake, why?"

Churchill-Butler hesitated, then continued:

"My head was all over the place. David was putting pressure on me. Francesca was also putting pressure on me."

Tom interrupted and asked:

"Francesca... David's Italian lover? I'm aware of Francesca's role in the European project, but what was her current involvement in this mess?"

Churchill-Butler replied:

"She is up to her neck in this mess. Francesca might be a glamorous seductress, but she is also an ice queen capable of cold-blooded murder who comes from a Mafia family. She planned and personally undertook the arrangements to lure the other journalist to Brighton and have him killed. It was meant to look like suicide, by jumping from the top of a hotel, but the police quickly established it was murder. Francesca has been arrested along with the hired killer, who she knew previously from her Mafia connections."

Tom continued to shake his head in disbelief and responded:

"Why was it necessary to enter into this mission?"

Churchill-Butler continued:

"Both were saying if drastic action wasn't taken soon, our property empire in Europe would be ruined and we would all be exposed and locked up. The stolen Mercedes was locked away in Manchester, waiting to be used by the two foreign guys, but there was no one able to make it legitimate. So, I did an Internet search for an identical car, which was located several hundreds of miles from Manchester. According to the law, a new set of car number plates can only be legitimately made up after the garage has seen the car's registration documents. Since we didn't have documentation for the stolen car, I had to persuade, with a backhander of £500 cash, a friendly backstreet garage owner to have the cloned number plates made up. I have a horrible feeling that the bearded detective already knows what I've done."

Tom remained silent for a minute and then responded:

"So, firstly, you were aware that a Mercedes had been stolen. Then you undertook an Internet search to facilitate having an illegal set of cloned number plates made up. Yes, there is a good chance that the police will follow that trail to the end. And where will that lead? Straight to the murder of the Winchester journalist, which is linked to the murder of the second journalist in Brighton, *and* their investigation into the criminal activities of your brother David and the exposé of his property empire in Europe and beyond. Larry, I must warn you that your activities, if identified by the police, have the potential to suck you into criminal charges including an accomplice to murder."

Churchill-Butler nervously asked:

"Accomplice to murder! Bloody hell. What advice can you give me if the police come for me?"

Tom replied:

"Remain polite and act as though you are mystified by their interest in you. If they arrest you, just say you are completely innocent of any wrongdoing. You will be entitled to have a solicitor present when they formally interview you. Ask for me to attend as your legal representative. Then make no further comment. On my arrival, I will request the interviewing officers to outline the case against you. Then, I will likely advise you to make 'no further comment' until you have had an opportunity to speak privately with me."

Churchill-Butler, with increasing panic in his voice, asked:

"Tom, should I leave the country and fly to somewhere that doesn't have an extradition treaty? At short notice, I should be able to shift a few hundred thousand pounds to a safe country."

Tom, also sounding concerned, replied:

"To suddenly flee the country would immediately indicate your guilt to the police. Before they begin digging into your affairs, make sure any and all incriminating evidence is destroyed or hidden. Do you have any incriminating paperwork, contact details, mobile telephones or computers with information that would link you with David's criminal activities?"

Churchill-Butler responded:

"The paperwork is all tied up in the company portfolio we have for David under his false name. It's worth many millions and pulled together in a series of complex and multilayered transactions involving many companies and several different countries. I use a separate iPad to deal with David's transactions and a separate iPhone when I need to speak with him. Both I keep in my locked safe at home."

Tom gave his advice:

"Larry, destroy as much of the incriminating evidence as you can. What you can't destroy, make sure it is secure and hidden well away from your home or office. I suggest with your iPad, if you need to retain the information, download it onto a stick. Then either have the iPad professionally wiped or, even better, destroyed. Likewise, 'lose' the iPhone. Destroy it and deny it ever existed."

Churchill-Butler, sounding even more nervous, replied:

"Tom, if it comes to me being arrested, I don't think I can hold my nerve. What a bloody mess. David was always my big powerful brother. He knew I dabbled in the odd stolen car and used that against me to persuade me, against my better judgement, to set up companies to launder money from his drug dealing operations. Then suddenly, he drops the bombshell - he's ordered the killing of that journalist and forces me to help in sorting their transport. Tom, do I have any defence?"

Tom responded with his glum opinion:

"No. No defence whatsoever. You are an intelligent professional savvy businessman. Firstly, you have no defence to your active participation in setting up false companies for the prime purpose of money laundering the profits from illegal cocaine smuggling. Secondly, on your own admission, you knew two hitmen had entered the UK illegally to murder a troublesome journalist, and you helped facilitate their transport. Larry, you have just got to pray the police don't find out about your involvement with David and, at all cost, you hold your nerve."

During the following days, Churchill-Butler's concern and paranoia increased. He made futile attempts to liquidate a number of property assets and transfer money to overseas bank accounts. His telephone and Internet transactions were monitored by the police, and he was also put under covert surveillance, with photographs taken of people with whom he came into contact.

Within the week, he would be arrested, charged with serious criminal offences including being implicated in the murder of the investigative journalist Max Bowman, and remanded in custody pending a Crown Court trial. His financial affairs, both in the UK and abroad, would be the subject of intensive investigation by the Economic Crime Unit.

At the same time that detectives were involved in the arrest of Lawrence Churchill-Butler at his company office in Leeds, two other detectives had visited the plush office of Thomas Bluewater.

The two officers were DCs Dave Hooper and Michael Sharp, the same two officers who had undertaken the initial visit to Churchill-Butler. From the outset, the atmosphere in the office between Bluewater and the detectives was cool, to the point of being unwelcoming.

When the two detectives first arrived at the office reception desk, they gave their details to the receptionist and asked to meet with Thomas Bluewater. The officers remained seated in the reception area for twenty minutes.

They were then escorted into the office of Thomas Bluewater. The solicitor remained seated behind a large impressive wooden Victorian desk. In front of him, on the desk, sat a four-inch-high polished wooden and brass name plate: 'Thomas E Bluewater – Solicitor at Law.' The officers were left in no doubt that this was the man they wished to see. They took their seats behind the desk directly facing Bluewater. He was dressed smartly in a dark grey three-piece suit. An arrogant individual, he did not welcome the visit and remained silent.

The receptionist, standing next to his desk, politely enquired whether Mr Bluewater wished tea or coffee to be served. Bluewater, in a brisk voice, replied:

"No. These two didn't have the courtesy to make an appointment. I'm very busy. This meeting will not take long."

He stretched out his open right hand and asked the officers for their warrant cards. He took both, which he placed on the desk in front of him. He carefully examined both, then, on a notepad, made a written record of the details. He handed the warrant cards back to the officers. No pleasantries were exchanged.

During their conversation, he repeatedly addressed each officer as 'constable.' His arrogant and conde-scending attitude towards the officers was clear. He was conveying that he considered his position superior to theirs. The experienced officers were not about to give ground or be intimidated by his attitude.

Bluewater continued to address the officers in his brash style. He demanded to know the reason for the visit. DC Sharp explained that Operation Goldfinger had been established to investigate the alleged serious criminal activities of David Evans and his associates. Was the solicitor aware of David Evans?

Bluewater gave them a disdainful look with a single-word reply:

"No."

DC Sharp continued:

"Do you know Larry Churchill-Butler?"

Bluewater snapped back:

"Correction, constable. Do you mean Lawrence, Mr Lawrence Churchill-Butler?"

DC Sharp nodded and continued:

"Yes. Do you know him?"

Bluewater continued with his short snappy responses:

"If you've done your homework, you would know I'm the company solicitor for Churchill-Butler Property Management Company Limited and have been for many years."

DC Sharp added:

"And personal friends, who often socialise together?"

DC Hooper smiled and quietly said:

"Both members of the local Masonic Lodge, so I'm given to understand."

Bluewater looked even more annoyed but did not respond to the comment. He expressed his frustration with the officers and demanded to know details of the alleged crimes they were investigating.

DC Sharp continued with his line of questioning:

"You have said you do not know a David Evans, but you have confirmed you do know Lawrence Churchill-Butler. Were you aware that David Evans is the older brother of Larry Evans, who you know as Lawrence Churchill-Butler?"

Bluewater responded:

"No, I wasn't. I don't ask people to give me details of their family background. As far as I am concerned, I undertake work for Mr Lawrence Churchill-Butler and his company. Full stop."

DC Sharp looked directly at Bluewater and asked:

"You acknowledge you have undertaken work for the company for many years. So, may I assume you are fully conversant with the affairs and financial dealings undertaken by the company?"

Bluewater continued in his combative manner and responded:

"Constable, you are evidently confused and don't know the difference between an accountant and a solicitor. As their solicitor, I give advice on legal matters. I do not audit the company accounts."

DC Hooper raised his voice and replied:

"Sir, my colleague is an experienced detective with several years as a member of the Fraud Squad. We both understand your role. We are not confused."

Bluewater snapped back:

"Constables, I demand to know the specifics of the allegations you are investigating and how they might have any relevance to my client, Mr Lawrence Churchill-Butler. I intend to terminate this meeting. Get your senior officer to send me a letter with details of the matters being investigated, together with a list of the questions you wish me to address."

DC Sharp smiled and politely responded:

"Mr Bluewater, we haven't quite finished."

Bluewater interrupted and shouted:

"Well, I have. What is the name of your Chief Constable? I intend to make a complaint!""

DC Hooper turned to face DC Sharp and made a mischievous comment:

"Constable, I don't believe our Chief Constable is a Mason."

Appreciating the increasing tension in the office, DC Sharp quickly interjected:

"I must ask, have you had any contact or discussion with Mr Churchill-Butler about his involvement with David Evans? And second, have you discussed with Mr Churchill-Butler the recent meeting we had with him?"

"No." Was his single word response.

DC Sharp repeated:

"I'll ask you again. Have you discussed our investigation with Mr Churchill-Butler? I would ask you to think about what I have said. Please answer very carefully."

Using several expletives, Bluewater said he wasn't prepared to answer any further questions. He stood up, pointed to the door and demanded that the two officers leave. Both remained seated and were not disturbed by the man's behaviour. It indicated to them that he had much to worry about.

DC Hooper opened the folder he had resting on his knee and read:

"Official police log. Verbatim covert recording of conversation between Larry (Lawrence Churchill-Butler) and Tom (Thomas Bluewater, solicitor). Commenced at 19:10 hours and concluded at 19:43 hours."

The officer looked up at Bluewater and continued:

"I will just refer to highlights from the detailed transcript. There are thirty-three minutes of recording. The recording begins with Larry stating: 'This afternoon, I had an unexpected visit by two police detectives, who were part of the team investigating my brother David.' Larry is then recorded as saying: 'I said I rarely had contact with him.'"

Bluewater remained standing and silent. He was clearly taken aback by the revelation that his conversation with Churchill-Butler had been recorded. He was desperate to try and remember exactly what damaging evidence had been revealed.

DC Hooper continued:

"Larry refers to the bearded detective, which was me, telling him about the shooting of the journalist from Winchester. Larry says he was concerned, and I quote: 'He wasn't asking me questions, because I felt he already knew the answers.' You are recorded as saying, and I quote: 'Larry, if they start digging into your involvement with David, that could prove explosive.'

Bluewater remained static with sweat on his brow. DC Hooper continued:

"And later in the recorded conversation, you both talk about David and Francesca putting pressure on him. In the recording, there was acknowledgement that you both knew about the Winchester and Brighton hotel murders. You warn Larry he could face charges including accomplice to murder. Your advice? And I quote: 'Destroy as much of the incriminating evidence as you can.'"

DC Hooper looked directly at Bluewater and continued:

"You advised Larry to wipe all data from his iPad and destroy his iPhone. You are also recorded as telling him he: 'Had no defence' for his actions, and offer him, which I will quote: 'Larry, you have just got to pray the police don't find out about your involvement with David and hold your nerve.' You further advise him that if he was subjected to formal police interview, he should go: 'No Comment.'"

DC Hooper closed his folder and gesticulated, by raising his right hand, for Bluewater not to comment.

Bluewater slowly stepped back and sat down in his chair. Sweat now streamed down his cheeks and onto the collar of his white shirt. The arrogance had disappeared. His shoulders were hunched together, and he physically appeared to have shrunk.

DC Hooper continued:

"Mr Thomas Bluewater, I am now arresting you as an accomplice, with Lawrence Churchill-Butler and others, in the commission of serious criminal offences. You will be handcuffed and escorted back to our local custody suite where you will be formally interviewed. As a solicitor, I appreciate you will be aware of the rights of a person arrested. Nevertheless, I will formally caution you and inform you of your rights."

Bluewater stood up as if readying himself for the handcuffs. He looked at both detectives, appeared contrite and commented:

"Gentlemen, I believe I have much to tell you. I'm proud of my profession and have been an honest and good solicitor. However, as far as Larry was concerned, I allowed myself to be slowly drawn into corruption. It didn't start that way. Once trapped, I couldn't get out of it. My career is at an end. I'm ruined."

Bluewater stepped forward and offered to shake hands with the officers. He gave a light-hearted laugh and added:

"I've spent my professional life telling my clients, when interviewed by police, to say 'no comment'. That is not for me. I think it's best for me to express my sincere remorse and cooperate. Let's get it over with."

Chapter Thirteen

The End Game

Operation Goldfinger had been established, with a dedicated team of experienced detectives, to investigate the complex criminal activities of David John Evans and his associates. In recent years, the man, born into poverty and a family of petty criminals, had progressed through violence, extortion, and fear to create his own lucrative crime empire. He had become a major importer into the UK of the Class A drug cocaine.

He was arrogant and ruthless in all aspects of his criminal activities. He enjoyed the power he wielded and, increasingly, had been associated with the murder of his rivals and those who crossed him. Fear was his ultimate weapon. No one had been prepared to cooperate with the police.

David Evans had always been extremely cautious when undertaking his criminal activities. His use of telephone and internet communications was almost non-existent. Likewise, known documentation on his activities was negligible. In the UK, he did not hold any bank accounts in his name and all property was held in the name of his wife Fiona.

He had been referred to as the elusive Boss, who ran his criminal affairs from a safe distance and with a 'firewall' deliberately constructed between him and the people who carried out his orders. Evans was said to have been an admirer of the Italian Mafia-style running of an organisation and modelled himself on his perception of a Mafia Boss.

He had been known to refer to the small group of principal characters he relied on as 'The Committee.' There were believed to be five, perhaps more, individuals. Each had the contacts and ability to call on groups of criminals who would undertake the required task. He was known for his preference of 'importing' criminals for specific tasks. For example, 'hitmen' entered the UK illegally, undertook the killing and were out of the country later the same day.

He would only meet with 'Committee' members on an individual basis, infrequently and by prearrangement. The chosen locations would always be at a crowded public event, such as a football match or at a horse racetrack, so that it would be virtually impossible for a successful police surveillance operation.

MI5 had undertaken separate sensitive research in an attempt to identify members of 'The Committee.' The research was ongoing. However, the available intelligence was given in confidence, with certain caveats imposed, to the Operation Goldfinger SIO, DCI Graham Durham.

The five members of The Committee:

- Lawrence Churchill-Butler, his younger brother who lived in Leeds. It had been established that Lawrence was actually an important and major player in the organisation. For many years, his role as a major player in David Evans' criminal organisation had gone under the radar.

- Francesca Benedetti, David Evans' Italian mistress. She had been born in Naples and had grown up with active family association with the Mafia. A ruthless and determined lady, she would call on her contacts to undertake killings or whatever crime was required.

There were then three individuals whose full identity Evans did not know. This was often the case when dealing with Mafia-style criminal organisations. Both parties would gain additional security from their anonymity.

- A Polish national, only known as Jakub, who had residency in the UK, believed to be in Liverpool, and elsewhere in the country. He was known to be a major importer and distributor of drugs. He was said to own several villas and other dubious establishments on the Costa del Sol, on Spain's southern coast. The area was home to British expatriates and fugitives and, hence in the British media, had been given the name 'Costa del Crime.'

- Known only as Igor or The Warrior. Nationality not known. Believed to have been a former agent in the KGB and a veteran of the Afghan War. He would occasionally visit the UK using a passport with a different identity. Such passports were readily available from corrupt officials in exchange for cash. He was Evans' preferred choice if an assassination was required to be undertaken in the UK.

- An Italian known only as Salvatore. Believed to be a member of the Italian Mafia known as 'Ndrangheta and regarded as the wealthiest and most powerful crime syndicate in Italy. It was reputed to have over 6,000 members. The organisation also has a significant presence in America and other South American countries. 'Ndrangheta is said to control 80% of cocaine that flows through Europe and, in addition to drug trading, specialises in political corruption.

For their services, Evans paid handsomely in cash and, if requested, in cocaine.

Throughout his life, he challenged all types of authority. During the initial stages of Operation Goldfinger, he had shown total contempt for the police. When he realised he was under surveillance, he brazenly approached the officers and mocked them.

As the investigation progressed, a significant evidential file against Evans was developed, including important evidence ascertained from his brother Terry and his wife Fiona. The police investigation became ever more complex, uncovering more cases of serious crime and increasing the number of suspects.

With the frequency of arrests increasing, people had become more willing to cooperate, either to reduce their own culpability or because the fear factor had diminished. They began to disclose incriminating and vital evidence against David Evans.

A senior barrister with the Crown Prosecution Service had been appointed to work with the police to develop a strategy to prepare for the multitude of forthcoming prosecutions.

The CPS would work with the different police forces and law enforcement agencies to prepare for separate trials, which would be linked by evidence and the principal defendant.

Without doubt, David Evans would be linked with all the trials. The CPS would subsequently ask for an order to be made, under The Contempt of Court Act 1981, to prohibit the publication of reporting from each trial until all the trials had been completed. This would be made on the basis that such reporting would create a substantial risk that the course of justice would be impeded and seriously prejudice the jury in the later trials.

The police and CPS acknowledged that the separate trials would be complex and involve long Crown Court hearings. It was anticipated that most defendants would plead Not Guilty, requiring a full trial with a jury. The estimate was that each Crown Court trial would extend to between two to four months. In addition, extra precautions would be in place to negate intimidation of witnesses and jury members. The protection of witnesses and jury members would involve a major police commitment.

The Economic Crime Unit would assist with the investigation into the criminal financial dealings attributed, or potentially linked, to David Evans. A review would identify the scope and depth of the necessary investigation. The investigation into the illegal financial affairs would be complex and would take an extended period.

The initial cases for Crown Court trials would concentrate on straightforward serious crimes. The first would centre around David Evans, beginning with his attempt to leave the UK using a false passport and his escape from lawful custody, coupled with his involvement in procuring the hijack of the prison van by armed accomplices.

A second trial would deal with his involvement in the illegal importation of the Class A drug cocaine, valued at one hundred million pounds. The accomplices arrested by police when they raided the lorry transporting the cocaine had already been charged and remanded in custody to await trial. The evidence of the MI5 undercover officer, Julian Lawson, in the guise of Guy Hamilton, would form part of the prosecution cases.

David Evans would also face a further separate trial before the Crown Court in relation to the tragic case of the late DCI Donald Ferguson. When Evans had identified Ferguson as the SIO for Operation Goldfinger, he devised a plan to have the officer and, by association, his team, humiliated.

On the instigation of Evans, with the assistance of an unscrupulous solicitor who was on his payroll, Mary Jean Butterfield, a vulnerable individual and drug addict, was persuaded to make a false allegation of rape against Ferguson. The loyal and dedicated officer was suspended from duty and effectively excluded from having contact with his police colleagues. In a deep state of depression, although knowing he was totally innocent of the allegation, he had travelled to his birthplace in Scotland and committed suicide.

The murder of the investigative journalist Max Bowman would form the basis for a separate trial. The defendants would include the two arrested for the shooting. Their identities had now been established by Interpol. The activities of Lawrence Churchill-Butler would be included in the indictment. The formal accusation would also include charges relating to possession and use of firearms and the theft of motor vehicles.

The murder of Peter Dice, who was attacked and pushed over the balcony at the Brighton hotel, would form the basis of another separate trial for murder. The defendants would include Francesca Benedetti, Evans' Italian lover, and the Italian 'hitman' Emiliano Gallo.

A further separate trial would also be undertaken for the two guards responsible for the kidnapping and imprisonment of the three people in the ex-nuclear bunker. The identity of the two men remained unknown. They were known to have entered the UK illegally and were likely from a former Eastern Bloc country. Enquiries continued to be undertaken by Interpol.

Five county police forces were separately investigating undetected murders, where it was strongly suspected they had been committed on the orders of David Evans. With the recent arrest and incarceration of Evans, potential witnesses within the drug fraternity were becoming more willing to cooperate. It was anticipated, soon, that charges would be proffered in respect of the murder investigations.

During the working week, Julian Lawson continued to reside in the staff quarters located within MI5 HQ in Thames House, Millbank, London. He had a lot of paperwork to complete so began his working day in his office on the second floor at 07:00 hours. He logged into his desktop computer to register that he was on duty and working from his office. There were many emails to answer, which he undertook without delay, before typing up outstanding reports. The electronic diary for his department had a meeting scheduled for 09:30 hours with Director Jane Rigby, his Boss, in her office.

Lawson arrived a few minutes before 09:30 hours and was pleased to smell, and see, fresh coffee being poured by Jane Rigby into two large mugs. She greeted him with her usual pleasant manner and asked after his welfare before they took their seats to discuss the reason for the meeting.

Lawson updated her on the ongoing Operation Goldfinger investigation, which he said was progressing well with encouraging results. MI5's direct involvement had almost been concluded, but he would remain in contact with the SIO, DCI Graham Durham, regarding any further input that might be required.

Jane Rigby addressed the subject of Lawson's future safety. He smiled and responded:

"Over the past few weeks, I've given that subject much thought. In simple language, I'm not going to let that dominate my life. I have a special passion for my Petworth cottage and woodland. For many years, it has been my happy place and I'm determined for that to continue. It also has precious memories of my late wife. So, I intend to, again, take up full residence there. Life always has its dangers, and the fact that someone tried to kill me there is just another one." He addressed his last comment with a wry smile.

Lawson explained that at the end of the working week, he would be returning to take up residence at his Petworth cottage. He confirmed that he retained the authority to legally keep his handgun at his home, and that it was securely locked away in his study wall safe.

Rigby broached the subject of Lawson's future. He was nearly at the end of his four-year secondment with MI5. She said the matter had been discussed by the senior team, who were keen for him to remain with the service. Had he given any thought about his future career?

Rigby explained that should Lawson wish to remain with MI5, he would be offered a permanent position within the service and, on appointment, receive a promotion. This would necessitate him resigning from the police service. He had originally been posted to MI5 on a two-year secondment, which had then been extended for a further two years. Lawson said he was grateful to the service for the faith they had placed in him. Before deciding, he would appreciate having some time to consider his future.

Randolph Beaumont joined the meeting with Rigby and Lawson. Following the shooting of the unknown assailant at Lawson's cottage, Beaumont had been tasked by MI5 with reviewing the circumstances and liaising with the other agencies who would be involved, including the police, CPS and the Coroner.

At an earlier meeting, Lawson had quietly considered Beaumont as an extremely intelligent and eccentric character. In his update, Beaumont mentioned that
a date for the coroner's inquest had yet to be confirmed.
However, the Coroner had stipulated that Lawson would
be required to attend court to give evidence, with the
assurance that special procedures would be implemented
to protect his identity.

Beaumont continued with his update. Further genealogical DNA analysis had confirmed that the dead
gunman had been raised in the former Soviet Union
republic of Kazakhstan. Extensive enquiries had been,
and continued to be, undertaken by Interpol and in
liaison with other official security services within Europe.
The assailant had now been identified and was strongly
suspected of having undertaken successful assassinations in Europe on behalf of international crime gangs.
The weapon he had used was a military GSh-18 9mm
semi-automatic pistol previously issued to Russian
special forces for close-combat fighting. The evidence
suggested that he had, at one time, been a member of
such a unit.

Lawson asked:

"With me having shot and killed the assailant, what are the chances they will send a further person to avenge his death?"

Beaumont didn't feel this would be the case. He responded:

"He was a hired killer, tasked with undertaking a specific job. He failed. The loss of his life won't be mourned. His fee will just not be paid out. So, the chance of seeking you out for a revenge attack is minimal. We still haven't identified who originally ordered your assassination. Will they order a second attempt? That's possible, but in their world of violent international crime gangs, there's so much in-fighting, they will have moved on and you will have dropped off their radar. No promises, but, from my experience, that's how they operate."

Beaumont said his team had confirmed that the magnetic GPS tracking device which had been recovered from the pocket of the deceased man had been fixed to the underside of Lawson's Land Rover Defender truck. They had not yet established when it had been fitted. Many enquiries still require to be completed.

As the meeting concluded, and Randolph Beaumont left the office, Rigby requested Lawson to remain behind.

She poured two mugs of fresh coffee, handing one to Lawson and said:

"So much has happened in the past couple of months and we have all been busy. Have you had an opportunity to contact Sally? I know Sally was very concerned when she was told about you being shot. She came to see me shortly after it happened. I reassured her that you hadn't been badly injured but, in the circumstances, and with your involvement with Operation Goldfinger, it wasn't a practical proposition at that time for her to contact you."

Who was Sally? Sally Chambers was a fellow MI5 officer. Their first meeting had been rather pleasant. Their second meeting had been explosive. However, attitudes had slowly thawed over the years to the point of a close friendship.

Four years ago, when Lawson was on the MI5 induction course, and at home for the weekend, he had helped an attractive young lady whose car had broken down. He had then taken her to a nearby pub for lunch. He was smitten by her but gave away very little about himself. Only later, he was told it had been an MI5 'sting' to test new recruits to see whether they would disclose details about themselves. He had passed with flying colours.

However, when they next met, he was angry, and they didn't part on good terms.

During the next few years, in the course of their work, Lawson and Chambers would occasionally meet. They were respectful meetings between work colleagues. Shortly before the recent shooting incident, they had unexpectedly found themselves paired together on a case. It involved dealing with terrorist activity on the Cunard liner Queen Mary on the Atlantic crossing from America to the UK. The operation had been a success, and they found they had much in common. Personal relationships between MI5 officers, for reasons of security, must be notified and approved by senior management. That was the point the couple had reached just before the day of the shooting.

In response to Rigby's question, he confirmed that he hadn't been in contact with Sally but now, with the end of his direct involvement with Operation Goldfinger, he was keen to do so.

At lunchtime, Lawson decided he would benefit from some afternoon sunshine. He took a short walk along Millbank towards the Houses of Parliament into Victoria Tower Gardens, which overlooks the River Thames. He sat on a wooden bench, loosened his tie, and stretched out his legs in a relaxed posture.

He desired to have his lunch break alone to contemplate his future career. Jane Rigby's offer to appoint him a permanent member of MI5, with the prospect of further promotion, was worthy of serious consideration. Lawson had always enjoyed working in a busy and challenging environment and MI5 had certainly supplied him with that, as had his career as a police officer.

What were the minus points? As an MI5 officer, he effectively always worked undercover. He operated with a cover name and a false identity, as did all the people he worked with. His position with MI5 was not known to his family and friends, and his social life with his work colleagues was almost non-existent. Indeed, they were colleagues and not friends.

Lawson thought a positive reason to remain with MI5 was his future security. Was he still a target for assassination? If so, staying with the service, he would continue to operate in the 'shadows' with the service better equipped to deal with the possibility of assassination.

In the role of an operational senior police detective, he would constantly be on public view in media reports.

If he remained an assassination target, he would be easily identified and traced. On the other hand, back being a police officer, he would regain his freedom with his own identity and a social life. The police service is a close-knit family with much camaraderie and social activity. This was something he had missed during the last four years.

Then there was consideration to be had about his cottage. Should he continue to live there? Would it be responsible of him to entertain family and friends there, knowing there was the possibility that a 'hitman' might have a second attempt at assassinating him? Likewise, could he, with a clear conscience, sell the property to an unsuspecting buyer knowing there existed the possibility that an assassin might return?

At 18:30 hours on Friday, Julian Lawson departed the MI5 Headquarters, London, and drove in his car towards his home in West Sussex. On entering the small rural town of Petworth, he continued his normal routine, parking in the high street outside the late-night general store to purchase provisions for the weekend at his woodland cottage. The ever-cheerful assistant Brenda greeted him with her usual: "Good evening, Ben," before discussing his requirements.

Her greetings triggered in him the reminder that he was back home; back in the world of Ben Swan. Normally, when collecting his weekend provisions, he would purchase a bottle of single malt whisky.

"Not tonight, thank you, Brenda. I've knocked whisky off my list of requirements. I have decided to give up alcohol."

He arrived on the driveway of his cottage and parked his car. The external floodlights switched on automatically, sending a reassuring beam of light over the front gravel paved yard.

He remained in his car, tapped the security app on his mobile phone to confirm the cottage was secure, which included having an internal view from the cameras located in the ground floor rooms. All was in order. He unlocked the front door, entered and relaxed.

The Julian Lawson documents were placed in the open wall safe, and he took out his own documents. Ben Swan was home for the weekend and feeling relaxed and happy. Breaking with his old routine, he decided to cook himself a proper evening meal. He then relaxed in his favourite casual leather chair, turned on some soothing music and began to read a newly published book on the

Battle of Trafalgar. He was keen on researching history and famous historic military battles.

Ben woke early. It was a clear sunny morning. He felt that he wanted some physical exertion, perhaps to release some of the inner frustration he was feeling. By 07:00 hours, he had walked down the woodland path to his log cabin. He made himself a large mug of black coffee and stood looking around, taking in the quite tranquil and natural beauty of his woodland, and weighing up the jobs he needed to do. He decided the almost empty log store needed to be replenished. He slipped into his forester's trousers, put on his safety helmet and gloves, and pulled the starting cord on his petrol chainsaw.

The machine spluttered into life. With a gentle squeeze on the trigger, he revved up the engine and cleared the carburettor of surplus smoke, until it reached the operating speed. From long thick branches, several dozen logs were cut and laid on the ground in a rough pile. After a short rest, with another mug of black coffee, Ben put aside the chainsaw and picked up a large axe. The logs were split down the middle, and he stacked them in the covered log store which was always a pleasing sight to see. Feeling refreshed and satisfied with his work, he walked back to his cottage and cleaned his tools and boots.

Back at the cottage, he took a long relaxed hot shower and, wearing his dressing gown, walked into the kitchen to consider making himself lunch. His personal mobile phone was on the kitchen table. It vibrated and made a buzzing sound. He had been sent a text message. He picked up the mobile phone and read the message:

"Very attractive lady is seeking lunch from a grumpy man. Suggest White Hart Inn in 45 minutes. OK?"

Ben responded to the cryptic text:

"I don't know a very attractive lady! However, will be there for a Ploughman's lunch!"

The lady who'd sent the text was his friend, Sally Chambers, a fellow MI5 colleague. He now thought of her with affection. When he had joined MI5 four years ago, using his cover name Julian Lawson, Sally had been a member of the 'sting' who had tested his ability not to disclose details about himself.

The 'sting' had taken place at the White Hart Inn. Subsequently, when he was advised of the 'sting', he had been extremely angry. Their working relationship had remained very cool, until recent times when they had worked together on an operation. They had then had a return visit to the White Hart Inn to seal their relationship.

The day before he'd been shot during the assassination attempt at his cottage, they had discussed their possible future together and, with some humour, had divulged their true identities. Sally Chambers was actually Emily Braithwaite.

Ben arrived at the White Hart Inn, which was located on the outskirts of Pulborough, West Sussex, and parked his car. The rear garden of the public house overlooks the river Arun. From his car, he could see Emily sitting at a table in the garden area. On seeing him, Emily ran towards him. They met halfway, stopped and engaged in a long, silent and emotional embrace. She then quietly whispered:

"I've missed you. I've missed you so much and have been so worried."

They cuddled up together and walked back to the table Emily had reserved. They ordered a Ploughman's lunch and, with good humour, joked about their previous two visits to the pub. They had much to reflect on and to discuss about the future. From their last meeting, Emily had been aware that Ben's secondment with MI5 was almost up and that he was considering resuming his police career.

Emily appreciated, and had understood, his frustrations of living with a covert identity. She had similar concerns about her career and future. Likewise, because of restrictions, she missed the ability to socialise with long-term friends and the need for living in 'the shadows.' In a recent long-running Crown Court trial, she had explained the pressure of arriving each morning in a closed van at the rear entrance to the court. She had remained isolated until called into the witness box to give her evidence behind a large screen, with her identity being protected from the jury and the public. Then, she'd had to spend two more days being challenged by an aggressive defence lawyer. Throughout, she had been identified only by a letter - D. Emily had previously confided in Ben that she felt she: "Was always present, but somehow, never there."

Emily and Ben were to spend over two hours at the table talking and enjoying each other's company. Both had previously arranged evening commitments. Ben said he was scheduled to have a meeting with Director Jane

Rigby the following Monday morning to give his decision on his future career, which he was still weighing up, but had almost decided. Ben and Emily agreed to make contact by telephone later on Monday evening, and then arrange a dinner date.

09:30 hours Monday, MI5 Headquarters, London. Julian Lawson was scheduled to have a meeting with Director Jane Rigby in her office. He did not arrive. The appointment had been logged in his computer diary some days previously. Lawson was known for his punctuality. His office and mobile telephones went unanswered. His mobile telephone had been switched off. It was subsequently confirmed that he had not logged on for duty that morning. The MI5 building security system showed he had last left the building at 18:30 hours on the previous Friday. There was concern expressed as to his whereabouts.

At 13:45 hours the same day, along with two colleagues, Jane Rigby was standing in the study of Lawson's Petworth cottage. When they had arrived at the cottage, it had been found locked, with the alarm set. His VW Golf was parked on the driveway. The car was locked. There was no sign of Lawson. They had forced an entry and deactivated the alarm. The interior of the cottage was neat and tidy, with no sign of any disturbance or that Lawson may have left unexpectedly.

Rigby stood for several minutes looking around Lawson's well-equipped and tidy study. On the left-hand side of the leather-topped wooden desk sat a full-size dark green and gold leather-bound Bible. It contained several bookmarks, and throughout the Bible, many handwritten post notes were attached to various pages.

A closed laptop computer occupied the centre of the desk. A pewter mug containing a quantity of pens and pencils was positioned on the right of the desktop, next to a brass table lamp. A framed photograph of his late wife, Lucy, had a prominent position on the desk.

The bookcase displayed a good cross-section of books which indicated he had a keen interest in sailing and navigation. He enjoyed history and studied great leaders of the past. There were also various books on woodland management.

On two shelves were half a dozen-coloured photographs of happy gatherings with family and friends, including Lawson sailing with a group of male colleagues. There was also a small photograph of him in uniform as a young police constable. Two electric guitars stood on their stands in the corner of the study, next to an expensive-looking Marshall amplifier.

In an unlocked outbuilding, located in the rear garden, was a wooden bench on which sat a petrol chainsaw, together with various handsaws and axes. A small oil dispenser, oily rags and sharpening files rested on the bench next to a recently cleaned and polished pair of walking boots. Friends would say that whenever he'd finished his day working in the woods, he would always clean his tools and boots in readiness for the next occasion.

Jane Rigby returned to the study and sat for a moment in the leather office chair. She looked around the study and quietly thought. She had known and worked with Julian Lawson for four years. He was a conscientious, loyal and effective MI5 officer but, in truth, she knew very little about him. Was he religious? She didn't know. Neither did she know that he played the guitar or was a keen sailor.

In the five minutes she had spent in the cottage, she had learned more about the real man, and what made him tick, than she had known in the previous four years.

Previously, Jane Rugby had just known Julian Lawson. The MI5 office of Julian Lawson was, in accordance with strict Security Service policy, sterile and devoid of any personality. The study of Ben Swan was full of his personality and showed an interesting character.

She had now got to know Ben Swan. Ben Swan was missing, in unexplained circumstances. Where was he? Director Jane Rigby was concerned for his safety.

THE END

Made in the USA
Columbia, SC
13 February 2024